BORROWED TIME

ALAN HRUSKA

BORROWED TIME

THE DIAL PRESS
DOUBLEDAY & COMPANY, INC.
GARDEN CITY, NEW YORK
1984

ACKNOWLEDGMENTS

I wish to express my gratitude to my wife, Laura Chapman Hruska, and to my friends, Laurie Colwin, Juris Jurjevics, and Paul Saunders, for their encouragement, support, ideas, and emendations.

I want also to acknowledge a debt to two books, *The Origin of Consciousness in the Breakdown of the Bicameral Mind*, by Julian Jaynes, and *The Dancing Wu Li Masters*, by Gary Zukav. I should note, however, that neither Professor Jaynes nor Mr. Zukav has endorsed, or should otherwise be held responsible for, any whimsical notions expressed herein.

Library of Congress Cataloging in Publication Data

Hruska, Alan.
Borrowed time.

I. Title.
PS3558.R87W6   1984   813'.54   83-18859
ISBN 0-385-27923-X

Published by The Dial Press
Copyright © 1984 by Alan Hruska

All Rights Reserved
Manufactured in the United States of America
First printing

To Laura

BORROWED TIME

PART ONE

CHAPTER ONE

One raw February afternoon in the city of Philadelphia, several extraordinary things happened to Briton Bell. For one, he became left-handed, although he had never previously shown even a tendency toward ambidexterity. For another, he met Katie Dunston.

On the face of it, becoming left-handed was the more remarkable of the two. But this was not so. Both events were part of a larger, still more exceptional occurrence of which Katie was unwittingly the cause.

Philadelphia, it might be noted, was not a city which either frequented by choice. What drew Briton Bell was a musical that had opened there in tryout the night before. He had come to view it, and having viewed—and heard—to obtain the publishing rights to the score.

Briton Bell was the proprietor of an old-line music publishing company, one of the most profitable in the country. At thirty-six, he hardly looked the part; in fact, owing to a family trait of preternaturally youthful complexion, he looked almost ten years younger.

He was also long and lean in face and body, conservatively tailored and undemonstrative in style. In a business dependent on flamboyant presentation, his underplayed aptitude, his lack of self-consciousness, were conspicuous.

Now, having concluded his venture, the ink on the deal just dry, he left his attorney's offices to check out of the Sheraton Hotel and return home as quickly as Amtrak permitted. He was not someone who took pleasure in the kind of escapes from reality that adventures in another city might offer. Or, for that matter, in careless departures from the routine and satisfactions of his life. Yet, as he waited that afternoon to descend to the streets, a unique feeling of anticipation began to tug at him in a strangely unsettling way.

Katie Dunston, at age twenty-six, held a highly responsible job at United States Computer Corporation as a computer architect and programmer. On the afternoon in question she was on the fortieth floor of the "Tower of Light," delivering a flip-chart presentation to the principal executives of the Mid-Atlantic Electric Company.

Katie, too, was strangely exhilarated, but not by this role, which she performed in similar circumstances almost daily, and not by the prominence of these executives, whom she regarded as a doltish lot. Katie, uncharacteristically, was moved by the weather, or at least by the sense of expectancy it seemed to bring.

As the meeting broke, and she funneled her charts into their carrying tube, she stopped a moment to observe out the window the drama of clouds bunching purple and turning black. From the ground, sixteen blocks away, Briton also gazed up to watch it, before stepping into the limousine that would return him to his hotel. It was as if night had fallen without the streetlights going on.

Given the temperature, it should have snowed, but instead it became a rainstorm of torrential proportions. It announced itself with a lightning crack that illumined, then shook, the city—certainly his car, and even the Tower of Light. The streets emptied as in an air raid, and promptly turned into rivers as the deluge poured down between the towers and spires.

Though the traffic rolled, all sound was the storm's. Briton felt as if he were in a bathysphere. Then suddenly, just for a moment, it stopped. Emerging like a laser, through a pinhole in the clouds, shot a beam of piercing quality. Surely it pierced him: in one instant he experienced a curious weightlessness; the next, a loss of consciousness; then a single hard surge of strength. All around him the avenue glittered.

Katie missed it, being en route to the lobby, and by the time she dashed the several blocks to her hotel, the storm had resumed its force as if never interrupted. But to Briton it now seemed no simple act of nature—for he scarcely felt such a radiance could have existed in the midst of a storm without a city to turn into gold and himself to see it happen. There was now in it, therefore, an element of human involvement, as in some portentous biblical event.

Upon arriving at the hotel he reached for the limousine door handle with his left hand. It was unnatural for him to do so, particularly because the door was on his right side. Yet his instinct was to use his left hand, which was alarmingly disorienting.

The lobby was astir. People were shaking out their clothes and drying their hair or just waiting for the rain to let up. He strode briskly past them, mentally shaking himself as he went. And there in the open elevator car, standing alone rather impatiently, was a very pretty, rain-bedraggled young woman.

When he saw her it was like the beam.

For a long moment they stared at each other, almost in recognition and with surprise. Her eyes were brown, very large and uncompromising. She began to speak, but then, with a small shake of her head and slight blush on her cheeks, silently acknowledged the error.

He was not so sure. He couldn't place her, but couldn't shake the feeling he soon might.

As the doors closed, making them for the next moments solitary sharers, she stared at the numbers they had lighted on the board, and he, since quite a bit taller, at a tangle of wet chestnut curls.

Her face was a small oval; her skin, clear white; her nose, which bore round, gold-rimmed glasses, lightly freckled and snub. There was a chip at the corner of one of her front teeth. She clutched a wet cardboard tube and a file envelope of papers, and her raincoat was soaked. Beneath it, in her black turtleneck sweater and pleated gray flannel skirt, was, from the waist up, the body of a gymnast, and down, one seemingly more womanly and plump.

He spoke—with a catch in his throat. He said, "Whom did I remind you of?"

It was no less ordinary or grammatical a question.

But she gave a start. And her brown eyes flashing up, disproportionately large in so small a face, unaccountably turned Briton Bell into jelly.

He was not normally given to spontaneity. He was the sort of man who saw rather clearly the consequences of decisions and thought them through thoroughly first. Yet her stare—at once vulnerable, challenging and eerily familiar—made him say what he would never have dreamed it was possible for him to have said, and so fast it was totally garbled.

"What?" she responded, sensing madness afoot.

"I said . . ." He swallowed hard. "I'll get off this elevator with you."

She turned whiter by a shade.

The door opened at 10—his floor. They stood frozen, gazing into the hall. He felt himself being drained down it into a suddenly dangerous, bottomless abyss. Silently, painstakingly slowly, the door crept shut.

"Okay," she said, flaring crimson, and not looking at him at all.

Katie Dunston was not promiscuous in the least. And she was as stunned by her own apparent acceptance of this proposition as he was at himself for having proposed it.

Unknown to him, he could not have made a more clever advance. For Katie believed, at least theoretically, and without prior experience, in impulsive adventures. She did not much like admitting this, and was startled at times by what her imagination cooked up. She would also have reviled with scorn anyone who suggested she was even romantically disposed. But if there was ever a young woman to whom, in precisely the right circumstances, such a rash scheme might have deeply appealed—at least once— Katie Dunston was she.

Briton's appearance was surely part of those circumstances. Definitely nonthreatening, she thought. In fact, now he looked as if he might be regretting the whole thing.

At 14, which was really 13, he followed her down the hall. The full implication of what she was doing finally hit her, as if she had wakened from a daze. My God, she thought, he'll expect me to take off my clothes.

She stopped. He stopped too. The hall was dim, shabby and scented. She studied him up and down, as if reconfirming her data. He tried to appear friendly, although his knees were now shaking. Somehow his seeming so unsure, the feel of the storm outside, the fact of being in another city, made the situation almost plausible.

Oh well, she thought, continuing down the corridor, I'll turn out the lights.

In her room, she had a conversation on the telephone he couldn't overhear. For while he had closed the door, he hadn't advanced more than two steps from the threshold. This context was far different from the elevator and the hall.

On hanging up, she draped her raincoat over a chair, looked at him somewhat apprehensively across the room, and twisted her mouth reflectively.

"It was your idea," she finally asserted.

"Yes." He came forward boldly, despite feeble knees.

The bed was between them, as crude a symbol as one could hope for.

"I suppose you've done this sort of thing before," she said more loudly than she intended.

"Actually . . . I haven't."

"Well," she said. "You know the conventions."

"Isn't it more or less ad hoc?"

"Jesus. Latin yet!"

"Shall we talk . . . first?"

"Wha'd'ya mean, 'first?' " she exclaimed, in a voice suddenly high-pitched and nasal. "What's second?"

"If you've changed your mind . . ."

"I never made up my mind."

"You said 'okay.' "

Another mouth twist. "To what? If you won't name it, I won't do it."

"We get undressed?" he said.

"In cold blood?"

"It won't seem so cold in a minute."

"Oh boy, this is unbelievable," she said.

"I think it's rather essential."

"You know something—you look terrified."

"So do you."

"I *am!*"

"I could leave," he said. "No hard feelings."

"Are you kidding? I'll never get this far again. You stay where you are!"

"Right."

"I want to know nothing about you, you understand, least of all your name."

"Agreed."

She took off her glasses and placed them on the night table. She folded the bedspread to the foot of the bed.

With a fleeting look at him, she turned off the lights. The city of Philadelphia shone ghostlike through the windows.

Though it was now dark, and they were on opposite sides of the bed, he could see her face was again aflame.

"I'm certainly not going to . . . do it first," she said.

"Understandable." He took off his raincoat. After standing there a few moments he took off his jacket and his vest. Again, the dominant hand was his left one, but there was more to disorient him at that moment than that.

Her lips puckered, she started to say something, then stopped.

He yanked down his tie left-handedly, slipped off his suspenders and removed his shirt. Then he just looked at her, swallowing again with a very dry mouth and standing awkwardly naked to the waist.

She gave him a small frown. His chest was wiry, smooth-skinned and hairless.

In a quick, impatient movement, she crossed her arms and pulled her sweater over her head, then stood challengingly, arms akimbo.

He let out a gasp. She was braless and small but perfectly formed. He smiled lopsidedly.

The trousers were more difficult, no less than five buttons plus a zipper involved.

"My God. It's like a vault," she observed.

"London tailoring."

"Oh I see."

He went to a chair, tugged off his shoes and socks, stood up and pulled down his shorts and trousers.

Eyes on eyes, she let down her skirt.

Cotton underpants, he exclaimed to himself.

Her body, divested of these, was splotched with small islands of pink embarrassment around a dark center, no less chagrined. She was in fact more mortified than he, which partially restored his self-confidence.

She dived between the sheets. He got in too. They lay side by side without speaking.

"Jesus," she said, looking wildly at the ceiling, "I must be crazy."

He pulled her against him, her body as cool as his.

"You're trembling," he said.

"So are you."

He reached down her and squeezed.

"Ohmigod!" she said.

Then they made love. For it was love. They simply didn't know it yet.

CHAPTER TWO

When Briton Bell woke up in his own bed in his New York apartment and looked out his tenth-floor window on Central Park, he saw a gray day with brown trees and yellow and brown grass. He had never quite appreciated leafless tress before. He had never quite seen the soft, rich contrasts the color brown is capable of displaying. He was profoundly moved. For him there was lacework of infinite precision, not branches or twigs.

Briton's wife, Mary Jo, was his good friend. She had great common sense, feet on the ground. He shared everything with her. He wanted to share his experience in Philadelphia, but knew he could not. So he brought her to the window and showed her the trees.

"Very nice," she said.

She was already dressing. Her mind was not on lacework trees but on rousing the children, making the breakfast, making the beds.

Mary Jo had a gangly, sturdy body of better than middling height. She had long, straight hair that was once very blond—now would have been called, unattractively, "dirty blond," had it not been touched up. Touching up was Mary Jo's secret vice, for her long hair was her secret vanity; a definite chink in her otherwise impermeable no-nonsense armor. Her brow was wide, her nose straight to a ski-jump tip, her chin somewhat narrow.

She had clear, intelligent, no-nonsense blue eyes. But she cared nothing for bodies. One, to her, was very much like another. Functional. Thus she cared nothing whether Briton watched or did not.

He watched. Little known to Mary Jo, he really noticed her body for the first time in years. What he noticed, of course, was the contrast with Katie's. Katie's was a delight. But from Mary Jo's had come their two boys.

They had breakfast together as they normally did, each eating a different meal. Briton had eggs and bacon, Mary Jo, coffee and toast. Edward, age nine, had peanut butter spread on slices of apples, wheat germ dry with mounds of sugar, and a glass of chocolate milk which he stirred vigorously himself. Geordie, age seven, downed three sausages with a bowl of the sugar-crunchy cereal being advertised most frequently on his favorite programs and enjoying current vogue among his peers.

The boys had Mary Jo's body and Mary Jo's hair, but their faces were Briton's and they could pass for fraternal twins. Yet they were very different. Edward was serious, concerned, extremely acquisitive about knowledge and prone to test what he felt he knew. He would conjure up the most original, extraordinary or sometimes simply outrageous propositions from his incomplete understanding of the facts and state them solemnly as revealed truths. He expected to be challenged; it was his way of refining his data and theories; and then you would hear him days or weeks later, patiently expounding the revised propositions to Geordie or his friends.

Geordie, on the other hand, was funny, musical like his father, relatively carefree and, by his lights (yet with some justification in fact), the boss of the known universe—namely, his family and his second-grade class.

Both boys had remarkable IQ's. Years ago, based on those scores, they would have been referred to as geniuses. As it was, the admissions office in the private school they now went to regarded their applications with awe.

"Finish that last slice of apple," said Mary Jo.

Edward observed it morosely.

Briton said, looking up from the *Times,* "Knicks won last night, Eddie."

"They make the play-offs?"

"Not yet. But they have a shot."

"If he's not going to eat that apple . . ." said Geordie, shiny blue eyes coveting the slice.

Edward viewed it in a new light, but instead of taking the expected sibling, territorial course of action—one small bite with the remainder left spoiled on the plate—he pushed it negligently over to his brother.

"Did you know," he said to his father, "that there is a black hole in this galaxy, and our solar system rotates around it?"

"That's just a theory."

"I know."

"Good apple," said Geordie.

"But it's probably true," said Edward.

"What do you think?"

"We have to rotate around something. And did you know that the density of a black hole as big as my fist would be a billion times greater than the sun and all the planets put together?"

"That's crazy," said Geordie. Then to his father: "What's density?"

"Come on boys," said Mary Jo. "Skedaddle. Get your ties on. You're going to be late."

"I think I may have a sore throat," said Geordie.

"Oh sure. Open up."

"Ahhh."

"Nothing wrong with that throat."

Look of fiendish delight. "Might have been."

"They're your boys—both of them," said Mary Jo to Briton.

But Briton was thinking something was strange. It was the sky, which should have been blue and clear, not gray, after an East Coast storm that violent.

Mary Jo said, "It was considerate of you to call last night from Philadelphia. When did you get home? I never heard you come in."

Briton looked at her blankly.

"I would have stayed up worrying about you—Briton, what is it?"

He reached for his coffee cup with, he noted, his right hand.

"Are you all right?"

"Of course."

"You sounded funny on the phone, I was about to say."

He sipped. He recalled making no such call. "Did I? How so?"

"Well it may have been the connection. Your voice was . . . well, dull, blurry. I'm sure it was the connection." She laughed. "It made you sound like a zombie."

*   *   *

Katie Dunston lived in three small rooms on Ninety-second Street between Columbus Avenue and Central Park West. On this particular morning she sat on the edge of her bed in her shortie nightgown, tingling from her scalp to her toes. Had she really done what she was remembering?

She had never done anything even remotely like that before.

She had gone to bed, just once, with her high school steady in North Stonington, Connecticut. It was such a breathless, bumbling comedy of errors it hardly counted. She was not even sure she'd been "penetrated," as the saying goes.

She had gone to bed quite a number of times with a coworker in New York, a programmer like herself, a mangy, brilliant boy who now lived in Los Angeles. She'd been penetrated by him good and proper every time, but it had been very systematic.

Yesterday afternoon had not been systematic. It had been—indescribable. Her stomach sank to the floor.

She got up and went to the window. Pretty, tree-lined street. It was sinking, too.

If anyone had previously suggested she was capable of doing what she had now apparently done she would have immediately branded him crazy.

"Holy Mary," she said. "Don't I know who I am?"

This question was not entirely rhetorical. It was one—along with, "Where did I come from?"—that Katie had been asking since childhood, and not because of any confusion either about the biological process involved.

Katie's family was decidedly nonintellectual. Her father, when working, was a mechanic at Electric Boat in Groton; her mother, a part-time checkout lady in Almac's, a supermarket in Mystic. She had one brother, who was younger, who worked in the construction trade when not collecting unemployment. He was lovable, but hopeless and ordinary. As were, truth to tell, her parents.

Katie looked enough like them that there was small possibility of her being a changeling or secret adoptee. And in school she did sufficiently poorly as to raise no question along those lines.

The trouble began when the grade school she went to in North Stonington started giving standardized tests. Katie's mother one day got a call from the school principal that shook her very badly. It seemed that on the arithmetical parts of these tests Katie had been scoring perfect 800's. There could be no question of cheating, for no one then in her class, or, for that matter, in the recalled history of the school, had ever tested at this level. And her verbal scores were average.

What disturbed the principal, and hence Katie's mother, more than this was Katie's explanation of how she had done so well. She said there was something, or "someone," in her mind that showed her the answers.

With worried parental consent, the school psychiatrist took over. He was a man who practiced at the New London Hospital and actually knew what he was about. But, after administering a battery of tests, he was at first confounded by Katie. She was not schizophrenic, although that was his original hypothesis. Schizophrenics heard "voices"; some saw "pictures"; but all had other symptoms that Katie did not share. In fact, she was perfectly normal in all traits but this one.

Nor could he pronounce her an *idiot savant*. She was plainly far more intelligent than her class work would indicate, even in nonmathematical fields. Her verbalism, given her background, was simply latent.

He finally concluded quite reasonably that there had been in her case a remarkable genetic leap. She was just plain smart. And her intelligence derived from an unusual, if not unique, development of the left hemisphere of her brain—the hemisphere (which in Katie's case, she being left-handed) was the source of original intuitions and abstractions.

In most people, the psychiatrist explained one evening to her parents, this off-hemisphere works unconsciously. It contributes to thoughts—has, indeed, a strong influence on them. "But we are not aware of it," he stressed. "Katie is. She gets messages that she can recognize as such, as independent communications. This is rare," he said solemnly. "You must get used to the fact you have a gifted child."

Of course, they never did. They treated her like an odd duck. They saved to send her to the University of Chicago, which had a special scholarship program for young geniuses. Perhaps in reaction, her grades were deplorable, and but for the intervention of another psychiatrist—a former professor of her New London doctor—she would have dropped out. She never fit in until she went to work at USCC. She had never met a young man whose brain worked like hers; she despaired of a satisfactory relationship.

Now she thought of the man—whose name she did not know—of how embarrassed and surprised he had been. He had definitely been something new to her experience. As for his mind, however—their actions were hardly conducive to reaching conclusions on that subject.

On the other hand—his body!

Let's face it, she thought, he was beautiful, and he caught me just right. She shook her head. Too simplistic.

I was feeling sexy. Hotels do that.

No, no, no! I am a very private, modest person. It's impossible. A man I never saw before? A tawdry hotel room? I even arranged for a late checkout!

Am I going nuts again?

She flung her nightgown off over her head, let it lie on the bare wood floor. Naked, she felt sexy once more. She fought an impulse to observe herself in a mirror. Something very odd, she thought, is happening to me.

The dresser drawer almost landed on her toes, she opened it with such unconscious abandon. All her underpants were rumpled and torn. I need new ones, she decided. She carried a pair back to the bed, sat again on the edge, got the briefs to her knees. They're plump, she thought. How could he have liked me?

More tingles.

Who was he? I don't know where he lives, anything about him.

Oh God!

He's probably married.

*   *   *

Throughout the day Briton thought about the girl in the Philadelphia hotel. He thought about her through breakfast, going to work, in his office. And he thought about the phone call he had not made to his wife.

His firm occupied four rooms in the Chrysler Building, the largest being his own, which was old-fashioned and immense. Each room had a glass-plated door on the corridor with the name of the firm, Bell Music, Inc., stenciled in black on its face.

Briton was fond of this building and these offices to the point of nostalgia, though he came to them almost every day. The art deco style stirred something within him; the large half-moon windows of the suite, its high ceilings and huge, darkly stained oaken furniture were just what a music publisher's office should be. He remembered coming here when his grandfather held forth, and later his father. It looked the same to him now, for he'd scarcely changed as much as a filing cabinet or a chair. Same outsized desk and conference table; same black upright piano. Only the mammoth Oriental rug had been replaced since having been worn tackily bare; but Briton had shopped for weeks until he found a near replica. Though he could certainly afford more elegant offices, they'd have to tear this building down before he would move.

The company had been founded by his grandfather in 1911. It was nurtured by his father for twenty-five years. In seven, Briton had doubled its catalog and tripled its earnings. Given the copyright laws of the United States, membership in ASCAP and association with music licensing societies throughout the world, it was a veritable gold mine of a business.

Briton got up from behind his desk, opened the giant armoire in one corner, and scrutinized himself in the full-length mirror. He had never done this consciously before. He was not vain. What he was looking for was how he would have appeared to her, and how, if at all, she might remember him.

His nose was aquiline, long and thin. His forehead and cheekbones were broad, tapering to a roundish chin. He held a tan so well that a weekend in Harbour Island three weeks ago had left him as brown as a jet-hopping playboy.

He concluded that his appearance must be Caledonian. He cared little for ethnicity, but a good deal for history and geneology and knew the roots of his family tree.

His grandfather, Briton I, had been the immigrant—in 1906—the fourth son of an impoverished laird in a family that traced back past the Union, into the Highland mists. He had left Glasgow bankrupt, at the age of thirty-two, as a piano player on the *Lusitania*. He was also a card player who won or lost in streaks. At the top of one he invested $25,000 in the first Ziegfeld show and got the publishing rights to the music. At his death, he owned one of the finest old-line catalogs in the country: Kern, Gershwin, Porter, Rodgers and Hart.

His son, Briton II, had done a competent job of protecting that investment, while adding little to what they had. Briton II was a lawyer, a partner in a Wall Street firm. He administered the family publishing business as he administered trusts and estates. He took pleasure in books, paintings and a swift set of tennis, but for music he'd a dead ear.

Not so Briton III. Like his grandfather, he played a mean and hot piano. Like his father, he went to law school, but his eye from the start was on the publishing business.

He had the knack.

It was rare, and he had it.

Somewhere inside his brain was the prototypical construct of a successful, commercial tune—when he heard it, he knew. This was his edge against the conglomerates. There were no wasted energies or money on scores that didn't pan out.

The intercom buzzed. "They're here."

That was Miss March. She'd been with the firm forty-one years. Originally hired as his grandfather's secretary, she had been made a vice president by Briton, but still occupied the same desk and chair. She knew everyone in the business and treated all democratically. All were "they" to Miss March.

In moments the office was invaded. He saw three or four composers or performer-composers a day. The present "they" were Leah Gestalt and her arranger/producer, Herbie Glass. They came in with Miss March and Soupy Selinger, accountant, promoter and general factotum for the firm.

"Brit baby! Congratulations on Philadelphia!"

Briton jumped out of his chair. Then he realized Glass was referring only to the news, appearing in the trade press that morning, of his signing the rock musical he had gone to Philadelphia to see.

"Thanks, Herbie. Hello, Leah."

Her head jerked; she withdrew, looking elsewhere, had difficulty arranging her spiderlike arms. Leah was tall with coat-hanger shoulders. Her hair was blond and unstylishly ironed; her face, angular, with cheekbones so prominent as to make Tartar slits of her eyes. She was too shy to perform

without a nose full of coke, but with that—an old story in this trade—
could electrify a hall.

If the people in it emitted the right waves.

That was always a problem with Leah—another trade cliché.

"I'm somewhat pressed today," said Briton Bell.

"So what else is new?" said Herbie.

Briton always said that. From other publishers, producers or record
company executives, this short-circuiting of the ritual exchanges and
harangues would not be tolerated by artist or manager. They knew their
due. Besides, a preliminary, emotion-letting half hour got everyone in the
right groove for either performances or negotiations or both.

Briton was the oddball. Soupy wore the velvet jumpsuit and did the
warming up. But Briton heard the music. With three hit shows and seven
gold records, he could be as "pressed" as he liked.

So Soupy smiled and winked and Herbie sat at the piano and Leah
stood there, as usual, looking scared.

Her real name was Lila Blair. In the market values of the day, it was
obviously insufficiently ethnic. She had broken in with a group that called
itself, In the Buff, since that's how they generally performed. She had to
be doped plenty to do that.

Briton thought, Leah is a cartoon. But she could write music. And sing
it in a pure resilient tone.

They were putting together material for a concert tour and album.
These were the last three songs. As she sang, Leah stood as still as a choir
girl. No expression. Her lyrics were bad poetry, very naive. But Briton
never listened to the words. He barely even looked at her or the sallow
Herbie. He listened to the music. It fully vibrated within his prototypical
construct. It made his skin shrivel and bump.

He saw the girl in Philadelphia listening too. She probably knew nothing about music. "That's pretty good," she would probably say, before
changing the subject. She hoisted her sweater over her head.

*   *   *

Katie Dunston spent the day in Stamford, at the USCC Account Engineers' Building on West Avenue, attending flip-chart presentations on a
new line of minicomputers. That's what Katie once had been, an AE, and

after that, a high-level programmer. Now, as a computer architect, it was her job to conceive of new hardware and software implementations that would make the systems more flexible and faster—and often to explain to customers and potential customers all the uses to which the new processors and peripherals could be put. She was better at it than almost anyone. It was something she understood at levels which even the largest and most sophisticated users rarely even approached. So she thoroughly enjoyed it. She enjoyed coming into offices with her insignificant physical stature and turning the operation inside out, like the bossy little terror she was. She made them hop. She knew software like Briton knew music.

And it was equally instinctive. In her mind's eye was an abstraction of the most simple and efficient system possible, from the programmer's point of view. They had picked her as a natural right out of the first indoctrination course, and put her in the middle of future product development.

Her regular office was at 325 Park Avenue. But she was often in Stamford, and most people at the AE building knew her. After some initial passes, the men, even the single men, gave her a wide berth, and she them. She was smarter than they and was known for her waspish humor.

At lunch she sat alone in the USCC cafeteria, facing the rear terrace, eating her peach yogurt, watching the rain which had just started.

She was getting angrier and angrier. She could not get that guy in Philadelphia out of her mind.

After that first garbled speech, he had said little and that in mumbles; yet she had convinced herself by now he was very bright. She had never liked aquiline noses; yet she was persuaded his was beautiful. Except for the few obligatory patches, his body was virtually hairless; and she now conceded she liked that too.

Jesus! she thought. I'm getting softheaded and depraved.

She scooped up the last of the evil-tasting yogurt and lit a menthol cigarette. It was a nonsmokers' table. So what. She was the only one there.

A voice on the loudspeaker demanded attention. The huge cafeteria fell silent. The roads were icing; if you must drive, take caution. Harumph, she thought, typical USCC paternalism.

The next day was Thursday. She had a presentation to make in the afternoon at some ritzy private boys' school in Manhattan. Just the kind of place that guy probably went to as a kid.

A shadow fell across the table. "Man trouble?"

Katie jumped. "That's funny as hell, Jeanie. Really is."

It was her friend Jeanie Scanlon, who occupied the office next to hers in the Park Avenue building and now, laughing, took the opposite seat with her own half pint of yogurt. Jeanie Scanlon was a tall, homely stringbean of a girl with a large bumpy nose and stringy hair. Like Katie, she was a computer architect, and a good one. Her main problem was that she thought she knew everything else besides.

"Usually means a man," said Jeanie, whirling boysenberry into yogurt. "That dreamy look you were wearin'."

"What're you doing here?"

"Taking Art Fowler's class. Can you believe this guy? He called me at home last night—all peekaboo and honey talk. Took me ten minutes to understand what the hell he wanted. I thought he was warming up to asking me out. The man has twenty-seven kids, for chrissake." She swallowed yogurt and made a face. "I think he's being raided."

"Art Fowler!"

"Why not? There're six or seven new companies opening up around here. You're probably next. They say that one in Croton—what's it's name?" She recalled in mid-mouthful. "Quantum Corp. *That* may be a hot one. Real mystery house, that one is."

"I've got enough mystery in my life."

This drew a look from behind Jeanie's spoon. "So, who is it? Man of your dreams?"

"Oh yeah, right."

"Then what ya worried about?"

"Who says I'm worried?"

"Look in the mirror, kid," said Jeanie, applying her napkin.

"You're a real smartass, y'know!"

Jeanie's lips puckered out. "Touchy, touchy."

Katie frowned.

"Does he put out?" asked Jeanie.

"You ever know a man who didn't put out?"

Jeanie reached for an ashtray. "Some," she said lighting up. "Unfortunately." Her smile was sardonic.

Katie jabbed out her cigarette. "Gotta get out of here."

"Hey, wait a sec. This was just getting interesting."

"Got a class."

"Well, so do I. It'll keep for a minute. The goddamn company won't fold. What I don't understand is, if he's not the man of your dreams, if he's just some ordinary make-out—"

"You wouldn't believe the man of my dreams."

Jeanie's eyes brightened. "Try me! Some cerebral type, hunh?"

"Are you off!"

"You're kidding."

"Muscle shirt. Muscle brain. Arrives on a motorcycle."

"Wow!" Jeanie licked her lips. "Real hunk, hunh? Tell me more. Rain always makes me feel sexy."

"You'll wet your pants."

"Let me worry about my pants." She flashed a look. "I once had a boy like that. Trouble was, the muscle brain part."

"Yeah."

"You?"

"Only dream about'em. Well. . . ." Katie bounced up. "Give'em hell, back to basics, other self-elevating thoughts."

"Sheeet," said Jeanie.

The two young women carried their trays to the disposal belt at the far end of the room. Katie was now feeling awful. The dream was no joke. She wondered why she had told Jeanie. The only person she had ever previously told was the college shrink who had wormed it out of her during sophomore year.

She split with her friend on the corner. Their classrooms were in opposite directions, each building several blocks away. Walking made Katie think more about the dream.

Nothing in Freud gave a satisfactory explanation for this one. The male figure was menacingly macho, an arrested-development type, with a muscled physique and long black hair, belligerent about his stupidity. What scared Katie was that, in this dream, she was no more intelligent than he. The dream was recurring in that the characters were the same—she, this boy, her parents and some friends—although the plot snaked around like an afternoon soap.

In her adolescent nightmares, she was actually sleeping with this creature, which was more frightening than erotic. By sophomore year of college she dreamed she had become his wife.

In real life she hated everybody then, which induced in everybody indifference or dislike. On top of other problems she was having in college— like persistent anxiety and total lack of concentration—she thought she had sleeping sickness, since she couldn't get out of bed. She finally roused up the energy to get a job as a waitress in a truck stop, without bothering to inform her parents or the university that she had stopped going to classes. She was also on the verge of involvement with a piece of rough trade reminiscent of her dream man—another near disastrous chapter of her life—when Marcel Vermeil tracked her down.

Marcel Vermeil was a chaired professor of psychiatry at the medical school of the university. He also taught a select undergraduate seminar in which Katie was enrolled. He was a jaunty, round, diminutive man of advanced age and deep ironies with a blue-eyed pitiless gaze, white beard, and the elocutions of his native Vienna. He knew all about Katie—from her childhood doctor who had once been his student. He thus thought her worth his time.

"Don't you think this somewhat of a waste?" he had asked across the formica counter of the diner. The presence of such an elegantly dressed personage in such a place was causing a considerable sensation.

"It'll do," she said. "What're you having?"

"Tonight I am giving," he said, and handed her a card with his address.

She was there two hours later, in truth quite desperate for help. And his seminar was the one class she liked.

Let in by his wife and led to his study, she saw her record spread out on his desk: medical history, SAT scores, test papers, school transcripts. "I have taken an interest in you," he acknowledged.

"I didn't give anyone permission to send you this stuff!"

"For one thing," he observed, "you have rather remarkable powers of erasure." He leafed out her SAT papers. "I note, for example, that you believed Chile to be someplace in Africa, and as to Boston, did not even hazard a guess."

"Where'd you get this?"

"Where would you think? The registrar. The ETS. The medical history came courtesy of your parents."

"You've been talking to my parents?"

"I haven't, no."

"I see!"

"Have we passed through hostility?"

"I don't know what I'm doing here."

"My dear girl."

She sat down. Her fingers twisted a slender chain of charms, a high school graduation present from her father. "Geography's not my subject. Boring stuff. Has nothing to do with me."

"Boston, I would estimate, is a two-hour drive from your home."

"Never been there."

"Do you know, I doubt there are ten high school graduates in this country who could not have answered these questions. And you are now failing history here."

"What is this? You a psychiatrist or a faculty adviser?"

"Which do you think you need more?"

"Oh boy! All you guys do this? Answering questions with questions."

"Would you like to scream? It occurs to me you might wish to do that."

"What?"

"Come, we can scream together, if you like."

"Are you kidding?"

"Not at all." He got up, took off his jacket, raised his small arms through his double-breasted waistcoat. Katie, who was not tall, topped him by three inches at least. "Are you ready?"

"I'm not going to do this."

When he smiled, his face creased into eye crinkles and dimples beneath his white beard.

She let out a squeak, he started to roar, then she screamed at the top of her lungs.

"Ah," he said, when they had finished, and shook his round body all over. "Feels good?"

"It was okay," she said looking a bit defenseless.

He reseated himself like a white furry ball. "So. Now we know each other a little better."

"You always do this?" she said sinking back to her chair.

His lower lip arched in thought. "No. Shall we do it again?"

"When are you going to ask me about my dreams?"

"You have bothersome dreams?"

"You might say that."

"They are frightening you?"

She clammed up.

"So. Let's start there."

She arrived at the Account Engineers' building late, flashed her badge and went up in the elevator alone. This reminded her of the man in Philadelphia. He was scaring her more.

Thank God I'll never see him again, she reflected.

CHAPTER THREE

Briton was late for the executive committee meeting of his sons' school. It was the same school he had attended, and it was natural that he be a member of this committee and the board of trustees. Particularly if he was going to be as large a contributor as the school expected.

When Eddie had been admitted three years ago, the headmaster, Mr. Sturbridge, had called Briton, and they met at the Union Club for lunch. The head, who was then in his seventies and about to retire, had always looked and acted like the president of a European state. This role assumption was quite deliberate. His helmsmanship for nearly forty years—in procuring grants, obtaining college admissions and disengaging warring factions of faculty or parents—differed little from the elements of statecraft by which Bismarck ran Germany or de Gaulle, France. And he considered Heycroft, which was the school's name, no less an imperial institution.

He talked a great deal at that lunch about educational freedom and the preservation of values. He spoke of the importance of continuing to turn out "our sort"—by which Briton presumed he referred to the long line of lawyers and investment bankers for which the school was famous. Briton knew he was being looked over to see if he was "sound." So he said very little and passed. When the call came to serve on the board, he accepted immediately. If his sons were to go to this school—and it was still the best in New York—he wanted to know firsthand what was happening there. And he would, as he told himself, "work from within."

When he arrived at the meeting, the executive committee members were still milling about with cheese, crackers and drinks in the new head-master's office which, in the manner of successor regimes, had been thoroughly redecorated. Several of them greeted Briton enthusiastically. He neither saw them nor heard what they said.

Standing near the coffee urn, deep in discussion with the new head, was the girl from the Philadelphia hotel.

As she concluded this conversation with a series of cordial smiles, the ice forming around Briton's heart got colder and colder. He felt faint. He felt as if he were disintegrating. She put her coffee cup down, which was fortunate. For when she turned and saw him, she staggered as though hit, her hand moving to her mouth, her face turning redder than it had in the elevator.

The meeting, to Briton, was a blur. There was considerable confusion at the start when Jock Talbot, chairman of the committee—and a man with the sensitivity of a boulder—evidently misascribed her blushes to shyness. Katie could deliver this presentation in her sleep. After Jock finished a rambling introduction, repeating several times each bit of information supplied him by USCC, Katie spoke briefly and well. She told them how the equipment they ordered fit into the hierarchy of System/880 machines, in terms of storage capacity and processing speed. She told them what it could do, both as an educational tool and a replacement of the school's present record-keeping approaches. She informed them of educational programs available from USCC and others. She closed with a personal judgment that the children's study of the machines and their learning of computer programming would teach them more in the end about how to think than would using the equipment simply as a means of feeding the students information.

At that point, Jock said in effect, "Yeah, but how does it work?"

"On what level," said Katie, "do you want it?"

"Oh, I guess pretty simple."

There were in that meeting a number of business executives who had been relying on computers for years, but they could not have come close to answering that question, or to admitting they couldn't. It was therefore with thinly disguised excitement that they attended to what she said. Katie opened their minds.

She briefly explained the binary number system of zeros and ones, which was familiar to most. She then described how the basic electronics —"and," "or," and "not" circuits—could be made into "adders" or other miniature arithmetical computation machines. She then took them through the entry of data in zeros and ones (signified by current being partially off or fully on) onto the wire registers of a terminal; how they were moved on these wires like trains on tracks, switched in their course by other zeros and ones that were emitted to track junctions by the "control" electronics, which received the program to do that from "memory," and were then pulled through the "adder" or other processing circuitry of the "logic" electronics, and the answer sent back to the terminal screen, a printer or some other "output" device.

Through all this she did not look at Briton once, although he sat in a chair directly opposite. She also had occasion to draw diagrams on a pad. Toward the end of this tutorial she realized what she was doing. She was writing right-handed. It felt as if nothing were wrong. It felt as if she *were* right-handed. And then she noticed from the way people reached for the diagrams, mixed sugar in their tea or simply oriented their bodies that she was in a room filled with right-handed people.

She almost screamed. She knew the mind played funny tricks, and she attributed this one to her Philadelphia friend—to her reaction to being with him in the same room. She thought of the monograph she'd once read, authored by Professor Vermeil, of how lifelong stutterers would speak normally in a new language while learning it, then stutter as badly as ever when fluent. But she had been feeling strange since she walked into this school. *Before* he arrived. She had suddenly felt like a pointillist painting, all insubstantial, incorporeal dots.

They detained her with questions. They thanked her excessively. She got up and left them to the rest of their meeting.

Briton excused himself at once.

"We're always meeting at elevators," he said to her at the landing.

"This is not funny," she said, tight-lipped with impending rage.

"I'll go down with you."

"Like hell you will."

As they stood there glaring, three ninth-graders, as tall as Briton, strolled past, eyeing Katie appreciatively. He realized that among his other problems he did not like men looking at her like that, even if they were only boys.

"Let's walk down."

"Go back to your meeting!"

"I know who you are now, Katie Dunston. I can find you anytime."

She made a face, and produced a finger. The elevator came, and she got on it. He boarded too. The button panel was very low, adjusted for the smallest children.

"Why didn't you look at me in there?" he asked.

She did now. "You have a child in this school?"

"Two."

"So you're married."

"Right."

"That's what I thought."

Disembarking in the lobby, Katie got her coat. Briton's was upstairs, but he followed her outside anyway.

"Where will you be tomorrow at lunchtime?"

"I don't have lunch with married men—not those with your ideas."

"We have to talk."

"I do not want to talk to you. I do not want to see you."

"Katie—"

"Oh Jesus, go back inside. You'll freeze to death."

"Lunch tomorrow. Where?"

"I can't. I have another meeting like this."

"Where is it?"

"First Boston."

"I know it."

"I'm not going to meet you, and I'm not going to stand here."

"I'll see you tomorrow—around noon."

"Oh, you fool," she said whirling about and walking away.

She realized she was talking to herself about herself, for she had deliberately told him where she'd be. He realized he still hadn't told her his name.

CHAPTER FOUR

Broad Street was cold, scoured by a stiff wind off the bay. Katie had declined a late lunch with the First Boston director of computer services and his colleagues and felt like an idiot for doing so. By the time she reached the lobby, she was furious with herself for thinking that "he" just might be crazy enough to have shown up and to have waited.

He had. In his black Chesterfield topcoat, looking thin and chilled. He's done it again, she fumed with her heart leaping all over her chest.

Before he saw her, Briton knew she was coming. He felt that same disintegrating sensation.

"I thought we might have lunch in the park," he said.

This threw her completely. She was prepared to say something dismissive, but instead found herself exclaiming, "What park?"

"Battery Park."

"You *are* crazy!"

"No one will be there."

"Of course no one will be there. It's freezing."

"No. The water warms you. You'll see."

"I could have lunched at the Broad Street Club."

"You wouldn't have liked that. It's on Beaver Street now."

"Does that change the food?"

"Must have. Also, the Wall Street Club's on William. It's all mixed up down here now."

At the foot of Broadway there was an old German cafeteria with big fogged windows, and inside, steaming trays of knockwurst, pig's knuckles, pot roast and the like. They bought two hot pot roast sandwiches and containers of coffee, and with their brown bags walked into the park.

Miraculously, there was only a breeze. Gusts of it eddied into the mouths of Broadway and Broad, Water and South, and as those streets narrowed, were whipped by Venturi effect into veritable gales. But here, in Battery Park, it was as he had predicted—almost warm.

They picked a bench, so they could look at the bay. They ate their sandwiches and drank their coffee, watched the gulls and pigeons and said little. Every now and then, people passed by, but very few, and those, walking briskly. There was something odd, something he could not place, about this scene.

"Were you wearing that coat in Philadelphia?" she suddenly asked.

"No. A raincoat. Don't you remember that?"

"I can see you now, when you're sixty years old, thin and haggard, wearing that coat, and a vest with a silver watch chain."

When that did not produce quite the intended effect, for he merely frowned, she went on.

"What do you do? Are you a lawyer? A banker? Do you work down here? You seem to know all about the clubs. You—"

"Stop!"

She did, frowning herself, sitting back hard on the slatted bench.

He knew her nervous attack for what it was, and this was not what troubled him, made him so uneasy he needed silence for a moment to gather himself in. It was something else, something so disturbing his conscious mind was not accepting it, even as his stomach was sinking to the ground.

When he saw it, he wished he hadn't.

It was nearly 2:30. They were facing south. The sun was over his left shoulder. It was descending in the east!

Jesus, he thought, this isn't happening. It's my reaction to her.

He scanned the horizon. The Bayonne oil tanks were there; Staten

Island was there; the Statue of Liberty raised her torch on Bedloe's Island. And the sun was slanting over Brooklyn in the east.

He shook his head to clear it and made to glance at his watch. Instinctively he had raised his right wrist, but his watch was on his left.

Oh Jesus! I always wear my watch on my left wrist. Because I'm right-handed!

Later! he thought. I've got to think about this later. I can't let her believe I'm going crazy.

He turned his glance to Katie.

"You all right?" she asked.

"Of course."

"It's cold," she said, folding her arms belligerently.

"I'm a music publisher," he said, refusing to look at the sun.

"You're joking."

"No. That's my trade."

"How peculiar."

"I'm very good at it."

"I wouldn't have thought you had the time."

He took a deep, salty breath. "My name," he said, "is Briton Bell."

"I know what your name is."

"You do?"

"They told me at the school. You have boys in the second and fourth grades. And your wife is a class representative. I received considerably more information than I wanted. I only wanted to know your name. And this is becoming ridiculous."

She swung about with a menacing look. "And trite. It's a cliché. Do you realize that?"

"Calmly!"

"Are you calm?" she demanded to know.

"No."

He was certainly far from calm, but as long as he looked only at her, he could appear to be so. Understanding this would have to wait.

"So why're you telling me to be calm?"

"One of us should be."

"Oh great! Another cliché. You get that from one of your songs?"

"I'm going to kiss you," he said.

"Perfect. It's just what I need. Maybe one of these gulls will bomb us, too."

"Unfortunate allusion."

"Listen, my friend. You don't even know me. I'm full of unfortunate allusions."

"Do you want to be kissed or don't you?"

"What do you think? What do you think I'm here for? Do you think I'm freezing my ass off in this park—in the middle of winter—because I don't want to be kissed?"

He kissed her. Salt air was good for kisses. It made them warmer and sweeter. It was a very wet, warm, hungry kiss.

He almost died of it. That's how he felt.

"Oh, bloody, bloody, bloody, hell," she said.

"Where do you live?" He was dizzy with love; it was that simple.

"Yes, yes, I knew that's where we'd end up."

"So let's go. Is it far?"

"Too damn far."

"We'll take a cab."

"Of course we'll take a cab. You think I can keep my hands off you in a subway?"

*   *   *

He felt his shoulders being pushed.

"Wake up, Briton."

He hadn't thought he was asleep. But the last thing he remembered—Katie in his arms, his thinking how that and this room seemed wonderfully familiar—was no longer happening.

She was sitting up against the headboard, pillow propped behind her, sheets pulled to her neck. She had the air about her of having been, until then, deep in thought.

"It's over," she announced.

That stirred him to an elbow, though he was groggier than he thought. It made him smile rather inappropriately.

"I don't do this to other women," she declared. "Especially class representatives."

"Wait a minute," he said, rubbing his face.

"You awake now?"

"Yeah."

"Did you hear what I said?"

"You're always telling me things you don't do."

She glared at him. "Don't you think I know it? You're a menace. You're a dangerous person."

"It's not me."

"Well, it's certainly not me. I don't go around seducing people, making them crazy. I've never acted this way before in my life. Not even remotely. I don't recognize myself, and I'm very unhappy."

"That's not what you said before."

" 'Before' was pure lust. That's my point!"

"It's not me, it's us. And it's surely not only lust."

"Oh no? What do you call it?"

"Enchantment," he said with a smile even more foolish.

"Oh boy! Now I've heard everything."

"The way we met—I could not possibly otherwise have proposed what I did. I could not even have spoken to you. And our meeting again, so soon. The odds against that were astronomical."

"Don't you quote odds at me. I'm a mathematician. And mathematicians don't become enchanted. Frogs become enchanted."

"Katie, from the first moment I saw you . . ."

"No lyrics, please."

"Katie, I love you. I feel no guilt. You will say it's because I'm a monster, but I'm really not a monster. If this were blameworthy, I would feel the worst possible guilt. I am as amazed by it as you are. You just saw what happened. We were both absolutely out of our heads."

"Lust."

"You know that's not true."

"It's a trite situation, Briton! And I hate it."

"The very fact that you've never acted this way before—doesn't that tell you something?"

"Damn right. To get out of it."

With that she burst into tears. He tried putting his arms around her again but she squirmed free, still clutching the sheet.

"I never felt so stupid in all my life."

"It has nothing to do with intelligence."

"You're telling me!" she cried.

"Katie, we're going to work this out."

"Idiot! People have been working on this particular problem for three thousand years. There are no solutions."

"We'll find one. Trust me."

"You're a lunatic. Why should I trust you? I don't even know you."

"We know each other very well."

"Yeah! Biblically."

"I didn't mean that."

"What other way? You know nothing about me."

"Let's get up and make dinner."

"No! No more meals. I do not eat meals with somebody else's husband."

"We have to plan."

"I have a plan."

"I'm not fond of it."

"You will be. Long-range."

"I'm not going to do it, Katie."

"You're not going to have much choice about it."

Her small face was grimly determined.

"Katie," he said, "what do you feel for me?"

She shut her eyes and swore.

"That's an ambiguous answer."

"It's an ambivalent feeling!"

"There's no ambivalence in me."

"Well, there damn well should be."

"Maybe so. But there's not. And I want to know precisely how you feel."

"Briton, don't be dumb."

"It's important that you tell me, Katie."

"Well, what in the hell do you think? Do you think otherwise I'd be sitting here like this without my clothes on? I am actually, believe it or not, a very modest person."

"I know you are."

"So go. Leave me alone. You are plaguing me."

"All right."

"Good."

"I'll tell you exactly what's going to happen. I'm going to get up, get dressed and leave."

"Right."

"And in two or three days I'll be back."

She shook her head.

"Katie, to stay away from you that long . . ."

"Make it three weeks."

"Why three weeks?"

"Because, damnit, by then I'll be cured."

"Of what?"

"Will you stop asking me stupid questions!"

So then he did get up and put his clothes on, and she watched as though in a trance. When he kissed her good-bye, she barely responded.

After he left, she went to the bathroom. Then she went into the kitchen and sat there thinking a long time. She thought: I have not had the dream since I met him. Then she went back to bed without having eaten. It was dark in the room. She put her head back, but could not close her eyes. Nor could she complete any thoughts. Presently she started to cry. I never do this, either, she thought, and then cried herself to sleep.

CHAPTER FIVE

It was Sunday. Briton was in the Ninety-eighth Street meadow of Central Park with his two sons playing touch football. The sides were Briton and Geordie against Edward. Edward, who was fast and shifty, was winning by a lot. He had just scored his sixth touchdown, and Geordie, who had run as fast as he could and not caught him, was furious and close to tears.

"You're not trying," he accused his father.

Briton collapsed to the ground. "Well, I'm running pretty fast."

"No you're not!"

They were all very sweaty, for it was unseasonably warm. Since it was late in the day, they had the meadow practically to themselves.

Edward, returning, was tossing the ball up to himself. "Let's run some patterns," he said in the manner of one bored with easy conquest. He tossed the ball to his father and shrugged off his winter jacket like a Dallas lineman getting back on defense.

Patterns was a game Briton had introduced several weeks before. It was already accepted by Edward, who appreciated the intricacies of the sport and believed strongly in establishing routine. Now, after touch football, came patterns. That was that. Geordie was less sure.

"All right," said Briton, rising and shucking his own outer jacket. He handed the ball to his younger son, while Edward assumed the appropriate stance at a mythical line of scrimmage. "On six."

Geordie looked confused.

"Means hike the ball, when I count to six."

Geordie remembered and shrugged, as if to say, "Pretty simple-minded."

"Post pattern," called Briton, and then, gave the cadence.

On the hike, Edward dashed to the sideline, then cut smartly to midfield. The pass led him a little too much but he caught it diving, making two unnecessary rolls on the ground for flourish. He returned with a swagger, the stadium roaring in his ears.

Geordie's turn. Briton called a sideline pattern, which he then had to explain. Grudgingly, Geordie aped his brother's stance. With the ball in the air, his face was expectant. When it bounced off his chest, he looked surprised, then hurt as if he'd been tricked. The ball was, after all, as large as his chest. He had to be coaxed to continue.

They ran several more plays, Edward catching most of his passes, Geordie none and becoming progressively angrier—mainly at his brother.

"Post pattern," Briton said, and Geordie went out.

"Cut now!"

He did; the ball was there, and Geordie caught it. He hid nothing. No controlled swagger, his. As he returned with the ball, his entire small body rocked from side to side, swollen with pride and pleasure.

Briton loved Geordie and Edward almost more than he could bear. It made him think again of Katie, of whom he'd been thinking on and off all day. Thinking of Katie and thinking of his sons almost tore him in half.

He said to himself, I wish I could be two people. That would solve everything.

*   *   *

It was Tuesday morning and Katie was talking to Jeanie Scanlon in Katie's office at USCC.

It was a fair indication of the state Katie was in that she finally confided in Jean about Briton. Ordinarily she would not have told anyone anything that personal about herself. But she had reached the point where she had to tell someone or burst.

"Never fool around with married men," was Jean's immediate pronouncement.

"Shit, Jeanie, if I'd wanted conventional wisdom, I'd have gone to a priest. It's not like that."

"It's always like that. He's got kids, right?"

Katie nodded glumly. "Right."

"Always the same. Hackneyed situation."

"No. Different."

"Can't be different. How's it different?"

"What I feel."

"Oh, you always *feel*. That's part of it. But it only ends one way. You holding the stick."

"Even so, it's different."

"What you feel is different?"

"Yeah."

"What makes you so special?"

"Dunno. But I'm going to die of it."

This gave Jean a jolt, for Katie was not given to dramatic declarations. It made her reassess the situation.

"Who'd you say this guy was?"

Katie sighed. "His name is Briton."

"What is he—some Greek god type?"

"Hardly."

"What then?"

Katie's eyes filled with tears. They'd been doing a lot of that.

"Jesus, girl! You better get a grip."

"Yeah."

"They all look the same with the lights out."

"Yeah. Thanks."

"Well, I mean, I don't know what I can do."

"Nothing!"

"Look, I got a cousin—a bachelor—who teaches math at Rutgers. He's no beauty, but a decent guy. Wha'd'ya say I fix you up?"

Katie started laughing. It was semihysterical, which frightened Jean even more. While she was debating whether to slap her into placidity, Katie stopped.

"Boy, I'm a sad case. Just listen to me. I scarcely know the man. He scarcely knows me. The second time I saw him I thought I was disintegrating; I was so upset I started writing right-handed. He says we're enchanted. Can you beat that? I'm beginning actually to believe it."

"That's quite a line."

"It's not a line! *He* believes it."

"Jesus!"

"I know, I know."

"Look, when you're that crazy over a guy you hardly know—it's not the guy. It's you."

"I've thought of that, too."

"Well?"

"It's not like that."

"You keep saying that. What is it like?"

"I can't describe it."

"Try for chrissake."

"I just ache all the time."

"Wha'd'ya mean, 'ache'? Like a headache?"

"No. All over."

"Maybe you got the flu."

Katie, who was becoming increasingly regretful at having launched this conversation, now became morose.

"All right, I'm sorry," said Jean.

Katie said nothing.

"Look, Katie, you're a hardheaded girl. Face the facts!"

"I am facing the facts. I ache all the time for a man I barely know. I must be going crazy."

"Those aren't the facts."

"What are the facts?"

"The facts are you've got the hots."

"But I was all right before I saw him."

"What did he look like when you saw him?"

Katie's mouth opened, then shut hard. "It's too ridiculous."

"All the more reason to say it, I'd say, in present circumstances."

Katie then did something else she hated: she blushed crimson to the roots of her hair.

"Wow," said Jean, "must really be something."

"He sort of glowed."

"Jesus!"

"Yeah."

"You have got it bad."

"Yeah."

"All right. Advice time."

"To the shrink."

"Waste of money."

"What then?"

"Go away with him. Take a month. You haven't had a vacation in two years."

"And then he'll stop glowing?"

"You bet he will."

"I can't ask him to leave his wife and children for a month."

"If he's as loony as you, right now, he'll figure out something."

"I don't know."

"What can you lose? Be a hell of a month."

"Suppose it gets worse?"

"Can't. That's against human nature."

"I'm not sure it's against mine."

"Rent a house somewhere. A small house with one bathroom. Nothing could be romantic after that."

At least that made Katie laugh. Then, at the thought of such a month, she grimaced with ecstatic anticipation.

*　　*　　*

Briton was at a bimonthly meeting of the ASCAP board at the new ASCAP building on Lincoln Plaza. He was standing at the window, gazing out, doused in the sun. It was where it should be, setting in the west. Where the sun sinks in the east is not this world.

Standing there, firmly anchored in the here and now, in this world, he saw himself with Katie. They were on the side of a very steep green mountain overlooking the sea. Although their breath frosted, far down, near the water, there were palm trees, and not quite so far, the cottage to which they were returning and some cattle and sheep grazing nearby. For an instant he was actually on that hill—alone. It dissolved.

He felt he was being stared at. He looked up. There were twenty-three faces. He had drifted off in the middle of an important litigation report. Apologetically, he returned to his seat.

"How do you vote, Briton?"

"Pardon me. On what?"

"Are you all right?"

"No. I don't think so." He again got to his feet. "I'm not very well at all. Please excuse me," he said and went directly out the door.

*   *   *

That night, as they were reading in bed after the boys had gone to sleep, Mary Jo asked him the same question.

"I am feeling a little strange," he admitted.

"You haven't turned the page in a half hour."

"I know."

"Are you coming down with the flu?"

"No, it's nothing like that."

She made the face she usually made when the boys said "nothin' " (on being questioned, for example, about the events of a seven-hour school day). Her eyes reverted to her book, but she didn't read. With a sidelong glance she watched. Her husband had gone again—to wherever it was he traveled. Consciously, he wasn't there.

This, she thought, is getting to be a problem.

She could tell when he did it from the rhythm of his body. He left it, and it went slack. Practically lifeless. And this time he was troubled. There was a slight catch to his slowed breathing, a real blank, gone look in his eyes. She wanted to think about this very hard.

It's me, she thought. He's escaping from me. It's been eleven years and he's bored.

Am I boring? she asked herself. So contented I've turned into a cow?

With a determined, lips-pressed-together expression, she got out of bed, went into the bathroom and turned on the light. It was a large room with a sauna, a sunken oversized bath and mirrored walls, all put in by the previous owner. She tossed her nightgown off over her head. She raised her arms and rocked her hips. She threw her whole body abandonedly into an undulating dance, then suddenly stopped and made a "wild things" face in the mirror.

Contented I may be, she thought, but definitely I am not a cow.

She covered herself, returned to the bedroom, and stood, arms akimbo, looking at him from across the room. There he sat, unnoticing. What was worse, while he stared at his book, still not reading, a secret smile played on his lips. Ironically, a warmth for him spread through her. In repose he looked many years younger. He looked just like their elder son.

She sighed audibly, and got back into bed. Am I the right woman for this man? Ballast to his ethereal nature? Earth to his fantasy world? Is this a proper mating? To be ballast was hardly exciting, and exciting was what she wanted to be.

Do I? Do I really? she suddenly asked herself. Contentment reared its head again, but not so unattractively.

It never occurred to her to ask whether he was the right man for her. Not in eleven years. At least not seriously. No more than she would have asked him what these deep fantasies were about.

Tells you something, she concluded. We're not so terribly mismatched.

"Are you happy, Briton?" she asked quite loudly.

The question startled him out of his trance.

"I asked you whether you were happy."

"You never ask that," he said.

He hadn't, she thought, the slightest notion of how much time had just passed.

"I know. Sometimes I think perhaps we're too happy. We live in this great sprawling apartment like a family of bears. Does it get to you—being a papa bear?"

He shook his head and rubbed his eyes.

"What are you reading?"

"A book about Ghengis Khan."

"So naturally you think my life should be filled with dash and plunder," he laughed.

"Naturally. Would you like to get away for a bit, on your own?"

"Of course not! Mary Jo, what are you imagining?"

"Nothin'."

"That's what the boys say."

"Hmm. So they do." She sighed again. "I don't think I'm very exciting."

"Why on earth should you want to be?"

"Well, I guess that's what I think."

"So let's read our books."

"That's fine for me. But you're not reading."

"It's all right. I was thinking."

"So," she said, wriggling with anticipation, "give!"

"A perfectly infantile thought."

"Share it anyway."

"If by some miracle you had the chance to be two people, would you take it?"

"Oh dear. Worse than I thought."

"No it isn't."

"I really like my life!"

"So do I. It's precisely because I like it so much that I think about what it would be like having two of them."

"Maybe you should do something else. It's all so easy for you, Briton. Maybe you should practice law."

He shook his head.

"Take a mistress?"

With a dry laugh, Briton jumped from bed, switched off the lights, dove back again and grabbed her.

"I'm not the least distracted by the dark in this room," she said, "from the subject we are discussing."

"Nor am I."

"Briton," she exclaimed, affecting a little squeal, "what are you doing?"

"What you like."

"Our trouble," said Mary Jo in all seriousness, "is your gargantuan—"

"No anatomical similes, please!"

"I was only going to say—"

"Don't!"

"Appetite? Pride?"

"Shh!"

"Oh dear, oh dear!"

"Baby, it's me!"

"Ghengis!"

"There is a likeness."

"I must be more exciting than I think."

                          *   *   *

At four that morning Briton was wide awake. The apartment was making its usual incorporeal noises. For a long time he had been somewhere
else. He had been in the place he'd imagined at the board meeting that
day. And this was not, he now knew, a dream.

He went to the window and raised the shade. At night the park, with
the lights circling the reservoir and on Central Park West, looked even
more beautiful. Across it, he could pick out Katie's street. He questioned
whether, in this world, she was there.

"Briton," Mary Jo called sleepily. "What is it?"

"Nothin'," he said.

He was trembling with discovery. Yet he could no more explain it than
he could have explained how, at the age of five, he could sit down and play
the piano.

The feeling of disintegration, the switch to left-handedness, the sun on
the wrong side of the world. Katie's world. It was like suddenly seeing the
grid of your city from 10,000 feet in the sky, or the vein of a leaf at 500
magnification. The veils of familiarity, the illusions with which you have
stored these things in your subconscious, are torn away, compelling you to
glimpse, if only for an instant, the true complexity of natural laws which
all things are obeying.

There was, indeed, a mirror world that he, Briton Bell, had entered.
And what about Katie? Was it his world in which that meeting at the
school took place, or hers, or still another to which they both had traveled?

The trick was to go with it, not to think about it overly much. It was
just something he could do.

Holy Jesus!—he felt like opening the window and shouting into the
streets.

Control!

He had wished it; he had willed it. Something wonderful and radiant
lay in his life. It was, after all, powerful enough to have split him.

CHAPTER SIX

Katie stood alone at the bus stop on Central Park West receiving an icy blast in the face. It was 7:15 in the morning. The windchill factor, her radio had informed her, was minus seventeen degrees. In her mood, this weather seemed vindictive. She shivered in an old Navy pea jacket, peered up an avenue devoid of buses or cabs, and felt once again like crying.

It had snowed heavily that night, blanketing the park, and the flakes were still falling and gusting. A ground mist forced from the still-warm earth rose cloud upon cloud amid white-laced branches. The effect was spectral, for the trunks were obscured, and these lacy ghosts themselves dissolved and then reemerged from the mist. Anything this beautiful was to her sharply painful. The tears came and froze on her lids.

The pea jacket she wore had once been her brother's, inherited when he outgrew it in his large-growth year and sported by her through high school and college. To have taken it from her closet after years of neglect was an act of pure regression.

Why can't we have snow days? she brooded, joylessly contemplating a morning of meetings for which she hadn't prepared. The first was with Mike Hoag, USCC's chief patent counsel, who would expect her revisions on a draft of affidavit she had yet to read, for a Patent Office proceeding she knew nothing about. Then there was Art Fowler, her colleague on Advanced Systems, which was her major programming project. Next was a meeting at Union Carbide. . . . She wanted to scream.

This reminded her of Marcel Vermeil. He was at Yale now on a project teaching computers how to think like humans, and she had a meeting with him the next day. The project used USCC equipment. He had called the company and asked for her. She had not seen him since Chicago. It made her angry that she would now meet him when she was again in a desperate state.

As for this day, she saw how it would be—exactly how it had been for the past week and was likely to be for at least two more. All day long she would see Briton's face, and Briton's body. "How can I let anyone do this to me?" she ranted furiously to the cloud-covered heavens.

The buses were coming. In caravan. There were no less than four. How typical! she swore to herself. How goddamn typical of life! I've been freezing to death for twenty minutes—now there are three buses I don't need.

As she boarded the first, she ruefully reflected: love makes you crazy. It makes you see everything as a metaphor of itself!

*   *   *

"Mr. Bell!" shouted Miss March for the third time.

He dully looked up from the desktop.

"There's nothing there! You've been staring at nothing!"

He opened a drawer, put a catalog on the blotter, and stared at that.

With a skin-shriveling gesture of withdrawal, such as is made in the presence of the mad, Miss March uneasily stated, "I should like to go over your schedule of meetings."

"Cancel them," Briton said.

"Cancel . . . ?"

"Yes."

"I can't do that."

"Why not?"

"There's a group coming in ten minutes. I can't reach them. I think they call themselves, The Last Hurrah, or some such thing."

"Ask them to leave."

She pondered this pleasurably, seating herself with a slight rubbing together of knees. "Are you feeling quite all right?"

"Only a bit strange, thank you."

"If you don't mind my saying—"

"But I do."

"You're here, Mr. Bell, but you ain't here!"

"It's probably the flu."

"Then you belong in bed."

"No doubt," said Briton, feeling the irony of this acutely.

When she finally left, Briton picked up the thread of the thought he'd been having: that one of the many peculiarities of his present situation was that a passion so desperate for another human being seemed not to affect his feelings for his wife. Indeed, one seemed to have nothing whatever to do with the other. When with Mary Jo, his thoughts (he thought) were mainly about Mary Jo, their life and their children. He felt no guilt; only contentment. Once out of her presence, passion flared up. He could not work; he could not eat. He could not think about anything but Katie.

He could not even think about what he regarded as the true, incredible cause of his condition. It was as if all existence as he knew it was shattering around him while he clung maniacally to one idea.

In this respect, the deprivation of Katie centered his life, like a tooth pull. He not only probed this center for the novelty of its emptiness, but jabbed it repeatedly for its pain. In the same way, he had started listening to lyrics; had even been moved by what he'd heard.

He lit a cigarette and inhaled. It was the first pack he had bought in ten years.

Two more weeks. Maybe by then this fever would break. Maybe he could never again get into her world. He opened the catalog, read the lyrics to the first song he turned to and felt nausea sweep his body, sweat break out on his brow.

I can't go on like this, he concluded, writing the music to those words in his brain.

*   *   *

Katie drove to New Haven in a rented car. She could easily afford to keep a car of her own but would not do so despite her frequent need for such a vehicle. This had to do, superficially, with her aversion for maps, which made her think of those places—and all those lives being lived in those places—that she had never been to. Such thoughts made her queasy and dizzy. She had a theory for this, that it was connected to her recurring dream, which in turn was derived from her fear of being a changeling. In one of those places, the "real" Katie Dunston might live. Should she ever meet such a person, she feared she might explode, evaporate, or simply cease to exist. So Katie was unusually insular. If she didn't see it, it wasn't there. For essentially the same reasons the back of her hair was often uncombed. She could go nowhere without maps, for she effectively refused to remember where any place was. Buying a car, she perceived, would commit her to a map-reading future.

New Haven was approximately a one-hour drive from her family's home in North Stonington. She had been there, however, only once in her life and now, after finding the exit off I-95, she got lost in the downtown area. A succession of directions finally brought her to the campus and from there to the Payne Whitney Laboratories where, in the parking lot, she plowed into a snowbank half blocking the one open spot.

Marcel himself came down to the security guard's desk, stuck the visitor's badge to her blouse and escorted her back to his office. He had not visibly changed, looking quite natty and medically professorial in a white smock over his double-breasted Glen plaid vest. Until seating himself behind his desk, he had forborne from giving her the sort of close inspection she expected. When he did, she felt like a specimen on a plate.

"I look awful, hunh?"

"I would say, tired . . . worried, perhaps."

"Well . . . got news for you. I'm doin' just great."

"Would you like to talk about it?"

"I thought I came here to help you."

"We can't help each other? Isn't that what we've always done? So. Right, laugh! Would you like to holler?"

"Jesus," she said, cheered immeasurably by this man. "I told you, I'm terrific. Haven't even had the dream for a month."

"So, that's good, no?"

"Sure. That's what I'm saying."

"Why haven't you had the dream?"

"I thought we were going to talk programming?"

"We will, we will. Are you in a rush?"

She shrugged. "How should I know why I haven't had the dream?"

He sat back and mused.

"Unfortunately, you know all my tricks. It is here I would ordinarily gaze upon you in silence until the pressure to speak became unendurable."

"You're just nosy!"

"Correct."

"All right, all right," she laughed. "Something has happened. A man! Okay? There may or may not be a connection."

"You have formed an attachment?"

"Boy! I don't know what to call it."

"An inappropriate attachment?"

"Pretty inappropriate, all right. Wife and two kids?"

"Hmm."

"You betcha, 'hmm.' "

"So . . . you will get yourself out of this?"

"I'm workin' on it."

"This may be progress," he said.

"Yeah."

"So now we talk programming."

"You're a goddamn tease Marcel! Y'know that!"

"Back to the man."

"Programming!"

He spread out his small hands.

"You're out of your depth, right?" Katie glared at him.

"No doubt."

Katie looked down and decided.

"Okay. Programming," she said.

"Whichever you prefer."

"Programming."

"Have you got the day?"

"I've got the month, for what you guys are paying for this system."

"Good. There's another man I want you to meet, a professor of physics, named Hanratty. He runs a project more ambitious than mine. It time-shares the equipment. Before he comes in, I should tell you . . ."

The door eased open. "That he is a prodigiously brilliant scientist," announced a large and shaggy intruder. "A man of parts, difficult to work with and altogether a pain in the ass. I also listen at keyholes," he said pumping Katie's hand. "I find it exerts a certain deterrent on the proclivities of one's colleagues for slander. Hanratty's my name. Tom Hanratty. And you, I suppose, are Miss Dunston."

"Good God," she said, looking up to this black-bearded man of enormous girth and bloated face. "Are you always like this?"

"I'm afraid so, yes. Don't be alarmed. We will deal together quite nicely."

"What makes you think so?"

"Because you are smart." His laugh had a certain growllike quality. "No great powers of deduction there! You're too young for your job without being brainy."

A chair creaked beneath him as he sat down. In fact, his dimensions were barely containable by the room. "Shall we get down to cases?"

"Let's," she said.

"As the British say, at least in their films, I will put you in the picture."

"Where I long to be."

"Don't be obnoxious. These are serious matters."

"The picture."

"Quite. Vermeil," he said, nodding, "looks into the mind and he sees what? Mechanics? Electromechanics? Working parts? Biological equivalent of transistors, capacitors, resistors and the like? And he says, 'We should be able to make one of those! And when we do, and tinker with it, we will have a model on which to experiment . . . before we start messing around with the real thing.'

"My group and I, on the other hand, look into the same mind . . . and what do we see? The parts of the parts. In fact the *particles* and the forces they respond to. And we say, 'There is something very strange here. Each large working part is relatively stable. It looks the same, performs the same function, no matter when you observe it. But the particles of which it is composed are not stable at all. They are not merely changing, they are literally disappearing . . . every minute fraction of a second. And if that were not strange enough . . . for each particle that ceases to exist, a new particle or set of particles appears spontaneously generated and is totally different . . . in weight, mass, all characteristics, from the first. Also each such generation is different from all other generations, so the large working part, the molecule, which always looks the same and performs the same function, is, in reality, always composed of different particles and is constantly changing these.'

"So we say, 'We will never understand anything about the mind—about matter itself—until we learn where these particles go when they perform their acts of disappearance—and where others come from when they spring into this world.'

"That, Miss Dunston, is the problem on which we are working. I should tell you, there are teams of physicists all over the world working on the same problem. So that you may properly enter into the competitive spirit of the venture, I will also tell you that, while we all have extraordinarily powerful computers at our disposal, not one of those teams has yet programmed this equipment to make even a dent in the solution of this problem.

"Now let me ask. Are you familiar with subatomic phenomena?"

"Are you kidding?"

"Good. No one is. I wanted to be sure you were not burdened with the presumption of expertise."

"I took two courses in physics."

"Well, somehow we will overcome that."

"Is this problem related to probability waves?"

"Possibly, possibly," said Hanratty musingly.

"As for my project," said Vermeil, "you, I think, are ideally suited."

"Your computer has gone nuts?"

"No, no," said Vermeil with a kindly smile. "It is simply a very dull fellow. Let me explain.

"For a computer to think like a person, one obvious programming need is to enable the computer to make various associations. For example, if I tell you I have gone into a restaurant, ordered a cup of coffee and paid the check, you will see hundreds of discrete facts and fact possibilities that my words imply, but do not expressly state. You will assume, for one, that I placed my order with a waitress or waiter. You will assume that the coffee arrived and I drank it. You will speculate on whether I added sugar or cream, whether these were brought to me, or on the table, and so on. The computer, of course, can make none of these associations, unless it is programmed to do so. Therefore, for several years, the many people working on this project have been feeding associations into the data bank for almost every conceivable human situation, every concept, every word. We have also developed many subroutines to allow the computer to select appropriate associations from these wide possibilities on the basis of certain probabilities clued by the precise words used."

"Another form of probability waves."

"In a sense, yes."

"You say associations?"

"Let me be more specific. We have broken the language down to a surprisingly few basic concepts. For example, because movement is one, all words having to do with the concept of human movement are clustered. When one of these words is used, the computer associates it with the concept.

"These concepts are also cross-referenced to certain human situations—going to the theater, riding on a bus, taking an interview, getting married—almost everything you can think of—and these, too, are programmed. We call them scenario clusters."

"What about motivations . . . plans . . . goals?"

"Yes, yes. Very good. These too. For years we have been inputting these patterns. And what we have is very useful, for some things. We are very close to being able to write a program in the English language—and have this computer understand it and act upon it. In fact, it is more like a librarian, than merely the library itself. But the librarian is still a robot—it does not literally *think*. It does not *imagine*. It is therefore not teaching us to understand the mind."

"Dull."

"Precisely."

"I think these problems are related. Yours and yours," she said to each professor. "But there's lots more I have to learn."

For the next four hours, in Marcel's office, in the dining room of Silliman College where Hanratty was a resident professor, and then back in the Payne Whitney Lab, they dealt with Katie's questions. As a late-afternoon snow was falling upon New Haven, Katie said, "All right, this is how we go. Simultaneous processing."

"That," said Hanratty, "is what we are doing now."

"And you are doing it wrong."

"You will advise me."

"That's why I'm here."

"I'm listening."

"We are talking about particles within an atom."

"We are indeed."

"There are a finite number of such things."

"At any given moment—presumably."

"All right. Take particle A. Particle A disappears and a variety of other particles or particle groups come into existence, although some are more probable than others."

"Correct."

"So you simultaneously process each such possibility, running the more probable ones with greater frequency."

"Which is what we are doing."

"But that's all you're doing. Look, you are trying to figure out where particle A goes to, and where its replacement comes from—right? The first step has got to be finding out the *cause* for each such event. The sequence you are running will tell you whether that cause comes from within particle A itself or from the events leading up to the creation of particle A. It will not tell you whether the cause is related to the existence of particle B or the steps leading up to its creation. So what you've got to do is simultaneously process the probability waves for every particle in the atom."

"Your machine can do that? That's hundreds of millions of probability waves being processed at once."

"What'y' think we're leasing you—junk?"

"Could you write such a program?"

"Not in a lifetime."

"Then what's the point?"

"The computer can write it."

Hanratty got up, sat on the desk, and made that creak too. He said with narrowing eyes, "What if the cause is none of the foregoing?"

"You mean, if A forms simply out of energy? Is at the threshold between energy and matter?"

"I assume that. I had in mind a different threshold."

"Yeah. I've been thinkin' about that. I guess, then, you'd better polish your speech."

"What speech?" expostulated Marcel.

"I think this young woman has made reference to my acceptance of the Nobel prize. Either that or my speech to a panel of psychiatrists when they are trying to put me away."

"Either one, right," said Katie.

"You will, I trust in due course," said Marcel with acerbity, "tell me what the devil you are talking about."

"Well, well, you don't see it either," said Hanratty.

"Stop, my dear friend, playing games!"

"It's very simple. This not particularly imposing young lady has, I believe, just intuited my favorite working hypothesis—one that no member of my team has yet to conceive."

"Which is?"

"Katie?"

"Look, I'm just taking this stuff on faith. I've got no idea whether the facts you're feeding me are right."

"But if they are?"

She looked apologetically at Marcel. "If what he says is right—if particle-energy combinations simply disappear, don't disintegrate into other such combinations, and if new ones simply come into existence, not formed by the disintegration of the first—then there may be another form of existence, which they are going into and coming out of."

"To wit," said Hanratty, "alternative or parallel worlds. You are familiar with the many-worlds theory of time?"

"I have," said Marcel curtly, "read H. G. Wells."

"A merger into science fiction. One of my avocations," said Hanratty, coloring beneath his beard. "I write such stories, although no one has yet seen fit to publish them. However . . . the theory I referred to has more accredited foundation than the writings of Mr. Wells. It has simply not previously been perceived to relate to the phenomena of subatomic particles."

"For good reason, I should imagine," said Marcel.

"We shall see—if our young friend here can provide the programming."

"I should like," said Marcel, "to bring this discussion back to reality."

"You see the problem?" said Hanratty to Katie. "When an eminent scientist, such as Dr. Vermeil, refuses to accept what logic may dictate—I fear the publication of my findings may well lead to commitment proceedings, rather than to the honors it deserves."

"Unless we aim to keep this girl here over night—"

"Your problem's a cinch," said Katie.

"I'm pleased to hear it."

"What you've got is a right-hemisphered computer."

"Yes, I know that."

"It's very logical and literal—it doesn't perform the function of the left hemisphere of the brain. And it has no subconscious."

"Yes, precisely."

"So that is what we must add, and process it simultaneously with the right."

"Excellent. That I know. And how do we do that?"

"We do that the way the left hemisphere works, of course."

"You can do that?"

"Marcel," exclaimed Katie. "What'y' ask me here for? You know I can do that—up to a point."

Professor Vermeil appeared extremely embarrassed. "I was not sure. I did not wish to take advantage . . ."

"I can do two things. They won't be a total solution, but they'll get you a lot closer than you are now. I can make left-hemisphere associations . . . you give me what you've now got in your data bank—your concepts and scenarios and the rest—and I'll give you the associations.

"The other thing I can do is give you the constant left-hemisphere patterns. At least my patterns. They're not likely to be everyone's."

"It will, as you say, bring us closer."

"There may be somebody else like me."

"Perhaps. I've not met him."

Katie laughed. "Well, if it's a him—especially if it's a him—and you do meet him. . . ." she stopped. Jesus, she thought, the implication of this line of reasoning now dawning. "Say, I've got to get out of here, or I'll never find my way in the dark."

It took her another half hour to leave. There were last-minute things to discuss, particularly arrangements for sending her written materials, and they gave her elaborate directions for getting back on the highway.

Driving home she thought very little about that meeting. It had been a temporary diversion and the beginning of a new project. The matter preoccupying her was again Briton Bell. She wondered whether his mind worked in the same peculiar fashion as hers, and whether that was the source of this outlandish attraction.

*   *   *

Thomas Hanratty dwelled far more on that meeting than did Katie, and on another, small incident that Katie forgot. They had left the laboratory building together, for Hanratty was already late for an evening appointment. He watched her car turn wrong at the end of the driveway, honked her down and pulled alongside. She rolled down her window.

"I've botched it already, hunh? Left turn, not right?"

"Follow me. I'll take you to an alternative entrance to the highway. It's on my way."

Two miles later, he stopped and gave her fresh instructions. "It's just two turns, now. Left and right."

"Got it. Thanks."

He parked and watched. She hesitated at the next corner and turned right. He gave a blast to the horn. She swung around, waving thanks through the window.

The next morning he bearded Marcel in his office. "Did you tell me that that remarkable young woman we met with yesterday was a former patient of yours?"

"Patient and student."

"What was her problem—perpetually losing her way?"

"She does seem," said Marcel with a smile, "to have . . . er . . . difficulties with spatial relations."

"Spatial relations! Last night, when we left . . . she couldn't find her way out of the driveway." He then told his diminutive colleague about the subsequent wrong turn. "She may still be driving around New Haven looking for I-95."

Marcel went to his file cabinet and in a few moments pulled out a reprint of a monograph he had authored.

"You may be interested in this. It's about Katie. Her name is not mentioned, but we discussed it openly in the seminar and I don't think she'd mind."

Hanratty accepted the reprint and read the title out loud. "What precisely do you mean by the term, 'bicameral mind?' "

"Are you familiar with the Penfield experiments?"

"Can't say I am."

"Some years ago a neurological surgeon named Wilder Penfield performed a series of studies with approximately twenty patients who required serious brain surgery. As part of the surgical routine, immediately before removal of the damaged tissue in each patient, various points along the temporal lobe of the left hemisphere were stimulated by a low electrical current. The results were extraordinary. Each patient reported hearing a voice or voices, generally resembling a parent's. The voices called or pleaded or issued commands. The amazing thing about these voices was that they were clearly perceived as *not* being the voice of the patient."

"I should think," said Hanratty, "that some memory had been stirred up. The resemblance to a parent's voice would reinforce that."

"So Penfield initially thought. And he examined those patients with that hypothesis in mind. It turned out the resemblance was merely that. In each case, the patient insisted that there was a difference. The resemblance derived, it seems, from the *feeling* the voice gave the patient—that he or she had been *directed* in some fashion. It was the same sort of feeling one senses in an actual admonitory experience.

"Since Penfield, a number of related experiments have been conducted. The evidence is developing that the left hemisphere of the brain operates independently of the right and performs different cognitive functions. In a left-handed person, as almost all of us are, the right hemisphere is logical, mathematical, analytical. The left is more flamboyant, and not necessarily rational. It is more intuitive, creative—it takes large leaps, sees more forest than trees, is receptive to symbols and is the repository of myths.

"We are not normally conscious, of course, of what our left hemisphere is doing—how it is directing our thoughts and our actions. What Penfield's patients may have been attesting is precisely that sort of direction, made auditory by electrical stimulation.

"Schizophrenics appear to undergo a similar experience. In fact, schizophrenia may itself occur as a result of an electrochemical overstimulation of the left hemisphere of the brain.

"With one notable exception, there are no reported cases among otherwise normal people of clear consciousness of left-hemisphere function—of direct *communication*, as it were, between left and right."

"The exception being, you believe, Miss Dunston."

"Read the monograph."

"Oh, I will! You can be sure of that. But tell me—if she . . . ah . . . has such a condition, is this—what you refer to as 'communication'—going on more or less constantly?"

"No, no. If it were, she'd be a very sick person—in fact, a schizophrenic. And to a schizophrenic, I should emphasize, this form of communication is not useful at all—it is an overload condition. The extraordinary thing about Katie is that she appears to have the power to control it. To *will* it, if that does not startle you too much. And at the risk of losing your attention and respect entirely, let me suggest this may actually be a mutant condition.

"But I believe that ability to control is attributable to some mechanism in both hemispheres of her brain—some transmitting and receiving units, if you will—that do influence her behavior. What I mean is that the left hemisphere function is closer to her consciousness than it may be in others —and it may in some respects *interfere* with the operation of the right.

"You saw an example of that, perhaps, yesterday."

"You refer to her persistent wrong turns?"

"Precisely."

"But you said, my friend, that the left hemisphere sees the forest for the trees!"

"Which is the point. Place Katie at a miniature maze and her responses will be faster than any recorded. So long as she can see the whole of it at once. Her genius at computer programming is doubtless related to this facility. Place her on the streets, and she is practically helpless."

"Extraordinary."

"So I said."

Hanratty, frowning deeply, leafed through the monograph on his lap, and seemed disinclined to end this conversation. "You refer in here," he said, "to a recurring dream."

"From which apparently she still suffers."

"Is that related to her . . . condition?"

"Indirectly. She is half-persuaded she is a changeling, and in a sense she's right. She has not been switched away from her natural parents—the physical resemblances are too plain. But they are very ordinary people with rather dull minds. She has developed some considerable guilt and insecurities on this score. She dreams, then, in a somewhat classic wish-fulfillment mode, of how it would be to live life on their level. The unusual thing about this dream, however, is that it is sequential. She dreams, as it were, in chapters, rarely repeating what she has dreamed before."

"Exactly how unusual is that?"

"It may be entirely unique. I am not aware, Thomas, of anything like it, and I have done substantial research on the subject."

"Is this also related to—what did you call it—her bicameralism?"

"Possibly, possibly. The dream may be a story being told by her left hemisphere. Remember, this is largely a nonvolitional, independent cognitive force."

"Absolutely astounding! Marcel, if you are right about this girl. . . ." He stopped and shook his shaggy head. "Let me ask this. You published this paper . . . you are a reputable scientist . . . what can I say? . . . you are one of the most distinguished psychiatrists in the world. Why wasn't there a stir? . . . publicity? Public reaction?"

"I believe, my friend, you know the answer to that."

"Other explanations for what happened."

"Just so. And mine appears on the surface to be a bit . . . oh . . . incredible? And as you will see . . . in the paper itself . . . I have hedged my bets a good deal more than I have with you this morning. After all, I have no wish to be the subject of the sort of commitment proceedings you referred to yesterday, when you were talking about a project of your own."

Hanratty took the monograph back to his office and read it at once. In the days that followed he was to read it often and to reflect upon it and trouble over it more often still.

He noted that in its report of Katie's dream, specific mention was made

of the Almac's supermarket in Mystic, Connecticut. This is where Katie
dreamed she worked with her mother in a line of checkout counters. He
thought long hours about visiting that place—the place to which he began
to believe the dream might actually refer.

CHAPTER SEVEN

Three days after the third week of enforced absence was a Sunday. They had had two rainy weekends in a row, so on that day Briton took the boys to the park for an hour of touch football and patterns. Neither his mind nor his heart was in it. He was thinking about the passport in his pocket—a passport, he mused, to another world?

On the way home he said, "You fellows go on up, I'll be there soon." He thought he might, despite the drumming of his heart, despite the arrangements made to clear his calendar for a month. Even while taking a cab to Katie's. It is not, he thought, as if I will really have left. On the sidewalk he felt so weak he could barely climb the outdoor steps of her building.

The front door was unlocked. When he knocked on hers, it fell open. There was a strange silence, as if the apartment were holding its breath. He stood at the threshold of the small living room until his eyes adjusted to the near dark. She materialized, elemental. Thank God! he thought.

She was sitting in the lotus position on the floor in the far corner of the room. He saw two thoughts revealed in her face: that, having wished for this so long, she might find she had conjured up an apparition; that by starting, or speaking, she might cause it to disappear.

Slowly she unfurled and glided toward him. He felt a sudden single hard pound of heart muscle.

"You bastard!" she howled.

He commenced to breathe.

She dove her arms inside his coat and dug her fists into the small of his back. Like in a mea culpa, her brow banged three times against his breast.

"You're three days late," she cried.

He kissed her again and again on her mouth and all over her face and ran his hands all over her body—which is what she did to him.

                    *   *   *

An hour later, in her bed, she was still holding on for dear life, but he, emptied of anxiety, was now filled with purpose.

"Come up here so I can see you, and we can talk."

"No talk." Her voice was muffled since her head was beneath the covers and his was not.

He pulled the sheet down. "You've changed your mind."

"I have no mind."

"Katie, Katie, I love you, too."

"It's not the same."

"Of course it is."

"You haven't been delirious," she said.

"What makes you think not?"

"You would have been here."

"I'm here now."

She let out a harrumphing noise, the breath of which he felt against his stomach. "For how long?"

"For as long as you want me."

She shimmied up a bit and poked out her face. "I won't be tricked into letting go."

"No trick."

She scowled with disdain. "In my lucid moments, I see again that this is disastrous." She released him. "I have no pride left. I have lost my cool and my pride and you have stolen them. I am miserable, I am happy. I am totally nuts."

"So am I. We're going away."

"Oh yeah? Where we going?"

"I'm not sure. You have to help me. It's a place that's very green—with palm trees—but it's not the tropics."

She sat up fully in her natural state and shrugged her bony shoulders. "You have failed to rule out at least one-third of the inhabited world."

"Well, in this place, your breath can frost, despite the weather being warm enough for palm trees. And what I see is this particular house— whitewashed stone—on the side of a steep hill, perhaps a mountain, that goes down to the sea. And there are lots of horses and sheep, whose rumps are dyed red or blue, and the hillside is covered with flowers."

From lids half-closed in thought, her eyes grew wide in recognition. "You've been there?"

He hesitated slightly. "No."

Her face was strained. "Wait a minute!"

She leaped out of bed, thoroughly unashamed, which was far more affecting than the strange feeling in his stomach and the crawling of his scalp.

She rummaged in the chest of drawers, upheaving piles of outers and unders, then shot up triumphantly, an album in her hand. On the way back to bed, she stopped. "Go ahead. Look. You see! No pride."

The pictures of her babyhood and adolescence stirred him deeply. He made her stop on these so he could study them at length. Impatiently she wrenched the book back, and turned to what she sought.

"There!"

"Yes . . . that's it." The world was toppling fast.

"Briton, this is Dingle, in Ireland. It's where my family comes from."

"Yes."

"You look sick." So did she.

"No. I'm fine."

"How'd you know about this place?"

He looked sicker.

"Well, there are lots of places like this in Ireland. You must have seen one in a travel ad."

"Very likely," he said without the slightest conviction.

Then he shook himself all over.

"Let's get going," he said.

"What?"

"To Ireland. There!" he said, jabbing the photo.

"Now?"

"Right now."

"Briton, that's absurd, we have no tickets."

"We'll take the next available plane."

"But that could be hours, days!"

"We'll get on, don't worry. Come on." He threw the blankets down. "Move it!" He was laughing now. He could be as free as he liked.

"I have meetings. My work!"

"Take a vacation. Send a wire. Call! There are telephones in Ireland."

Her expression, though still dubious, began to clear. Advanced Systems was now programmed. The Yale jobs were assigned. Mainly what she had for the next several weeks were appointments with customers. Jeanie could fill in. It was, after all, her idea.

"You do have a passport?" he asked, looking for his shoes.

"Of course I have! I travel all the time."

She jumped up. He already had his shorts and pants on. "But I have to pack. So do you. Are you going home?" She sat down again. "Oh God!"

"No packing. We'll just go."

"Just like that?"

"Just like that."

"Briton, for God's sake, what about your wife?"

"Mary Jo'll be fine."

Katie was horror-stricken. "You're not leaving your wife!"

He stopped buttoning his shirt. "No. I couldn't leave her."

She felt a surge of self-loathing. "This is awful! I keep forgetting how really awful this is. Briton, I've got to talk to her."

His face showed pity and despair. "I don't think that's possible."

"Why not?" she groaned. "You don't seem to understand the trouble I'm in."

"Katie, Katie," he said, sitting on the bed, holding her. "It's all right. Truly. Believe me. For now, we have at least a month. Maybe more."

"What did you tell her?"

"A story."

"Oh, Briton. Hateful!"

"No. A nice story. I won't be missed."

"And your children?" Katie cried, tears now brimming into her lashes.

"Nor by them."

"Oh, I am a wretched person!" she said, getting up again, wiping her eyes, pulling a brand-new pair of cotton underpants from her dresser. "Look at me," she said, stepping into their leg holes. "I am actually going to do it."

"I know," he said, trying not to cry himself, bending to unpeel a Bloomingdale's label from her pantied hip.

*   *   *

Thomas Hanratty, shoulders tense, stood alone in his laboratory, clenching and unclenching his fists. There was nothing to indicate a reason for such agitation. It was a Saturday morning, eight days before the scene just described. The room, a former attic of the building, was unlighted except for occasional bursts of sun through the dormer windows. Its elaborate equipment was in shadows. This consisted principally of a Hyzinger chamber, offered commercially only two years before, which combined the principles of emulsion, counter and bubble-chamber physics, so as to permit the tracking of subatomic particles in a vastly miniaturized machine. It still occupied three-quarters of the room, itself the entire length and width of the building, and resembled a giant intestine. Hanratty's eyes, however, were fixed on a far simpler piece of equipment —a man-sized bell jar—that stood in one corner of the room.

On closer inspection, the initial impression of a vacuum chamber was dispelled by the existence of a door having no special sealing. From the top of the jar a chromium tube welded to it extended through the roof. Inside was a switch that did nothing but power a plate in the roof so as to open the tube to the sky. Within the tube various polarizing screens had been affixed at different angles.

At once, Hanratty strode to this apparatus, stepped inside and closed the door behind him. Visibly trembling, he threw the switch. The jar was immediately filled with light of a slightly pink coloration. He stood there for approximately ten seconds. Nothing extraordinary appeared to happen. His brow creased in intense concentration and sweat erupted from the large pores in his skin. For a moment his body seemed to undergo a wave of convulsions, as if the tension in it was rippling out, and then suddenly was suffused in calm.

The Thomas Hanratty who stepped out of the jar was so unnaturally serene as to appear drugged.

*   *   *

At that moment, Professor Thomas Hanratty leapt up from the breakfast table in a small house in Cambridge, Massachusetts. His wife Faith, a handsome but sharp-faced woman, exclaimed at this eccentric start. Only once before had she seen on his face such a look of exhilaration.

Without a word, he gathered the car keys from the hall table, pulled a jacket from the hall closet and got into his car. By the time his wife followed to the door, the car was down the street and heading for the highway to Connecticut.

He made Mystic before noon. On the main street of the small town he parked in front of a stationery store called Gatch's and bought a Friday *Mystic Sun*, the paper not being published on Saturday. He read it in his car.

The front page was largely devoted to a wire service item he had seen covered by network news the night before last. His flesh crept at this identity of events, but even more so at reports of international incidents—a hijacking, a meeting in Europe, a guerrilla war in Peru—of which he had never heard, and the acts and statements of unfamiliar public figures.

On page four was a photograph of Katie Dunston. His excitement was so high he could barely read the print.

The story accompanying the picture was that Katie had returned that day from Armonk, New York, having been presented there with an award from a company named International Business Machines Corporation, which was said to be the largest computer company in the world.

Much of the remainder of the story seemed to be repeating old news. It reported that Miss Dunston, a checkout girl at Almac's, had won the award, which included a prize for $25,000 for submitting a logical schematic for the redesign of cash register computer systems used in supermarkets and department stores. An executive of the company was said to have expressed amazement that Miss Dunston had received no training in computer science and was not even a high school graduate. He was quoted as saying that the design was "inspired, utilizing a simplified, yet highly advanced principal of 'virtual memory' to permit market chains, such as her employer, to keep running totals of inventories, sales and other data, on-line, chainwide, and at price-performance levels not previously attainable."

The article then commented on the equally amazed reactions of Katie's family and noted that Katie's maternal grandmother had settled in Mystic in the year of the great hurricane, having come originally from Dingle, Ireland.

Hanratty marched back into Gatch's, obtained directions to Almac's from the elderly proprietor and got there in under five minutes.

The shopping center housing this supermarket could not be missed, occupying a full eighth of a mile on U.S. 1. It contained the usual assortment of local and regional stores, including a Penney's, a Friendly's, and a Walgreen Drugs.

Almac's itself was nothing short of gigantic. It had no less than a dozen aisles and fourteen checkout counters. But along these, Katie was nowhere to be seen. A dark and pretty young woman at one of the counters, who abruptly confirmed that Katie was not in the store, had no compunction in providing him with directions to her home.

This was a ramshackle two-story house on Long Point Road with three motorcycles parked on its lawn. The only person home was a young man, apparently her brother, who saw nothing odd in this visitation from a self-declared M.I.T. professor and volunteered that Katie had gone walking on Massachaug Point.

It was there he found her.

As suggested by the brother he parked his car in front of the Yacht Club cabanas, climbed the dunes behind the Beach Club and walked onto the beach. The sun was bright enough to take the chill from the air and quite dazzling on the water. He breathed deeply and felt his body fill with the strange sense of being of this world. The Point was a mile-long sandbar, a spit of land that curled into the Sound and sheltered the Massachaug Yacht Basin. At its end lay the ruins of an old fort, and strollers and joggers dotted the long crescent. Several were alone, and any one might be Katie. He kept on walking in the direction of the fort, on the hard surface from which the low tide had retreated.

After 200 yards he picked her out, stopped and waited. As she approached, eyes cast down to the clouds in the shore's mirror, he made his face friendly.

"Miss Dunston?"

Stopping dead in her tracks, she lifted to him a face innocent and shocked, one nearly identical to the memory he brought with him. Though expected, it curled his toes. She seemed about two years older.

"Don't be alarmed," he said soothingly. "My name is Thomas Hanratty. I'm a professor of . . . ah . . . psychology at M.I.T. Your brother told me I might find you here."

"You know my brother?"

How fascinating, he thought. The meekness, the insecurity. What a change in personality the lack of brilliance does create.

"I've just met him. I drove down from Boston this morning for the opportunity to talk to you. I think I can help you."

Her face changed. "Who says I need help?"

"You've had, I've read, a very unsettling experience."

"What're you? A shrink?"

"No, no."

"My mum put you up to this?" Her arms swung out. "Oh boy! You that guy from the New London Hospital?"

"I'm not a doctor, and I've not met your mother. I am a man who has had an experience—two, to be exact—remarkably similar to yours."

She glanced about quickly, reassuring herself that there were people within earshot in case she needed to call for help.

"I traveled here this morning expecting to find something extraordinary about you, and I've not been disappointed."

"Look mister, I'm kind of late."

She tried to walk past him but he snatched at her arm.

"Katie Dunston!" he bellowed, the sound punctuated by the screeching of gulls. "You have been to another world, and so have I!"

She didn't shout but simply stared at him. He released her arm.

"One moment here—then gone! Another place. A different mind, yet conscious of it. Then bang! You're back again. Am I right?"

Her eyes narrowed with suspicion. "Y'talk to Larry? Is that it?"

"Your brother? Not about this."

She scoffed. "My ex-husband."

"My dear young woman. I have never been in this town until this morning. I have never been in this world but once before. The world I've come from may have been the world to which you went."

"Jesus Christ," she said and sat down hard on the sand. He lowered his large body with difficulty beside her.

"I wish to know the . . . ah . . . details of your trip."

"You're crazy!"

"Think so? Then why haven't you run away?"

"Look, I don't know who you are—"

"I've told you. I'm a university professor. My interest is entirely scientific."

"I don't know why I should tell you a damn thing."

"Because you wish to know what happened to you, Katie—and I can explain it."

"Oh yeah? Then you tell me!"

"That's exactly what I'll do. But first I need to know what you . . . ah . . . saw. The sequence of events as you observed them."

She wrapped her arms around her knees. She leaned her head back, face to the sun. Her mouth twisted.

"If it will help," he said, "I will give you my word of honor that I will not tell a soul."

She studied him.

"Cross my heart and hope to die."

This brought a slight smile.

"Assume I'm a nutcake. What have you got to lose?"

Her smile turned frownish.

"Okay." She folded her legs beneath her and bent over, picking up a small stone. "I was home. It was a Wednesday afternoon; I work the night shift on Wednesday. I was watching TV, a soap. All of a sudden, I got to feeling very peculiar." She stopped and frowned again.

"How so?"

"Like . . . I was comin' apart."

"How long did it last?"

She shrugged. "Dunno."

"Then what happened."

She drew a deep breath. "Like you said. Bang!"

"You were somewhere else."

She nodded.

"I was in this room. I must have been dreaming, but it didn't feel like a dream."

"Were you alone in the room?"

"No."

"Who else was there?"

"Lots of people."

"Was it a large room?"

"Pretty large."

"And?"

"Well. . . ." She was having difficulty visualizing the event. "I was . . . giving a lecture."

"About computers?"

"Right." She threw down the stone. "You know how much I know about computers? Nothin'! That's how much I know. And there I was, the ideas just coming to me. Standing in front of a big easel, drawing on this pad, as if I knew what I was doin'."

"Then what happened?"

"I woke up."

"What did that feel like?"

"Like I didn't know I was asleep."

"Were you groggy?"

"Mister—I was just plain scared."

"Why?"

"Are you kidding?"

"What did you do then?"

"I got this notebook, one I had from school. I wrote out everything I could remember and drew all the pictures. Then I went to work. I work at Almac's."

"I know."

"Yeah. The newspaper articles. So you know I work at the checkout counter. Well, the machines we use there are IBM machines. So the next day I put what I had written out in an envelope and mailed it to IBM. I said in the letter, 'Does this make any sense to you?'"

"And, of course, it did."

"You better believe it!"

"Oh, I believe it."

"Yeah, well, plenty don't. They think I stole the idea . . . and I mean, Jesus, who the hell would I've stole it from? . . . and then other people . . . they jus' think I'm some kind of freak or somethin'."

"Neither, of course, is true."

"So what is?" she turned on him. "I've told you everything. Now it's your turn."

"Right." With strenuous effort he lumbered to his feet. "I can't sit like this."

"Mister," she said, scampering after him, "you promised."

"Exactly," he said, waiting for her. "And what I'm going to tell you, you had better promise to keep to yourself, or people will think you're crazier still." He pressed in at the small of his back and looked out to sea. "There are three things you're going to have to try to understand. They are not easy. In fact, no one in your world or mine knows anything about two of them—and no one before has ever put them together." He looked down at her.

"I'm listenin'."

"All right. You see the sun. Sunlight is made up of particles. Subatomic particles. They're called photons. You understand that?"

"Whatever you say."

"Right. You know how fast light travels?"

"Well, I learned it once."

"One hundred eighty-six thousand miles per second. That means that all photons travel at that speed. Correct?"

"I guess."

"Wrong! That's the first thing. There is a photon in light—we shall call it the slow photon—that travels at approximately one one-hundredth of that speed. So that in any beam of light there is a trail of slow photons in its wake. You got that?"

Again, the mouth twist.

"All right, try to stay with me. The second thing is this. All matter and all energy are composed of particles also. What some people understand— they're called physicists—some physicists anyway—is that particles may

be conscious—not conscious like you and me, but close . . . 'instinctive,'
perhaps, is a better word.

"And the third thing you have to understand is that there is a part of
the brain, almost certainly in the left hemisphere, that is conscious of that
particles consciousness.

"Now what does all this mean?" he rhetorically asked, talking no longer
to her, but to the sea. "All particles, like all other matter, exist not only in
the observable three dimensions, but also in the dimension of time. As
such, they are capable of being switched. At least two conditions are
necessary for this switching to occur. The first is the presence in high
concentration of the slow photon in light. That is so because only these
photons can selectively affect the time orientation of other particles without having the mass-energy to blow them straight out of the atom.

"The second condition—are you listening?" he said to her blank,
dumbfounded expression "—the second condition is the power of will.
The right hemisphere of the brain must be able to communicate with the
left—*consciously*. It must be able to communicate with that portion of
the left that is conscious of the consciousness of particles and—this is the
key—will it, absolutely drive it, to create the stimulus which will activate
their receptivity to switching. It is conceivable that the higher that consciousness, and the greater that receptivity, the lower must be the concentration of slow photons.

"Have you understood a single word I've said?"

She looked angry and confused.

"Good. I'm going now, Katie. Don't trouble yourself too much over
this. But there is one more thing I must tell you. In my world there is a
young woman just like you. Except that she is a computer genius. One day
last month—quite likely on a Wednesday afternoon—she traveled from
her world, possibly into yours. And you went elsewhere, through no fault
or act of your own.

"Oh, and another thing. This young woman has a chip on her front
tooth."

He seized her jaw, raising her upper lip with his finger. "Yours, I see, are
perfect. Good-bye, Katie."

Leaving a shocked and troubled young woman on the beach, Thomas
Hanratty clambered back over the dunes and drove the two hours to

Cambridge. He was recognized at the security guard's desk at the MIT building in which he worked and allowed to proceed to his laboratory on the top floor. In the corner stood a man-sized bell jar with a door and a switch and tubes going straight to the ceiling.

CHAPTER EIGHT

Briton and Katie took a cab to the International Arrivals building at Kennedy. Four jumbo jets had just landed, as several others were preparing to depart. The terminal was therefore a bedlam. People parted from luggage, families and homes were looking disoriented, intimidated and adrift.

The lines were appallingly long. But just as Briton and Katie cast about for the shortest, a pert attendant with carrot hair opened up another Aer Lingus counter. Briton was there like a shot, others forming behind him, the imagery in his mind Darwinian.

"Two tickets to Shannon?" she twinkled in an excessively cheerful way. "Hardly likely today."

She played with a computer terminal. With kelly green uniform and lettuce green eyes, she was a veritable salad.

"You *are* in luck!"

"Got 'em?"

"A cancellation a minute ago."

He handed his Air Travel card across the counter.

"You planned this," said Katie.

"Always carry my cards."

"Where are your bags?" asked the attendant, looking past him.

"No bags," said Briton.

She did a double take and laughed. In the din, it still jingled. "Well, you'd better hurry. They're boarding now. Gate twelve."

They ran. It was a Boeing 747, and it took off almost at once. There were two seats in the back by a window through which, minutes later, they watched the sun burn into the eastern sea.

The plane was full, the magazines out, the food inedible. Their actually being on this flight was a marvel so large that neither could quite begin to discuss it. Katie thought: Time . . . a whole month together! All those minutes and seconds, it seemed endless. At least the end seemed inconceivable, like trying to think about being dead.

And then she thought: I hardly know this man, yet I feel as though I've known him forever. She pushed the wonder of that down. It was another goblin at the edge of her happiness, which did not bear thinking of at all. Eventually they raised the armrest, covered themselves with a blanket and dozed on and off most of the way.

They awoke with the sunrise, feeling worse than if they hadn't slept. Yet Katie cast upon Briton a big, beaming, radiant smile that was the most open acknowledgment of possessive love that she had heretofore allowed him to witness. "Our first night together," she said.

The lavatories were odious. Breakfast hurriedly served. They were feeling claustrophobic. But the coast of Ireland soon appeared. It floated in their window. No prior description could have prepared them for this.

On Katie's lips, a silent, "Ohmigod!"

Briton thought, The boys should see this.

Katie said, "It's like Oz."

The plane was hushed, as in a reverent moment.

At the Shannon terminal, disheveled and half-awake, they booked a car at the Avis desk with another of Briton's cards. Outside, waiting for it to be brought round, they saw the land was flat and the buildings functional and commercial, like airports throughout the world; but the air was soft and exhilarating, the hills in the distance, gray-green.

Briton's heart sang. So did Katie's. Ireland! They looked for the little people to come out of the trees.

The car was a white British Ford with a sunroof and an unexpectedly powerful kick. They drove to Limerick with the aid of reasonably clear instructions and a decent map. Staying on the left was problematical, particularly chancy on turns, but it was still early morning and the roads were nearly empty. In place of conversation, they exclaimed at the fields, the flowers, the cows and the sheep. But the city itself was tawdry and drab, and so, a disappointment.

At an American Express office, Briton's card was good for 250 pounds. They bought walking shoes and a large tan canvas suitcase in one store, toiletry items in another, and underwear, bathing suits, socks, stockings and shirts in a third. There was one good store which took cards, where they both bought heavy white Irish sweaters, Katie a tartan kilt, and Briton gray flannel trousers and an oatmeal heather Harris tweed jacket. It was like Christmas, or a new life.

They arrived in Tralee in time for a late lunch at a family hotel, after which jet lag hit them with a vengeance. Katie called Jeanie Scanlon. Briton could hear her excited utterances vibrate in the receiver. But she would take up Katie's appointments. They booked a room upstairs, marched a bit around town, staggered back, toppled into bed and slept almost until the following sunrise.

*   *   *

By 7:30 they were back on the road, zipping along in their white British Ford along a spectacular peninsula shoreline. They were perched high, with sheer, rocky drops to the sea. Each turn unfolded new sights of fields —neatly divided by low stone walls, carpeted in emerald, quilted in butter-cups, arrayed with hawthorn, thatch-roofed cottages, horses grazing, herds of red- or blue-rump-dyed sheep—and below, the sea, sun glancing off it, and the soft air, the quiet, except for the churning sound of their motor. They passed through few villages, saw few faces; and these, mainly school-children or bicyclists or farmers with cattle, stared like still photographs, but were quick to return smiles and then to wave.

They were now oriented to time but not to place. Briton stopped once to leave the car, lean over the wall at the edge of the road, making a memory of what he saw. Katie watched and thought of his family. Her complicity was now equal to his. At Inch, they stopped for tea at a seaside inn, used the rest rooms, and ordered another cup. Katie had gone into an emotional tailspin.

"You're really regretting this, aren't you?" she asked.

"I'm not, no."

Her face was fresh from the drive. It made him smile to see her look so vulnerable and earnest in her newly bought white sweater and tartan kilt.

"Well, you ought to be. I am!"

He dismissed this, deepening his smile, but acknowledged, "Something strange has happened."

"You're telling me!"

He rubbed his chin in reflection. That's precisely what he decided he couldn't do.

He could not, reasonably, say—"Look here! My wish has been granted. I used to be one person, now I think I am two. For me, to be here may be as final as landing in heaven."

One did not believe in such things, much less discuss them.

"We don't have to go to Dingle," Katie was saying. "We could stay right here. It's lovely."

"Come on," he said with a comic face, finishing his tea. "Let's get going."

She frowned without budging. "Briton, why are we going to Dingle?"

"It'll be fun to find that house."

She bit her lip.

"Come. What's wrong?"

"I don't know. This is magic land. I feel I'm in a dream, but the trouble is, it's not even my dream. It's your dream. I'm having . . . it's like hot and cold flashes; joy one moment, the pits, the next."

"It's still the jet lag."

"No, Briton, it's not the jet lag." She pouted and pushed at her cup. "I'm just losing my marbles."

Dingle town was up and bustling as they drove down its principal street. It was a fine morning, the sun warm, the breeze from the sea soft and briny. The traffic, such as it was, consisted mainly of bicycles and horse-drawn carts, driven by men and women in tweeds and scarves; the pedestrians, predominantly tourists, identified by cameras, knapsacks or maps. The street was narrow, on a remarkably steep incline, both sides crammed with brightly painted shop fronts in small two-story stone buildings, centuries-old. There were hand-painted signs for a pork butcher, a greengrocer, a fishmonger, two chemists, several sweater shops and an Irish Tourist Bureau, already crowded with map-bearing, jeans-wearing people. At a black and gold sign reading, "Titus Doyle, Estate Agent," Briton pulled up to the curb. He immediately felt a strong sense of inevitability, of premonition. A small rail of a man, presumably the proprietor, stood in the open doorway, as if he had been expecting them for some time.

Mr. Doyle, for it was he, had washed blue eyes, a quizzical expression and a funny narrow head, its length and narrowness accentuated by his hair, which was closely shorn at the sides. He watched Briton decamp from the car, stretch, then tug at the young woman's arm to unfix her gaze from the dashboard. When Briton performed the introductions (Katie, by first name), a blush spread from Mr. Doyle's flat cheeks to his pointy ears and into his scalp like a flame. One could imagine him being the genetic residuum of intermatings between leprechauns and humans.

"You'd be Americans," he opined, bringing them into his office. "And you'd be wanting to rent?"

"For a month, yes," said Briton, for which Katie gave him a look of outright astonishment.

Mr. Doyle plunked behind a small battered desk, while they took seats opposite, and almost immediately began to fidget. Then, glancing from one to another, he suddenly and unexpectedly made his eyes flash. "Of course you'd be wanting a view of the bay."

"Of course."

"I have one such house. Like to see it?"

Briton felt as if he were swimming in current. He said, "Yes," and Katie, "No," in unison.

Mr. Doyle's blush seemed perpetual, varying only in degree. "Until now, I thought you two might be on honeymoon."

"No" (Katie). "We are" (Briton). Confusion and embarrassment reigned.

There was a pause, a watershed moment, in which stammering might have covered retreat. Katie looked as if she were about to acknowledge the false credentials they bore. But Briton interceded. "We have come a long way, Mr. Doyle, to see that house."

"Have you, indeed?" It seemed there was a trace of asperity to this little man.

"From New York City," Briton added irrelevantly.

But it seemed to satisfy Mr. Doyle. "Drove right here from the airport, did you?"

"Directly."

"Well," he beamed in high color, "you'll not find the equal of this house in Ireland!" He meant, this world.

*   *   *

Driving from Dingle, they pursued the agent on the winding coast road, every turn of which seemed designed for disaster.

"Look out!"

"I have it."

"Jesus, Briton!"

"I know."

"This isn't exactly I-95."

"I'm trying to keep up."

"He'll slow down, if you will."

So he did.

They both visualized what they might find. They visualized the photograph.

"I don't believe in coincidences," Katie pronounced.

"There aren't that many houses," Briton suggested.

"It's probably in ruins by now. That picture is ancient."

"So's this country."

"Or a high-rise."

Briton smiled. "Seen many of those, have you?"

"Let's turn back." She was serious.

"It would be rude."

"I don't care! Oh, Briton, I don't like this!"

Mr. Doyle's car, an old gray DKW, had slowed ahead and was grinding up an impossibly steep driveway.

"Briton, really. Let's keep going. I'm asking nicely."

"It's the house! It is! It's the same one."

"I can see that, damnit!"

He followed, shifting into first, gunning the engine, pulling in alongside
Mr. Doyle's empty car parked on a level place to the right of the house.
He yanked the emergency brake up hard. Katie sat as if frozen.

"We're here," he announced superfluously.

She was rigid, lips set, but she was peeking sidelong at the house.

"Looks charming," he said.

"Briton, did you set this up?"

"What?"

"You heard me. What'd you do? Sneak into my drawer? Find that
photo? I'll bet you did. And call that fellow. That fakir, that agent. This
isn't funny, Briton! This is damn serious business, mucking around in
somebody's ancestry."

At first bewildered, he started to laugh. "Katie, I didn't. I didn't even
know where it was."

"Then why aren't you spooked? You're acting much too calmly. You
drove right up to this man's office."

"Why is this something to be spooked about?"

"Holy Mary! I've been looking at that damn photo since I was a kid.
How the hell do you think I feel?"

"Overly excited. It's just a house."

"Is that what you think?"

"Let's look at it."

"Briton, why are we here? What is it? You're frightening me."

"Katie, please. I will tell you. Nothing bad. He's waiting."

Mr. Doyle stood on the porch like a wiry piper. If he was amused by
their disparate expressions, his face showed only a willingness to wait.

"As you can see," he observed, "the view, and air up here, are unex-
celled."

They could see, smell, feel, although to do so made them giddy. The air
was sweet with the smell of warm grass laced with sea salt and hawthorn.
As for the view, they felt they were flying. Their carpet was the sharply
tilted, vibrant green velour of the mountain, sectioned into small, flower-
filled pastures by a checkerwork of low stone walls. Almost straight down,
about a quarter of a mile, was Dingle Bay moving in a million coruscating
ripples to the sea. Across the bay was the Ring of Kerry, mountains of
purple and green, ringed, themselves, in ground fog, so that their peaks

looked, too, as if they were hovering. And above it all was the largest cloudless sky imaginable. Briton had seen it before, and it made his skin bump to be there. For Katie, it was like a prior incarnation.

Doyle gave them time to drink it in. Finally he said, "Should we look inside, then?"

The small rooms were cluttered and stale, but Doyle went around with his quick hands opening windows, turning up shades, and it brightened and became cheerier. The front parlor resembled an antique store, so many unassociated pieces had been collected, including a bulging over-sized sofa, two large wing chairs, an ancient foot locker used as a coffee table, a bombé commode, end tables, side chairs, and to Briton's delight, an upright piano. To the rear of the parlor was a dark bedroom whose windows were shaded by the steep rise of the mountain behind the house. The kitchen had the feeling of a cave, the walls and ceiling being slightly rounded, though it was larger than the parlor, extending the full width of the house, with a pump at the sink, soapwood counters, a real, if old-fashioned, refrigerator, and a Franklin stove (or the Irish equivalent) in the middle of the room.

Katie criticized everything. The living room was cluttered, the kitchen a pit. She pushed the pump and nothing came out, until Doyle pushed it further. She stood aghast at the stove.

"It works," said Doyle. "There is also electricity and plumbing. No central heating, I'm afraid, but all the fireplaces are in good working order, and there's plenty of kindling about."

"We'd freeze to death," she concluded. "How could people live here?"

"Very comfortably," laughed Doyle, "for many years. One family lived here for generations. It was sold to another about forty years ago and is now owned by an estate."

He guided them upstairs, all the while opening windows. In the master bedroom, he whacked the mattress of the big double bed. He was rather given to dramatic gestures. "Very little dust problem here," he noted. The room was as large as the kitchen, though it was over the parlor, and the view from its front windows was splendid.

"What are those?" asked Katie grudgingly, looking out the rear. When she turned, Doyle raised his eyebrows and flashed his eyes in that same startling expression.

"Those, ma'am, are a real feature of this house. Authentic beehive huts. There are three more of 'em further up the mountain. Know what they are, then?"

"Are you serious? Beehive huts are thousands of years old. On this land?"

"Yes ma'am. Of course before you get too excited, they're all over this area. Woman who lived here until recently put out a sign, in front of the driveway. Used to charge fivepence per head for people to park and take a look at the huts. Very popular with the tourists."

As they went down again, and outside to take in the full view, Doyle kept up a continuing commentary. "Plenty of dishes, utensils, bedding and the like. This time of the year, a fire at night should be ample. All the walls, as you can see, have been newly whitewashed inside and out." And so forth.

They stood on the porch, looking once more at the bay. Mr. Doyle coughed his dry cough. Briton said, "We'll take it."

Katie lowered her eyes.

Doyle said. "Two hundred a month. That's pounds of course."

"We'll pay in advance. Check all right?"

"You've brought your checkbook too?" said Katie.

He arranged to sign the lease that afternoon in Doyle's office and then give him the check, but Doyle handed the key over immediately.

As his car pulled away, Katie walked straight up the hill above the house. Briton watched her anxiously for a moment, then followed. They sat on the grass, Katie hugging her knees, while three cows grazed nearby in high stupor.

"You're angry," he said.

She frowned and said nothing.

"It's very lovely," he ventured.

"I can damn well see it's lovely."

"So?"

"It's not real. This hill, this view, this time. It's not real time."

"What's that mean?"

"A computer expression, not intelligible to you. Damnit, my grand-mother may have been born in that house."

"I expect she was."

"Well! This is all coincidence then?"

"That it was the one house he had, yes. But, after all, we came here to find it."

"You did! That's not what I came for. I don't know what I came for. I tell you Briton, I'm very mixed up. I think you have driven me too far. Not only do you have me acting absolutely gaga in my present life, but now you are trying to take over my past. I mean, when you think about it, it's fiendish." She turned to him with surprise.

"You," he said with a straight face, "have the same effect on me."

"Well, it's not natural."

"I agree."

"So what is it?"

"You are an especially lovable person."

"The hell I am. I am prickly and spiky and not very nice. No one could possibly love me the way you say you do."

"You're fishing."

"Oh Christ! I am. That's exactly right. You see the problem!"

"I have for some time now been familiar with the problem."

"And, shit, let's face it Briton, you're very sweet, and good-looking and all that, but you're not superhuman. You don't ordinarily go around driving women wild. I mean—do you? I mean, you're really kind of old-fashioned."

"Right."

"So what's going on?" she asked desperately. "Do you realize, before we got on that plane, I'd seen you only three times in my life?"

"Katie, let's let it be."

"I hate enigma!"

"Well, so do I."

"So think!"

"I have."

"And? And?"

"I'll let you know when I'm sure."

"You mean you have a theory?"

"Nothing so refined."

"Well! What is it? You think I need a doctoral dissertation? And—you did—you said in the car, there was something you would tell me later."

"It's too inchoate to explain."

"Bull!"

"It really is."

"Briton!"

He shook his head and laughed.

"I'm warning you! If you don't tell me your theory, I'll walk off this storybook hill, take the next bus to Shannon, and the next plane to New York."

He said the first thing that came into his head. "I think we're connected."

She viewed this with disdain. "That's it? That's what you couldn't tell me?"

"That's it."

"What'y' mean, 'connected'? We've been 'connected' good and proper. Four times to be precise."

"I don't mean that."

"So I gather."

He shrugged. "Katie, how do you do your job? How did the people at USCC know you could do it better than the several hundred people who started at the same time you did?"

She became fascinated with a clump of grass within reach of her left hand. She yanked at it. "It's instinctive, I feel something . . . see a picture . . . about what a system should be. How simple it can be."

"That's how I do my job. When the music is right, I know it. I don't have any question about it." He thought for a moment. "At college, you will be surprised to learn, I majored in mathematics. It was a very easy subject for me. I got very high grades on exams without going to class. And music is the expression in sound of mathematical relationships.

"It's a knack. A sense other people don't have. It's probably genetic. What's happened to us has something to do with that."

She was silent for quite a few moments.

"Well?" he asked.

"Briton," she said, stopped, took a very deep breath. "Have you ever heard the term, 'the bicameral mind?' "

"Yes, of course. I've read the Jaynes book."

"Jaynes? Who's Jaynes?"

"Julian Jaynes. A professor at Princeton. He wrote a book some years ago about the bicameral mind and the nature of consciousness."

"I've never heard of such a book."

"You were probably too young to have noticed it."

She looked at him very sharply. "If there was such a book, I would know about it. I am very interested in that subject."

"We can probably get it in some library here."

"Listen to me! When I was at Chicago, I went to a psychiatrist, a man named Marcel Vermeil. He believes that I'm a strongly bicameral person."

"You know Vermeil?"

"Briton, I'm telling you I've been through analysis with him. Three years. The whole thing. I'm a very strange character. Practically a freak." She stopped and gaped. "Where the hell did you hear about Vermeil?"

"The MIT project. Programming computers to think."

Her mouth fell open. "Marcel's at Yale."

"Is he? You would know better than I."

"Look, I just saw him there two weeks ago. I'm working on his damn project. I should be there now."

"I'm glad you're not."

"Jesus Christ, Briton. Where'd you learn about an MIT project? Where'd you hear about this project at all?"

"Some magazine or something. I probably got it wrong."

She stared for some time at the cows. "Well . . . let me tell you . . . your theory's probably right. It so happens I had arrived at the same theory. I think we're both bicameral."

"Quite plausible."

"I do so love to be humored."

"It's just a label, Katie."

"It *means*," she stressed with narrowing eyes, "the ability to communicate directly—at least sometimes—with the left hemisphere of the brain. Which in your case makes sense, because the left hemisphere is where we react to music."

"You say . . . the *left* hemisphere?"

"Well, for left-handed people. And since almost everybody is left-handed. . . ."

He raised himself upward, gaining torpid looks from the cows. It was one thing to entertain a theory this bizarre, quite another to confront it this blatantly.

"Briton, where you going?" She also got up, brushing her skirt. "We may have come upon a very exciting possibility."

"Let's think about it. In the meantime we have work to do."

She gazed at the house, as if it were an afterthought. "It's too expensive."

"As a matter of fact, it's dirt cheap."

"Two hundred pounds for my own house?"

"It's not," he said gently, "yours any longer. And we can't be absolutely certain it's the same one."

"Don't you think I know my own house?" She slapped her arms to her sides, and began descending the hill. "And I didn't bring *my* checkbook."

"I'll trust you for half."

"He says go to Ireland," she muttered, "and I go to Ireland. He says take this house, and I take the house. He says we're enchanted, and I'm beginning to believe even that. None of this is characteristic of me!"

Briton hugged her, and she shrugged away. Then she slapped her arms again and hugged him back. Walking to the house, their arms entwined, she sulkily hung her head. His was awhirl. He was as mystified as she but trying, at some cost, not to show it. It was 10:45 in the morning, and the sun was still rising from the west. He would just have to stop thinking about this.

*   *   *

This time they inspected the house more thoroughly, Katie approaching everything as if it were alive. "Do you realize I may have been conceived, derivatively, in that bed?" He did. "Look at this bed linen. It's actually linen, for chrissake. I'll never be able to sleep on that." He thought they could. "These pots and pans are ancient. It will take us a week to scrub them." He offered to find a maid.

"No maids," she decreed.

"Then I'll do them myself."

"Oh sure. Did you ever clean a pot in your life?"

"You need experience to clean pots?"

"Damn right. Just like you rich kids not to know that. How'd I ever get mixed up with you?"

"I've told you."

"Oh right!"

They made a pass at cleaning the kitchen, gathered all the bedclothes and towels, and drove into Dingle for lunch. While they ate it, at an indifferent tea and sandwiches place, and then shopped for food, wine, kindling, cleaning powders and utensils, their linens went through wash and dry at a laundromat near the harbor. Upon retrieving them, they spent some time gazing at the boats, then executed the necessary exchange, check for lease, with a fully prepared, efficient elderly woman in Mr. Doyle's office ("himself" being out "showing"), before returning home.

Though tired, they attacked the master bedroom and the living room with their newly purchased implements, until the place seemed tolerably inhabitable and their sense of proprietorship, instilled.

Eight o'clock, still broad daylight, found Briton stretched out on the sofa and Katie, bedraggled, her dust rag dangling to the floor, sitting on the antique trunk large enough to be a coffee table, for which, precisely, it was used.

"I'm too tired to make dinner," she said. "But I'll eat it, if you do."

"Give me an hour."

"In an hour, I'll be asleep." Then idly, "I wonder what's in this trunk."

"Wills," he said.

"You've opened it?" She tried, but it was locked. "How do you know it's wills?"

"Large chests in old houses always have wills."

A strange light came into her eyes. "Let's find the key."

"Tomorrow."

"Let's jimmy it."

"You didn't read the lease."

"It's normal wear and tear!"

"It is, hunh? More like breaking and entering."

At her deflated look, he staggered off the couch. "All right. You win! I'll make it. Dinner for two."

*   *   *

Later that night, after it had finally gotten dark, they huddled in the enormous bed beneath two quilts and as many blankets. Having consumed nearly two bottles of pretty good Châteauneuf du Pape they were still slightly drunk. After dinner, Briton had played the piano which, since it was dreadfully out of tune, sounded particularly honky-tonk. "How *can* you do that?" she had marveled. Briton, still playing, had given a look that said, "bicameralism," at which she blew up her cheeks. They had not made a fire, but they had just made love. "Fifth time," Katie murmured.

"Does your keeping count have something to do with your being a mathematician?"

"Naturally."

"Do you have a rating system as well?"

She shook her head and grinned into the pillow. "If I did, you'd go off the scale, Briton."

"In which direction?"

"Uh-oh!" She turned around and tried to see his face. "You're angry."

"Of course I'm not," he said, keeping his smile hidden.

"Your voice," she declared, "has an edge."

"All the better to cut you with."

"Oh Briton, don't mess with me when I'm drunk."

"I just did."

"I don't mean that. That you can do all you like. When I'm drunk I get very sentimental. I say soppy things."

"Good."

"Then you'll use them against me."

"Even better."

"I offended you, didn't I, this morning? On the hill?"

Silence.

"I didn't mean it, you see. You're not actually old-fashioned. And I'm sure you drive women wild. You do me. Is that all right, now? Briton?"

With a muffled laugh he gathered her back in and held her. What had he ever done, he thought, to deserve this?

Much later he thought, when he could not get to sleep, and how much longer will it last?

CHAPTER NINE

Katie dreamed she'd been abandoned. It was a murky, twisting, sinuous dream, cleverly wrenching the same denouement from different casts and times and places. At its recurrence at dawn she shot upright with a cry on her lips.

It was true; the room was empty.

She thrashed about for her nightgown, found it balled at the foot of the bed, tried to throw it on going down the stairs, and nearly killed herself.

"Briton!" she cried, one hand thrust through a sleeve and clutching the bannister, white-knuckled.

Not in the kitchen, not in the parlor, not in the house.

She ran outside, barefooted.

"Briton!"

Turning west, her eyes caught the sun.

He was silhouetted in it, a statue poised without breathing on the path leading up the hill.

She gulped down a mouthful of rage and humiliation. "Goddamnit!" She started to run.

Upon him, she was pale, febrile and in a sweat. "Goddamnit, Briton!" she beat his chest with her still-clenched fists.

"What?" Stirring dazedly from immobility, he smothered the assault. "I was looking around."

"You were gone!"

"I was here."

"Don't you ever do that to me again!"

He tried unsuccessfully to joke her out of it at breakfast, even rendering an omelet for two. "Not funny, damnit," she said poking at the food, her anger banking down to the sulks. He managed at least to induce her into clothes and then an expedition to the beach, but all the while she smoldered.

Across the road they took a trail which led latterly down the hillside through kissing gates in the walls, past horses and sheep herds, into fields of buttercups and daisies, through a thicket of pines, into a grove of palms, and from there to the shore. The beach was flat and wide, its sand fine and rippled hard, the bay water slapping with just enough force to indicate its potential for havoc. The air was salty enough to have seasoned their eggs. High above was the house, looking tiny. The sun, when not screened by puffs of clouds, turned the wet sand into a mirror.

In mid-step Katie stopped, shook her head and said quietly, "This is sick!"

It stunned him. Even on an empty beach. "Not again, Katie."

"You're out of my sight, and I break up. I absolutely go into a panic. In an ordinary relationship . . . ?" Her lips pursed and turned down. "You enjoy the absences as much as the presences. Right?"

"Okay."

"Well! We're not like that, are we!"

". . . Not yet."

"Ah! So that's where we're heading. Maybe you're there already."

He took a deep breath. "No," he said electing to lose on this score.

It was the right answer. Though partially mollified, she pulled free and kept walking.

They went another quarter mile without speaking. Then Katie said, as if in the middle of a conversation going on in her head, "And what's going to happen afterwards?"

They heard the water lap.

"After what?"

"Don't be stupid. We can't live in this fairy tale forever."

While talking, they both glimpsed in the distance, coming toward them, a solitary, very large man. He seemed to waddle. It was not the shimmering heat, but a definite waddle. Within fifty yards he stopped, exclaimed and started to jog. Right at them.

He burst upon them with a cheery look, expectant of recognition, on his bearded, moonish, heavily perspiring face. He yanked his soft tweed hat off in delight. He did a dance step—heavily, for he was enormously fat —clicking his heels in midair.

Katie, her heart sinking with recognition, exclaimed, "Hanratty! What're you doing here?"

"Vacationing. Just vacationing. How delightful to see you both."

"You know Briton?"

"Of course. For years."

"I beg your pardon," said Briton Bell.

Katie glanced from one to the other. Briton looked as if he'd been struck.

"I'm sorry," he stammered, "but I don't think I know you."

The man seemed uncertain, then roared. "Oh my dear fellow! You will doubtless? . . . when you have concluded this joke? . . ."

"I really am dreadfully sorry. . . ." Briton was absolutely white. "It must be some mistake."

The man's eyes, which had been gleaming, turned dark. He observed them shrewdly, one at a time. "Of course. My error. Sorry. Don't let it disturb your day." He then smiled, doffed his cap and waddled purposefully back where he came from.

Katie gasped. "He knew your name."

"So it seems."

"Briton!" She peered at the receding figure. "I think you know that man!"

"I swear I don't. I have never seen him before in my life."

"How'd he know your name?" she insisted.

"I can't imagine. It could be anything. He might have heard it in town. He may be crazy. Who knows?"

She started walking back toward the house.

"Katie, believe me," he said, catching up. "I really don't know who the hell he is. That was a very creepy experience."

"You know what I think, don't you?"

"Well you're wrong!"

"Am I?"

"Yes! I'm hiding nothing. If I'd known that man, I would have . . ."

"What?"

"Well . . . you seemed to know him . . . I was going to say I'd have . . ."

"What, introduced me?"

"Yes."

"As what?"

"As my dearest love."

"I'll bet."

"And you'd lose."

"Yeah. Some chance."

Climbing the hill, Briton said, trailing behind, "Well, who is that man?"

"A professor at Yale." She turned back and said sharply, "Where Marcel Vermeil is."

As they trudged up the driveway, they saw Doyle's car, then Doyle himself on the porch, in medium blush for his intrusion.

"Morning, Mr. Bell, morning, ma'am." He said that he'd just thought he'd drive out to see how they were getting on.

They brought him into the newly cleaned kitchen and boiled water for tea. As Katie selected cups and saucers from the cupboard, Doyle laid two rings of keys on the table. "They come with the house, ma'am. Don't know what they're for—probably closets and cabinets and such. Meant to give them to you yesterday."

Her eyes lit up. All thoughts of Hanratty and tea were forgotten. Briton, left with the latter, brought a tray into the living room, and Katie, having snatched both rings, had the chest overturned and was plowing through a huge stack of papers. Briton, sipping his tea, idly turned over old bills, policies, letters and magazines, then picked out a backed document with a faded red ribbon sewn into its spine.

"This is it," he said and started to read.

The testator was Sheelagh McLanahan. The beneficiary, Mary McLanahan Dunston.

Katie tore it from his hands.

"A relation of Mrs. Bell's, is it?" asked Doyle, all eyes over his teacup at Katie's white-faced perusal and the trembling of the papers she was trying to read.

This was doubly awkward.

"Mr. Doyle, we should tell you. Katie's name is Dunston. We're not married."

Doyle's cheeks ignited, and the conflagration spread up his scalp. "If you think, Mr. Bell, I've a judgment on that—" his flash of eyes helped here—"well, you're wrong." He put his cup down and thrust his hands in his pockets. "You know, sir, we're not quite so backward in Ireland as you might have been led to believe."

"You're a gracious man, Mr. Doyle."

"Not a bit of it."

Briton then explained that they'd just found a will from Katie's great-grandmother which confirmed what they'd suspected right along. Doyle allowed that, as youths, he and his wife had known Mrs. Dunston as Miss McLanahan, before she'd emigrated to the United States. She had been the music teacher in their school and had been studying to be a concert pianist. "A genuine local talent. She gave concerts here, pieces she composed. But then, you'd know about that."

Katie hadn't a clue.

He then surprised them with an invitation to dinner the following night, which he declared was another purpose of his visit. Briton accepted for both. Throughout it all, Katie looked fierce and said nothing. Doyle left, after having arranged to collect them at 6:30 the next evening. Katie then said without a trace of humor, "This, Briton, is getting out of hand."

"Let's look at the huts," he suggested.

"Why the hell should we look at the huts? I want to discuss this."

"It will give us perspective."

"I have all the perspective I need right here."

"Do you?"

"Yes!"

"Then stay," he said, going outside.

"You're a goddamn bully!" she said, nevertheless following.

Furious, she skulked behind him past the first two huts, came astride at the two above those, and stopped complaining when they got to the fifth, the largest of the beehive encampment. It was a knockout, a giant igloo of flat stones.

They crept in, for the entry tunnel was low, and sat, backs to the wall, gazing up through the circular hole in the ceiling. It was a perfect half-sphere, except for the lopped-off roof, closing them off from the world, with an outlet to the heavens.

"Feel it?"

"What?" she asked half-cowed.

"The weight of three thousand years."

"Oh shit," said Katie. She simply could not shake her feelings of oppression, and did not want to play.

"There are places in the universe," Briton expounded, "where what was happening here three thousand years ago is, in their time system, happening now."

"What's happening to us? That's what I'd like to know."

"Nothing bad."

"That's what *you* say! Oh Briton, who are you? What are we doing here? What happened to you this morning?"

He put his finger to his lips. "Look through the roof."

"The hell with the goddamn roof."

"Shush. Concentrate."

She bit her lip and folded her arms. She dropped her chin to her chest. She was, despite everything, still quite totally consumed with love for him. Had he told her to walk through the wall, she would have tried it.

It was strange. Strange! He was a million miles—or years—away. She had no more explanation than she had a month before, and the facts had grown more complicated. Still, she thought, when this is over it's going to hurt me a lot.

The sun popped out, beat down on the roof, and cast a spotlight on the ground before them. It spread to cover them, producing not warmth, but shivers. She felt as if she were freezing and melting at the same time. Miraculously, her oppression lifted; every muscle pleasurably uncoiled. What a marvelous sensation, she thought. She was drowsy; she felt free.

Free of my ego, she thought with sudden inspiration. It was as though that part of her which depended upon being smart—on being, for example, a computer architect—was simply melting away.

Slowly she got up and stood within the center of the sun spot in the ground. She was not quite sure at first what she would do.

She started taking off her clothes. When she was bare, she did a brief instinctive dance. None of this was completely under her control, nor did Briton seem to take especial notice.

She undressed him like a child. She felt now, somehow, he would always be hers; she felt ageless, and this place a part of her.

Somewhere in the process, he came back. "You see!" he said.

"I think so," she said.

"It's possible."

"Yes."

It was like making love at one remove, watching yourself do it, with someone also out of sync with time.

Weird, but definitely exciting. They then slept an hour in each other's arms.

*   *   *

"I've never slept so much," said Katie, forking an enormous oyster from its pan of garlic cream sauce. "And we'll both catch colds."

They were lunching in Dingle's three-star restaurant, a small seafood establishment named Doyle's. "The remotest relation," Titus had said, recommending it, the blush rising, as he had left their driveway.

"Have you? Slept this much? This is brilliant!" she said, mouth full.

Briton mumbled an unhumorous pun on the word "sleep." She wanted to talk about it; he did not. This dragged them both into long, separate thoughts, upon which only each excellent course intruded.

To arrest any postprandial plunge, Briton cashed a large check on the Bank of Ireland, on the security of his Visa card. They thereupon embarked on another spree of shopping: at the clothing shops, the pork butcher, the fishmonger, the greengrocer and the wine merchant, to which, this time, Katie made no objection. "Since none of this," said Katie, touching Briton's card wallet, "is real."

When they arrived home at about 4:30 and unpacked the haul from the car, Katie said, despairingly, "I can't believe it. I need more . . . sleep."

"Meaning what?"

Her face fell further. "Meaning just what you think."

CHAPTER TEN

The next day it rained and it was cold. They spent the morning opening flues, lighting fires and scouring all the dishes and utensils in the kitchen. They also lined the kitchen drawers, beat cushions on the porch and took down all the draperies and curtains for cleaning.

Near noon they took a break, sprawled out in the living room with their respective cups of tea.

"You didn't know you'd fallen into the clutches of a drudge," said Katie ventilating her blue cotton workshirt, for now the house was warm.

"You are a bit compulsive."

"If we are going to live in this house, Briton, we are going to make it a fit place in which to live."

"We have to do this every day?"

She treated him to a semi-pleasant smirk.

"I think we should get a maid," he said. At her frown of displeasure, he undauntedly added, "We are, after all, on vacation."

"No maids."

"It would help the local economy."

"*No maids!*"

"All right," he laughed. "But why? We can surely afford one."

"You can afford one."

"We can. Don't you hire someone to clean your apartment in New York?"

"That's different."

"Okay. Why?"

"Damnit!" she said, rattling her cup down in the saucer. "I *like* cleaning this place with you!"

Oh God, he thought, stomach sinking.

Her eyes were hurt now and angry. "Pathetic, hunh? Playing house! Is that what you think?"

"I'm sorry. I was stupid. I like it, too."

"Saying it now doesn't count!"

"Katie, it's not so bad—admitting sentiments like these. I'm not going to '*use*' it. I can't. I'm in the same boat."

"I hate it, I hate it! Go on. Hire a maid. Today! At once!"

"I wouldn't dream of it."

"Well, you'd better, Briton. I'm not going to lift another goddamn mop."

*   *   *

Briton went to town alone. Not to hire a maid. That argument, he hoped, was behind them. It was his intention, the next day, simply to start washing the dishes or making the beds or mopping the floor. Katie would then mutter some crack about his incompetency, snatch dish or mop from his hands and direct him to do something useful. That at least was the plan.

What he went to town for was to get away by himself for a couple of hours. He would deliver the draperies and curtains to the cleaners, pick up more wood, buy some shirts and possibly ties to replenish his meager collection. Katie, as he expected, chose to stay at home. They had been in each other's pocket constantly for four days.

He missed her immediately upon turning out of the driveway. The rain had stopped, the sun now shone, the blacktop glistened. He saw her face in the reflection, felt her presence in the front seat. She was, of course, right; this was not a natural relationship. But he couldn't think about that or, for that matter, about Mary Jo and the boys. Literally he could not focus on these sources of wonder or sadness; his mind would not work when he did. Thoughts of Katie were preemptive.

He made his first stop at the cleaners, then drove to McCormack's Hardware and Lumber on the northern outskirts of town. It was there he had the first of two strange encounters. This one was to disturb him more on later reflection, but it was odd enough when it occurred.

Two old men, very like in appearance, were seated at a potbellied stove in the middle of the store. One's face was especially craggy and gaunt, the other's more bloated, his nose spread out in soft, porous, red excrescences. The clothes of both—jackets, flannel shirts, sweaters and caps—fit them loosely. The one with the nose had bloodshot eyes; the other's were teary. Both pairs fixed on Briton from the moment he walked in and widened as if visualizing a specter.

Somewhat uneasily he wished them good day, inquired as to the whereabouts of the proprietor and was informed by the gaunt one in a stammering brogue that McCormack was "in the back."

Briton browsed the merchandise as the men's stares roamed with him. It was overpoweringly warm and close in there, so he took off his jacket and folded it under his arm, and the two watched every movement.

They thereupon conferred, obviously about him, for each turned to gape again several times during the course of their discussion.

"Something wrong?" he finally asked.

They got to their feet, the boozy one with a cane, and they were quite bowlegged. He realized with a shock that both were dreadfully frightened.

"I say!" said Briton. "What's the matter?"

"You from the States, then?" asked the caneless man, his voice thin and quavering.

"Right."

"Your people from Dingle?"

"Scotland."

They jumped as if prodded, making faces that were positively grotesque, shuffling to the back door. "We'll tell McCormack."

Briton was sweating. He pulled out a handkerchief and mopped his face. His hand was actually shaking.

McCormack appeared, a round, smiling man with a mop of brown curls whose eyes immediately sought Briton's as if expecting someone larger than life. He seemed, in the event, disappointed.

Briton stated his errand, but also asked about those two men.

"Brothers. They're all right. A bit breezy if you know what I mean." He touched a finger to his temple, indicating the source of the breeze.

"I seem to have had a remarkable effect on them."

McCormack's laugh rattled glass. "So it appears! You scared them witless."

"Did they tell you why?"

"Oh, I wouldn't take it too seriously. They seem to think you're the image of some man who once lived here."

Briton loaded his car up in the yard, paid and left. It was like waking from a nightmare whose wraiths cling. Then he had another. Driving through Dingle, having forgotten the need for shirts and ties, he spotted from the rear the man from the beach waddling along the pavement.

He drove past him, pulled his car belligerently to the curb, got out and waited.

The man saw him too, gave a start at his expression, hesitated, then approached. He was wearing a Burberry over a jacket and an open flannel shirt. He smiled with the evident intention of being gracious. "We meet again, as they say. I'm Tom Hanratty, from New Haven. I take it you're also American. My apologies once again for the . . . ah . . . gaffe on the beach."

"How did you know my name?" said Briton tautly, with very little color in his face.

"So." He contemplated that question. "You are also named Briton Bell. How curious."

"You thought you knew me."

"Yes, well, the man I know, who . . . ah . . . bears a remarkable resemblance to you, is a former student of mine—perhaps, a cousin of yours? He lives in New York, I believe."

"I have no relations having my name, so far as I know. Not in New York, certainly. In fact, I am reasonably certain there is no other Briton Bell in the phone book."

"Hmm. I've never had the occasion to look him up. He may be unlisted. Could it be a relation you're unaware of? Another branch of your family. These things do happen."

"Anything's possible."

"But you think it unlikely. Or worse? Look, my dear fellow, I assure you the mistake was quite innocent. I am not tailing you; I'm not a gumshoe or a suspicious character. I've recently come here with my wife, and we've taken a house in which we are vacationing quietly. Perhaps we could have you and . . . Miss Dunston . . . over for a drink sometime? . . . and laugh about this? I'd name tonight, if we weren't already booked. What do you say?"

The man's good humor and sincerity were so perfectly evident Briton found himself agreeing in principle to this plan. "The fact is you gave me quite a shock," he explained.

"And myself! I'm as fascinated by this . . . resemblance? . . . as you. When you come I'll tell you all about your . . . long lost cousin?" He laughed, a slow rumble from his prodigious belly.

Briton told him where they were staying and they left it that Hanratty would send them a note. Briton returned to his car, and watched this large man continue his stroll, the meaning of his "mistake" having become all too painfully clear.

He closed his eyes and was vertiginous. He saw worlds within worlds. It was a long time before he had sufficient control of himself to start up his car and head it in the right direction.

*   *   *

While Briton was driving adventuresomely around Dingle, Katie was moping at home. Jeanie's advice about the cottage with one bathroom was plainly not working. They had the cottage, a single bath, and she was more distressingly in love than before.

She had said it was sick and unnatural, and so it was. When he went out the door, it was her immediately formed conviction she would never see him again. In the ensuing moments of panic, she almost ran after his car.

What, she asked herself despairingly for the hundredth time, was going on here?

Of course she had no index by which to judge. She had never had more than crushes before and these had not survived prolonged, up-close contact. But she read books, for God's sake. Saw movies and plays. Outside of a few hyper cases, as in Stendahl and Shakespeare, in which she always considered the heroines to be hysterical types, even fictional characters didn't act this way, let alone real people. Certainly not hardheaded realists, like herself.

It was truly outside her pattern of behavior. When she went to sad movies and saw half the audience around her dissolved in tears, she regarded them with disdain. She was moved—she wasn't inhuman—but not that much! And if she admired poetry or music, it was for the precision of its meter, the coolness of its voice. Its *mathematical* qualities.

That gave her pause. It was what he had said about how they were "connected" and her own theory about the peculiarities of their minds. But, Jesus! that didn't explain the storms of passion she felt.

Who needed this insane devotion to the mere presence of a beloved? This panic at his absence? These jags of crying at the slightest slight? It was destroying her self-respect.

She had always accepted as probable that she would ultimately get married to someone. Not a shining-knight type or even necessarily someone handsome in conventional terms. She hated conventional terms. And not someone who would drop from the heavens. In her mind's eye the man of her choice would simply be brilliant, nonromantic, tough-minded, self-made, very superior, non–suffering of fools . . . why was she going on? Was Briton any of these things? Was she?

She didn't really know what he was. She didn't care! That was the worst. No—the worst was that he was as far gone as she was. Together much longer, they'd be institutionalized at the end.

They were even having mystical experiences. It was like shooting up or munching magical mushrooms—something else she'd never done. That scene in the beehive hut, for example. She still couldn't believe that had happened. She didn't even know exactly *what* had happened. And pretty much the same loss of reason occurred when they got into bed. She would remember little afterwards but the feeling she'd been dreaming in some prolonged ecstatic state. Normal people did not go through this sort of rarefied rapture, and now she couldn't live without it.

It was no good. She simply could not think objectively any more. He went away and she sat there like a quivering lump imagining disaster. She watched him eat, watched him make funny faces while thinking when he didn't know she was looking, heard him in that single bathroom—and still he glowed.

Real people did not glow! Especially when they have wives and children! Was he real? Not even that issue struck her as preposterous.

"I am truly going mad," she said. "I really am. I will not survive this one way or the other."

When finally she heard the car gunning up the driveway, she flew out the front door. When he started to relate the events of Dingle, she dissolved against his chest in tears. "It's just what I hate," she cried. "It is! It is!"

"No maids," he said. "I just got some firewood."

"Oh, I don't care about that! Damnit, Briton, here I go again! Get your ass upstairs with me in bed."

CHAPTER ELEVEN

Titus Doyle arrived at six, announcing, after they'd settled into his front seat, that another couple from "America" would be joining them for dinner. "Got here the day after you did. Very interesting people. The Thomas Hanrattys."

Doyle's eyes were on the road, Briton's on Katie, and Katie's inwardly directed. He had finally gotten to tell her that afternoon about his encounter with Hanratty. To Katie, it was all of a progressively outlandish piece.

As Doyle took turns on two wheels, he related everything he knew about Mr. Hanratty, which was that "he'd be" a professor of physics at Yale, who had come to Dingle to vacation and write, presumably (Titus ventured) "scholarly works." The evening now assumed for Briton the same aspect of inevitability he sensed upon first meeting Doyle.

His first reaction to Doyle's small fieldstone house was to wonder why a real estate agent would live in a nondescript insular place when there was available such a magnificent site as the house they had rented. It then struck him that Doyles might have inhabited this structure for centuries. It was easily that old. And on very high ground. The car had been climbing since it left the coast road.

Mrs. Doyle, Winifred (a.k.a. Freddie), was wreathed in smiles at the front door. She was handsome, as thin as her husband, not quite so twitchy, and taller by nearly a foot. Everything about her was straight: her face, her nose, her graying black hair cropped at the neck, her narrow-shouldered, bird-breasted carriage. And she was keen and quick. Later that evening they learned she was the superintendent of the local schools. She treated them as neither strangers nor adults: more, almost, as neighboring children.

While Freddie Doyle was everything she seemed, Tom Hanratty remained an enigma. He was standing when they entered, dominating the tiny parlor. His expression showed pleasure and chagrin at the humor of another unexpected meeting. He welcomed Katie and introduced both of them to his wife, Faith, who did not get up. He then treated the Doyles to the story of their chance encounter, a mention of the work he was doing with Katie, and the coincidence of his once having a student who so closely resembled Briton Bell.

Throughout, Briton reflected that Tom Hanratty himself had little connection with his physical appearance, like a radio voice one is shocked to see materialized for the first time on the tube. He was, of course, a fat man, with his features submerged in a fat man's face, darkly bearded, with a damp balding pate and large pores that ceaselessly emitted. His clothes were rumpled (though changed from that afternoon) and his fat man's shoulders slouched. Yet his manner, now that he was not dancing on the beach, was that of an elegant personage, self-assured in urbanity and the command of his presence. A sharp mind was evident; but his speech was hesitant and self-questioning, belying the boldness of what he said.

There was also to him a certain element of pathos, revealed as the evening wore on, as if he saw in himself some dispositive personal failing, although one with which he had long since been reconciled. This, curiously, made him more likable that he might otherwise have been, particularly to Briton and Katie, who he appeared to believe possessed in abundance whatever it was he thought he lacked.

Faith Hanratty, insofar as physical resemblance to her husband was concerned, might have come from a different race. It was difficult to imagine their attraction. She was slender and bladelike with fine bones, an elegantly beaked nose, and quick tongue. Underdressed in an old sweater and skirt, she somehow made you think there were designer clothes stuffed in her closet. She was effusive and charming, which ameliorated a dominating streak. On this, Tom and she had seemed to have achieved an accommodation, but as to other people, the trait was not so well in check.

They were drinking French red wine, not Irish whiskey, which was being handed around by Hanratty (who had brought it), not Doyle. The American couples swapped surface, informational items, during which Katie was led to describe her job at USCC, and Briton, his music publishing company.

"So you're that Bell," exclaimed Hanratty. "Even I've heard of Bell Music. I can still remember . . . learning pieces on the piano? . . . Bell Music Inc. written right across the sheet. For me the name is a slice of madeleine . . . although the memories it evokes? . . . massive, impregnable instrument . . . metronome ticking away . . . being incessantly pitched against a most stubborn lack of talent . . . ha! Not entirely pleasant!"

Freddie said to Katie, "We knew your grandmother, dear. She was my first-grade teacher. Later, perhaps, I'll tell you a story about her."

Katie wanted to know about this man who looked like Briton and had his name. Her face was set accusingly, as if the person of whom she inquired might have stolen both.

"As I suggested to Briton? . . . your Briton . . ." he laughed in that curious rumble and wheeze ". . . must be a familial connection. You might look him up when you get back. Very attractive fellow, actually . . . immensely successful . . . just started his second company and a damn fine engineer."

Tom was made, a little later, to recount the story of how the Hanrattys had first met: twenty-three years ago at a Turkish bath in Paris. He was in the Navy at the time and recovering from a binge; while she, clad in T-shirt and shorts, was in charge of dispensing towels. Until midnight, he took her to be a very funny, lower-working-class Parisian. Stripped of her disguise ("and everything else besides," Faith interjected with a wicked grin), she was revealed to be a Wellesley junior-year-abroad with a strange humor in part-time jobs. They were married two days later, their respective sets of parents flying in from the States.

On what they were doing in Ireland, Hanratty declaimed (although his tone turned statements into questions) that a change in location every so often contributed materially to maintaining one's sanity. "At least," he amended, "mine.

"The fact is," he went on, "there is an unhappy limit to what one can do? . . . if one does it entirely on a cerebral level? Creativity is a product of . . . instinct? So . . . one is better getting . . . what should I say . . . away from one's self . . . out of one's self?"

"I gather," said Briton, "you're . . . in the process of writing something?"

"Well, hacking about."

"Physics?"

"Hardly! Paraphysics, more like. Fiction. Sci-fi. Irresistible for people in my trade." He dabbed his forehead with a large linen handkerchief, an act he was to repeat more or less unceasingly throughout the night. "You know, theories one wouldn't dare write about seriously."

He gave Briton a look intended to be meaningful, which persuaded Briton he was not going to like what was to come. He was right; he would dislike it exceedingly.

Freddie Doyle, however, was asking, "Such as, Professor Hanratty?" encouraging him with the glint in her eyes.

"I advise restraint," said Faith, "in your expressions of polite interest."

"Shush," said Freddie. "I want details."

"An hour from now," Faith said with a perfectly pleasant smile, "your eyes will be glassy and your head, numb."

"Do you have any theories about time travel, Professor Hanratty? That is, by far," stressed Freddie, "my favorite science fiction theme."

Briton glanced at Katie and saw her turn to him uneasily, then clench at the look on his face.

"Revision!" said Faith. "Two hours at minimum. Catatonia at best."

"Why, yes, Mrs. Doyle," said Hanratty, encircling his wife with his rotund arm. "I have one that might amuse you, which is only moderately farfetched." His hand made a move to cover Faith's next interruption, and she bit it.

"Odd," he said, rubbing one finger solicitously, "the ways one has of appreciating brilliance?"

"Do go on, Professor Hanratty," said Freddie, passing a platter of hors d'oeuvres to Faith.

He folded his hands with effort behind his neck. "You all know the story of the astronaut who travels to and from a distant galaxy at several times the speed of light?" He studied each face, confirming its lack of knowledge of any such story. "So . . ." he continued with a smile ". . . on returning, this traveler would find himself—with no great surprise, if he'd studied his Einstein—in a period of time centuries after he left? We know, and he knows, why that would have happened—because time is influenced by physical forces, such as gravity and, in his case, speed? And if such a trip were actually to be made, it would be interesting to speculate, would it not, about the ruminations of the man who made it? One pictures him, for example, strolling along streets he'd never seen before, and meeting people older than he who weren't born when he left? Very likely this man would become convinced that *his* world was still going on—in a time frame from which he had somehow been . . ." he spread his hands out ". . . popped?"

"And you think," said Freddie breathlessly, "he'd be right?"

"Ah. It is, indeed, theoretically possible."

"Both worlds existing simultaneously in the same place?"

"Why both? If there were two, there would have to be many—an infinite number in fact. And, of course, it would not literally be the same place, would it, but an infinite number of places, each developing in its own sequence of time, influenced by its own events? And it need not be simultaneous, either, but only appear to have simultaneity."

To the blank faces around him, with the exception of Katie's, he said apologetically, "It's a crude analogy . . . to an extraordinarily high-speed computer? . . . operating in a time-sharing mode?"

She inclined her head, with a bit of a frown. If there was anything Katie disliked, it was being lectured to in her own field by someone outside it.

"You, I think," said Hanratty, "could explain this better than I."

"It's your theory," Katie snapped.

"But I'm happy to share the blame." He again looked about, his handkerchief swabbing. "Hmm . . . no takers. Very well. A computer? . . . *appears* to be able to do a multitude of jobs at once? In reality it performs the first step of each job consecutively? . . . then goes on to the second step of each job, and so forth? It only looks like it's doing all jobs simulta-

neously because it performs each operation at an unimaginable speed?
. . . a billionth of a second?

"Do I have that right, Miss Dunston?"

Another nod, frown intact.

"Similarly, our world has the appearance of being a solid block of time?
Suppose that within each piece of time a trillion times smaller than a
billionth of a second? . . . each zillionth fraction of that belonged to a
separate time world? If we were inside one, we would not see the others,
or have any sense recognition they were there. Would we?"

"Well," said Freddie Doyle, "that *is* fascinating. But how would it have
come about that we'd be inside one, rather than others?"

"Because"—he leaned forward, speaking directly to her—"we would be
composed of its time particles."

"Time particles?" they all said at once.

"Why not? Time is . . . a physical dimension? We are composed, just
like any mass, of separate particles? . . . down to the subquark and neu-
trino? . . . each of which has a length, height and width? It must also
have the dimension of time."

"Which, I should think, Professor Hanratty, would make time travel
impossible for anyone other than your astronaut—even if there were such
different time worlds. In fact, now, I don't see how the astronaut could do
it either."

"Why do you conclude that, Mrs. Doyle?" said Hanratty with a smile
to Briton.

"Why, I assume we'd just disintegrate, with all those time particles out
of—what's the word?"

"Synchronization."

"Precisely."

"Unless it is their nature to be capable of switching? To get off the
beat, as it were, of the first zillionth fraction of this basic time unit and
slip into the pulse of the second?"

"And how do you imagine they might do that?"

"Well, there are basically three possibilities, depending on your theories
of life and creation, determinism and free will."

"Oh, we come down to *those*, do we?"

"Profound questions generally do," he said with a laugh that again wheezed and rumbled.

"I am beginning to believe," said Faith, "that we are witnessing a routine. It sounds as unrehearsed as a talk-show interview."

"Oh, dear," said Freddie. "But I do find this engaging." Then, glancing at Briton, she said, "Are you feeling all right, Mr. Bell?"

He said, looking ashen, with a sheen of sweat on his face, "May I open a window? It's just a little warm."

"I'll do it. You're perfectly right." And on the way, "The three possibilities, Professor Hanratty?"

"If you believe in the divine, why then the first would obviously be divine intervention."

"I find that so unsatisfying, intellectually. Don't you, professor?"

He laughed, a near whistle, and his chair creaked in harmony to contain him. "It is at any rate . . . a somewhat larger subject? However, the other two take a branch. The first, continuing the analogy of the computer? . . . just as a computer in . . . what we discussed before . . . the time-sharing mode . . . can malfunction? . . . you know, because the software isn't debugged, or the hardware crosses some wires that ought not to touch . . . and starts transforming steps of the first job into the second . . . so, too, the time particles of a person might get out of sync with one time world and find themselves in another."

"I do find that a bit overwhelming," said Mrs. Doyle.

His face lit with mock surprise. "It may be a common experience. Haven't you ever looked in a mirror . . . you sir," turning to Titus, "when you were shaving . . . and had the feeling that you had just done and were about to do things you'd done before? Not simply *déjà vu*. Exactly the same acts . . . with another sensation of having been 'gone' for an instant? Consciousness lost?"

"All the time!" said Titus with his blazing, sudden smile.

"Well now!" said Hanratty. "And is it really much different from finding . . . in our universe of matter? . . . deposits here and there of anti-matter? . . . coming in from another system?"

"It takes one's breath away," said Freddie. "A system of universes, malfunctioning away, leaking people to and fro. Glorious conception, I say!" Her eyes alight, she asked, "What's the second branch?"

"Well," said Hanratty, with the sly look of one enjoying himself thoroughly, "this is a theory which presupposes that the . . . ah, transference? or leakage, to use Mrs. Doyle's term . . . comes in part from inside ourselves."

"We *will* it?" exclaimed Briton despite himself.

"Not exactly. Not totally, at any rate. There must be a force. And it can't hinge on the conscious, for we aren't aware, are we, of those other time worlds?"

"What force?" asked Briton, barely audibly.

"Genetic, perhaps?" Hanratty suggested.

Katie too, began to look ill.

"There's no such thing," said Freddie. "And you, of all people, Professor Hanratty, know that perfectly well."

"Do I, Mrs. Doyle?"

"A force is simply a word to describe how particles react to one another. There are only four forces. The two nuclear forces, strong and weak, electromagnetic and gravitational. Not only is there no fifth, there's no reason for one."

"If you will forgive me, Mrs. Doyle, that's dogma."

"We teach it in our schools."

"I daresay. So do we. But as you just pointed out, Mrs. Doyle? . . . we identify forces only after the fact, as it were—after observing a new interaction between particles for which there is no explanation but the exertion of a force? We don't even know what exactly causes the force. And who's to say we've found all the particles, let alone the reactions among them?

"We may very well discuss the nature of a stone in terms of the forces you've named. But the nature of a human being? There may be unheard-of particles and forces in the genes, the DNA . . ." he looked darkly at them ". . . the soul! . . . or in the other parts of the being about which we remain in a very primitive state of ignorance."

"If," said Freddie, dismissingly, "you're going to start hypothesizing all sorts of weird new forces . . . for which there's no need . . . I do say, Professor Hanratty . . . that's cheating a bit, don't you think? A bit bootstrappy?"

He made his face, his whole body, look aggrieved, while stealing another glance at Briton. "How so, no need? Think of the astronaut. How would you explain his predicament other than by the imposition of forces on particles?"

"Why you just postulated that he could be sent off into space and brought back again at speeds faster than light. If that were to happen there would be a need to explain the force that could do it. But now you're talking about a man switched to another time world while standing in his own shoes!"

"So I am. But if one is possible, so is the other.

"Remember, when we isolate those tiny bits, these subatomic particles of which we are all composed? . . . they are highly unstable? They disappear. Do they simply turn into energy?

"Inside an atom they are bonded together by a nuclear force? But out on their own they are hit with gravitational forces that are equivalent in relation to their mass to the force of a black hole on the fully integrated mass of atoms known as a human being! And a human being caught in the singularity of a black hole is almost certainly transferred to a different time system!"

Into the shocked silence that this produced, Titus Doyle cleared his throat. "I'll not pretend I've been following all of this, sir—but did I just understand you to say that a man can be . . ." he looked in their faces for the word ". . . disintegrated! . . . into his . . . particles! . . . and these sent scurrying off to another time world?"

"Yes," said Hanratty, grinning. "It seems I have said that."

"By what?" asked Freddie while Titus amusedly shook his head. "This mysterious force you keep dodging?" Her eyes narrowed with anticipation.

"I doubt that it would be only one. If this result were possible, and I can think of no reason why it would not be? . . . I would suspect a whole battery of forces at work, under . . . of course . . . ideal conditions. Some may be as seemingly simple and commonplace as the sun?

"After all," he added, "It was the rays of the sun that sparked the original conception."

"A moment ago," said Briton getting rather red in the face and feeling rather angry, "you said genetic force."

"I did. Force or drive. It may contribute, or be part of the . . . ah, necessary conditions? It is clearly a powerful influence on the way we act. There is even developing sociological evidence? . . . to suggest it is particularly influential on persons with specialized instinctive gifts? Who can be certain of the limits of its operation?"

At their look of consternation and Faith's I-told-you-so smirk, Hanratty roared with laughter, shaking so violently one feared for his chair.

Briton said edgedly, "You are doing what with this theory? A novel, a story?"

"A series of stories, I think," said Hanratty, his laugh cut to a sputter. "You think it's not salable. I'm afraid I agree."

"It's riddled with holes, and not only black ones."

"Of course. But poignant. The man caught up in such a transference! Could he remain of sound mind? To whom could he talk of what happened? Without fear of . . . ridicule? . . . worse? . . . being committed?" His expression entreated. "And holes there may be . . . but the theory cannot be disproved, either. There is really no physical law which precludes its validity."

"One could speculate on all manner of theories that can't be disproved," said Briton, bringing a sharp look from Katie.

"And a valuable exercise that is, too."

"Oh, I agree," said Freddie. "We are all rather hidebound, don't you think, to our notions of reality, limited by what we can see?"

"Precisely, Mrs. Doyle, the point."

They were sitting during this conversation in a circular arrangement of chairs. At its center, as Hanratty downed the remainder of his wine, a faint, distant roar seemed to form in the quiet to absorb their thoughts almost tangibly, as a blotter.

The silence was broken, after it became an embarrassment, by Titus Doyle. He said, "If you're wondering about that sound, that's the bay."

"Aren't we rather far from it here?" asked Faith.

"Several miles," said Doyle. "If you go outside and walk a hundred yards east or west you won't hear it."

"It's a sound tunnel!" said Faith.

" 'Tis that, exactly. A great feature of this house," he added, real estate agent to the bone.

*   *   *

Much later, in bed, the lights out, Briton repeated those words, for they heard in their own silence the sound of the bay. Katie, who had hardly spoken the entire night, said nothing, and the surf seemed loud enough to be lapping the hall.

At dinner, Freddie Doyle could forbear no longer from talking about Katie's grandmother, Mary McLanahan: "The most romantic story," she said, placing her cool hand on Katie's. What had befallen poor Mary was desperate love for a Presbyterian schoolmaster from Scotland. While the Dingle families had remarkably let this stranger teach in their school, they drew a line around their marriageable daughters. One day Sheelagh caught them in the hills, and dragged Mary home by the ear within the sight of the town. The Scotsman was fired and disappeared from Dingle, and Mary became "as the living dead." Freddie said, "You'll think that phrase overly excited, but I remember seeing her, and it was apt. I overheard my mother talking once. She said, 'She's here, but she ain't here.' It was months before she even talked again, and then the word went round, 'Mary McLanahan is back.' But she never played another note, the story goes. At least to the knowledge of people here. Perhaps she took it up again when she went to America. It was such a waste. She was frightfully talented."

Tom Hanratty proclaimed, of course, that the story reinforced his thesis. Katie, silent and unsmiling, removed Freddie's hand from hers.

Now she lay in the dark of their bedroom, head propped on her pillows, her large eyes unable to close. Briton did reach out, and she went to him and allowed herself for a while to be held, but stiffly.

It was not that she credited Tom Hanratty's theory. He did not, she thought, necessarily believe it himself. It was that, actually experiencing something possibly as inexplicable, she had lost the detachment and sense of humor with which such fanciful inventions must, to be appreciated, be viewed.

So, listening to the bay, in the place of this other story and past, Katie did not move or speak, but rather felt herself tunneling out with the sound. Though her wide-eyed staring seemed a call for help, Briton, more disquieted than she, could find no words with which to reassure or reclaim her.

CHAPTER TWELVE

He didn't have to; she helped herself.

Somewhere in that night her breathing slowed, grew rhythmic, heavy and at peace. He watched. When she's like this, he thought, the feistiness gone, the child inside comes out. He felt privileged and strangely moved, as if honored with a trust, that she would let him see her so unguarded.

For how much longer? He couldn't know.

He put himself in Freddie's story of the Scotsman driven from the town and walked it into sleep. It became a dream so real it might as well have been real. He plunged with it mazedly into the morning, as if years had gone by in the night.

The bedroom was flooded in sun. It blazed through the west window. She was stirring in it, dappling the beams, making small, waking sounds in her pillow. She thought at first she was in her apartment in New York. Then she remembered with a start that she wasn't. This gave way to resignation, then relief. Somehow in the night, in murky dreams now lost, the weight of this house, this place, had lifted. She turned to him still sleepily with a luminous smile as large as the sky over Ireland.

He said, "I've been thinking."

" 'S nice. I've been dreaming."

"I keep having this thought."

She got up on one elbow, yawned, laughed, covered her mouth. "Sorry." Her hair was in elflocks and ringlets.

"The source of our ignorance," he said, "of the physical world and of the world of emotions may be the same failed synapse of our minds."

Her face turned clownish with dubiety. "Just popped into your head?"

"Intact."

"You know what I think?" she said with a sly smile, infiltrating cold fingers to his ribs.

He positioned his hands for the counter. "Tell me!"

"Standoff?" she giggled.

"Remains to be seen."

"You think too much." Her fingers attacked. "We both do," she squealed, being tickled in turn.

She leapt from bed. "Look at that sun!" she said.

He did as it flamed in her curls.

*　　　*　　　*

With her first cup of coffee she became purposeful and intent.

"All right," she asserted with a pound on the table, "we still have three weeks, we're here, we're going to enjoy it. Right? One day at a time."

He readily agreed, smiling cautiously over his glass of juice.

"I mean it, Briton."

"So do I."

"Starting this morning. It's beautiful—sunny and warm—let's go for a swim."

"Great."

"Let's take long walks on the beach. Let's travel—see things! Let's have long, meaningful conversations."

"Marvelous."

"And when we get back—shortly after we get back—we'll say good-bye." She searched his face.

It had fallen.

"That's the point," she said. "That's how we are going to enjoy the time remaining."

She got up from the table in her shortie nightgown and went to the refrigerator for eggs, then to the stove to cook them. This was for him, because she did not normally eat eggs for breakfast, and he was moved again.

"And that's not," she said, facing the stove, "what we're going to have meaningful conversations about. We're not going to discuss that at all."

*   *   *

The bay was freezing, the beach, deserted. But sunny it was, and the air, warmer than at any time since their arrival. "That was wonderful," she said wet and glistening.

While he toweled off, she stretched her arms to the sun and he admired her, even while wondering at the intensity of his admiration. There was nothing, objectively, very special about her body. She was much shorter than he, wiry on top, compact on bottom, although in her skimpy bikini her legs appeared long. And she was covered with goose bumps. It was those which glistened. But, of course, he was not objective. He saw through the prism of his love.

"I have decided something else, too," she said, donning her glasses and spreading her towel. "I have decided that what we are going through is normal, healthy romantic love." She plumped down on the towel, clasping her hands beneath her head, as if to say, "So we'll have no more morbid discourse on that subject, either."

"In which case," he said skeptically, reclining beside her, "it will in any event cool down."

"Exactly," she said, then looked at him sideways, pushing her glasses to the top of her head.

"So we'll have had the best of it," he said.

"Yes."

They were nose to nose. Neither believed what they said for a moment.

*   *   *

That night they drove to Killarney, had dinner in the still-elegant dining room of the Great Western Hotel, and afterwards, leisurely strolled through the town. On the main street there was a small shop, kept open at night for tourists, with bolts of woolens and tweed jackets and caps in the window. "I would like that," she said pointing to a lavender heather tweed cap. She made the saleslady take it from the window and she tried it on, admiring herself in the mirror. "Very jaunty," she said and they bought it. "Just like I feel," she said.

Near the shop the main attraction was a singing bar whose music and laughter and noises spilled onto the street. "Oh Briton, let's go in."

Inside it was, of course, louder, and crowded and hot. They were seated at a long table with many others reveling in song, and ordered Irish coffees. Katie surprised him by knowing all the lyrics, even to songs that Briton had never heard of. They had two more drinks and a splendid time getting friendly with others at the table.

When the band took a break, Katie pulled at his arm, urging him volubly to go to the piano. Their newly made friends then demanded he do so and began to applaud, which was taken up by others in the room. It being less embarrassing at this point simply to perform, he went up to the stage and played "When Irish Eyes Are Smiling," and the audience roared back the words.

He tried to quit then, glancing menacingly at Katie, but was applauded back to the piano. He acknowledged this ruefully, thought for a moment, and started to play "Danny Boy," singing the first two bars himself.

The room was silent.

He stopped singing, not in any event remembering the words, and played rather rapidly to the end of the piece, comprehension eerily dawning. The applause, at first tentative, became louder and more enthusiastic than before. As the band came back to the stage, the leader said, "Lovely song. One of your own? You ought to finish the lyrics."

*   *   *

Later, while undressing for bed, Katie, who had been treating him, since his performance, to long, pensive stares, asked accusingly, "Briton, did you write that song?"

He admitted he hadn't.

"No one in that bar ever heard of that song."

"Must not be too well known, then."

"That crowd knew every Irish song that was ever written."

He shrugged.

Her eyes grew blank. She got into bed and turned off the light. This, he thought, is getting to be more than I can deal with.

*   *   *

She arose the next morning in far from the jovial mood of the morning before. Too many things were now fitting together.

Briton had conceded he did not write that song. It was unmistakenly Irish. He expected everyone in that bar to know it. That had been obvious on his face. The bandleader had never heard it, nor had anyone in that room. It defied rational explanation.

And another thing. Hanratty plainly recognized Briton, yet Briton claimed he'd never met the man in his life.

And a further thing. Briton seemed totally unconcerned about leaving his wife and two children for an entire month. He was not that sort of a person. And he was not very good about hiding what he felt.

And that, she thought, reminds me! What was that look on his face when I said practically everyone was left-handed? And, Jesus, she thought, at that school—I was suddenly writing right-handed! And in a room with right-handed people!

And then that morning on the hill! When he was gone—the life out of him! And then the beehive hut! The feeling I had—exactly what I felt when I went to that school!

She uttered no sound through breakfast but an occasional grunt. Without a word, she took her coffee out to the porch.

In a moment he followed, knowing the worst. "Speak," he said, leaning against the railing.

"I think this morning we should go into Dingle, and you should call your wife."

He said nothing.

"Okay?"

"Mary Jo is fine, Katie."

"How do you know that?"

"Trust me."

"Bullshit!"

"It's true."

"Tell me how you know."

"I just do."

She stared at him hard. "You know because you've seen her. You saw her the day before yesterday. The day we went to the hut."

He studied the planks on the porch floor.

"Briton!" she shrieked.

"Yes," he said almost inaudibly.

"Oh my God!"

"Easy."

"Easy? *Easy!?*"

"I don't think we should think about this."

"Briton," she said, palpitations in her voice, "are you left-handed or right-handed?"

"With you?"

"Oh Jesus, what have you left with your family? That zombie I saw on the hill?"

*   *   *

In all, they stayed in Ireland a month. They went to Galway twice, and once more to Killarney. One weekend they stayed in Dublin, at the Shelbourne Hotel, and visited the historical sites of that city. On a leaden afternoon in the Phoenix Park Zoo, Katie stood for some minutes, growing rigid, gazing at the kangaroos. When Briton touched her shoulders, she folded into herself and almost in half. "Goddamnit!" she burst out. "It isn't fucking fair!"

*   *   *

It was raining at Kennedy when they landed, a Thursday night in May. Driving in a taxi from the airport, the side windows pitted with rain, they listened to the windshield wipers metronome time as they had once listened to Dingle Bay.

They slept in Katie's apartment. On Friday morning, one filled with normality—of wives dropping suits at the cleaners or shopping for weekend supplies—Briton left for work, Katie watching from the door until he went out of sight at the corner.

The top of the Chrysler Building shone in the sun. Still there. So was his suite of offices. Not, however, occupied by Bell Music, Inc. A firm of patent attorneys, whose receptionist inquired of his business as if he, not she, were out of place, had been in residence, from all appearances, for years.

He went back to the elevator hall and stood there in a paralysis of uncertainty. It was too immense. When the elevator arrived, he got on it with inexpressible sadness.

*   *   *

On Saturday, they walked through the park, toward the east side. All green now. The sun was blinding.

Katie wore a denim skirt and blue-checked blouse. Her appearance seemed to him a miracle of simplicity, and even joggers ogled her.

All around them were families picnicking, hurling frisbees, flying kites, playing ball. They sat on the crest of the hill that Briton knew well. From here, after snowfalls, the children launched their sleds. Beyond, in the meadow, Briton had played touch football with his sons. He felt overcome with lassitude and fatigue. They watched the games below. He picked out one that intermittently came into view but which Katie could not see, albeit through no failure of her vision.

He watched it a long time, and as he did he felt, for the second time in his life, that he was being torn, quite wretchedly, in two.

"Briton?"

Her voice was faint.

She took off her glasses and peered, for at far ranges she could see better without them.

"What are you seeing?" Her hands, agitated, held his face, which he now felt disintegrating.

When he did not answer, although he tried, she began to shake him. "Briton!" Desperately she made a fist in his hair.

He tried to reach out, and his hand, the back of two fingers, glanced her white throat.

People were staring at them now.

"It isn't fair!" She may have been screaming, for all he knew, since only her lips gave him hearing.

"Oh God," she cried, "please don't do this to me! I'll do anything you want."

Strands of her hair stuck along her cheek and in her eyes and trailed over her ear. He wanted to tell her how sorry he was, that it was, after all, he thought, the first explanation, the one at which Freddie Doyle scoffed, but his attention was wrackingly divided.

Her lips read: "I can't handle this, Brit . . ." and she made a primitive gesture of bereavement.

It wasn't screaming, but keening.

It was the last thing he saw in her world.

*   *   *

Edward brightened at once. He was gazing at his father quizzically, as if seeing him anew. "You're off your form, dad."

"Got it now. On eight."

"Aw, do we have to?" said Geordie, still cranky, his small face sweaty and flushed.

"Get on out there. I'll lay it in your arms."

He did. The pass was perfect, and Geordie, beaming, caught it going away.

*   *   *

Upstairs, after Cokes, he found Mary Jo in the bedroom. Silently, she took him to the window and shared the view.

"It's very lovely," he said, holding on to her.

"Thank God, you're back," she said, bravely not crying, though her eyes welled with tears.

*   *   *

At Katie's buzzer in the downstairs entry two names were plated in place of hers. He called the USCC personnel department from a phone booth on her corner. They were pleasant but certain. No one by the name of Katie Dunston had ever worked for that company.

*   *   *

Miss March glanced up from her *Billboard*. "Well," she exclaimed. "You must be feeling better."

"What makes you think?"

Her mouth turned around the thought. "You look alive. You've been moping around here like a sick man for a month."

*   *   *

He called Jock Talbot, the chairman of Heycroft's board and an insurance broker who never forgot a name.

"Jock. I happen to have a computer problem. That young woman from USCC who gave us that presentation at the school? Remember her name?"

He didn't hesitate a moment. "Jeanie Scanlon." Then he said, "If she weren't so homely, Brit, I'd say you were a sly dog." He actually talked that way.

*   *   *

Irish information had no listing for a Titus Doyle. They did, however, for a Thomas Hanratty.

The line was bad, making everything echo.

"What did you say your name was?"

It came reverberating like a voice from the sky, as did his response. He waited for the echo to subside before adding, "We met last month at the Doyles'."

There was a long pause. "You mean the restaurant in Dingle?" Another pause. "This line's awful." The echo stopped. "Well, that's better."

In the interval, Briton decided. "That's right."

"I'm terribly sorry. I don't seem to recall. Are you sure you've got the right person?"

"Quite sure. Your wife's name is Faith."

"Well . . . all right. You have me, I'm afraid, at a deplorable loss of memory. What can I do for you?"

"I'm trying to find someone. A young woman named Katie Dunston."

"Sorry. Never heard of her."

"Do you know an old whitewashed farmhouse halfway up the mountain on the south road coming into Dingle? There are about five prehistoric huts on the mountainside above it?"

"I think so."

"Is there a young woman living there?"

"If I have the right house, a girl called Kathleen Taggart lives there with her mother. A schoolteacher. My wife and I just met them earlier this week, as a matter of fact."

"Could you tell me what she looks like?"

Static on the line.

Pause.

"I'm not sure. . . ."

"It's really quite important."

"Well. Pretty. Short. She wears glasses? Has very large eyes?"

"Thank you very much."

"Is she the one you're looking for?"

"Don't think so. How's the writing going?"

"Good God! How'd you know about that?"

*   *   *

One of these days, thought Briton. When Mary Jo might understand. And the boys had children of their own.

PART TWO

CHAPTER THIRTEEN

Katie did not leave her apartment for three days. She felt at first as if the conscious part of her were dead or at least so numb the difference hardly mattered. Her body, she relinquished to instinct.

Mostly, it slept. When hungry, it ate whatever was left from Friday's shopping that did not have to be cooked. When it had to go to the bathroom, it went. She had nothing to do with these things. She was numb and sad, but not otherwise materially involved in anything going on in her body.

Inevitably it healed itself. Hour upon hour of silence brought wave upon wave of shock, until each, slightly diminished, filled with cries and sounds from the street.

Tuesday night she got mad. It started as a slow-burning resentment, then stoked to a fury. She remembered when she was twelve being taken to a dental surgeon for the removal of impacted molars. The dentist worked her over for two hours. The pain was awful, but the indignity to her person was more than she could stand. Unable to speak afterwards, she wrote in block letters on his prescription pad, "I HATE YOU," and shoved it at him when she left his office. The message was for him and for

God. It was how she now felt. For this new mean trick, He had pulled out on her all of the stops.

She awoke Wednesday morning wanting a bath. Having that, she wanted a meal. Having coffee and toast, she became philosophical. Everyday life, she concluded, is founded on the premise that magic and enchantment are frauds. Once you learn that they're not, you are unfit for anything proper. It's as if you are sighted, and the world is blind. You have to find another place to live in. With people who can see.

Briton had said that he tried not thinking about it. She tried that too, but it was like a disease, the way it preyed in her mind. And the strange thing was, there was still part of her mind that could not quite accept it.

"What am I going to do?" she yelled. The telephone rang, kindling one mad glimmer of hope.

"Katie, you're back!"

"Oh, shit!"

"Katie?"

"Hello, Jeanie."

"You all right?"

"Terrific."

"You sure don't sound it. When'd you get in?"

"In. When? Last week sometime."

"Last week!"

"Yeah."

"Your cable said you'd be at the office on Monday."

"Oh, yeah, right."

"Katie, are you sick?"

"Yeah. Pretty sick."

"What the hell's wrong?"

"Briton's gone."

"Oh Jesus. Oh God. I'm sorry."

At this point, there was a very long pause.

"Katie?"

No answer.

"I guess I shouldn't ask how it went. In Ireland. Bad advice, hunh?"

"Went fine."

Muffled sounds.

"*Katie?*"

"I'm here."

"Katie, are you crying?"

"Balls!"

"He's just a guy!"

"Yeah."

"Katie, come to work. We'll talk."

"Good-bye, Jeanie."

"Okay! Then I'm coming over. You stay there."

"No!"

"Why the hell not?"

"Goin' out."

"Where? Where you goin'?"

"Just out."

"You're going to look for him!"

"Oh, right!" Katie said, both laughing and crying.

"Look, everyone's worried aboutcha. Mike Hoag's been in three times. You got a stack of phone messages, some Yale professors have called eight times and even Roy Sloane, for chrissakes. I mean, just cause this guy took a walk . . ."

"He didn't exactly walk."

"What's that supposed to mean?"

"Nothing, nothing! You wouldn't understand."

"Hey! Am I your friend, or am I your friend?"

"I gotta go, Jeanie."

"I'll be very sympathetic."

"Good-bye!"

"For pity's sake!"

"Look, you won't understand because I don't understand. There are things going on that nobody knows anything about. I tell you, Jeanie, it's not that simple! The world's not that simple!"

And with that, she hung up, stifling Jeanie's further protestations in the receiver.

She stared hard for a moment at the wall before her and bit her lip. Then she thrust herself up, brushed her teeth, threw her clothes on and marched determinedly out of the apartment.

*   *   *

The world was going on as before, not noticeably affected by her absence. This, unaccountably, was depressing; it would be at best a low-self-image day.

On the sun-drenched corner of Central Park West, she hailed a cab and got in it. Strangely, it did not go. "Where to?" This was grunted by the driver. It was the distinctively contemptuous tone New York cabbies take with deviant passengers.

From a surprisingly retrieved chance comment of Briton's, there appeared at the edge of her brain both an address and a floor. "Chrysler Building." It was a jolt to hear herself say that. She sat back and let it sink in.

She entered the lobby as if invading a dream. Her ears began ringing; her knees became rubbery and weak. She had trouble reading the directory. She tried the phone book in one of the booths, and there was no listing in that either. Just as she thought. All around her people were striding purposefully to places of whose existence they hadn't a doubt.

"What am I doing here?" she exclaimed aloud. Indifferent to stares, she boarded an elevator and punched the button for the eighty-eighth floor.

The doors opened onto a darkly wainscotted, carpeted hall. It was very quiet. She felt like Alice having emerged from the well. At one end were two enormous glass doors. Above them, in gold block lettering, the firm name: Parker, Pomerine and Fish.

"Are you expected?" inquired a housemotherish receptionist whose slack lower jaw managed somehow offensively to jut.

As Katie stammered over the potted plants between them, there appeared at her elbow a man who looked vaguely familiar. In fact, quite familiar. It was Mike Hoag, Chief Patent Counsel of USCC.

This, now, for Katie had the logic of a dream, where people having no apparent relationship to events suddenly materialize to control them. He exchanged brief words with the proprietress of this arboreal desk and then pushed Katie into a conference room with, of all things, triangular windows. She descended into a swivel chair.

"Well, did you or didn't you?" he was asking, apparently for the second or third time.

"Wha'd you say?" she said in total confusion.

"Jesus, where are you? Get my message?"

She gave him a look of such outright incredulity he was made to pause.

"If you didn't get my message, what are you doing here?"

"What am *I* doing here?"

His glance was now suspicious. "What the hell's the matter with you, girl?"

Her mouth crumbled.

"Oh, for chrissake," he said.

Mike Hoag was a short, chesty man with a face like a bouncer—more protuberant eyebrows than forehead—and tightly curled, graying blond hair. He was a widower with a brood of kids and a horse farm near the top of Putnam County, to which he commuted every day. From his appearance you expected him to be tough, not smart, which he was, and certainly not a worshiper of heroes. But he was that too, and of Katie's abilities he stood in awe. He also had for her a very soft spot he was not good at hiding. The way he tried was to become gruff and ornery.

"Do you realize I've been trying to reach you since Monday?"

"Mike, please, what are you doing here?"

He sat back, slapping his forehead. "Are you still sick, or something? This is a patent firm, right? I'm a patent lawyer, right? We have a meeting here with Francis Pomerine, our outside patent counsel."

"Is that why you've been calling me?"

His hands spread out in a congratulatory gesture. "If you'd answer your damn phone messages!"

"I've got a telephone at home," she complained, beginning to resent this.

"Do you, now? Except nobody in the whole goddamn company's got the number!"

"It's unlisted," she said, oblivious to the irony.

With a deep frown he glanced at his watch. "All right, Katie, we haven't much time for me to fill you in before this meeting. What is happening is this. There's some new company calling itself Quantum Corp., that's just set up shop in Croton, New York. Katie, for chrissake, are you listening to me?"

She got up as if trying to remember where she'd put the door.

"Listen, you little mick! Get your ass back in that chair!"

That kindled a spark. "I do so love," she said, eyes narrowed and lip curled, "being reduced to an ethnic slur. Particularly by one!"

He looked relieved. She'd finally come alive. "It just so happens I need you."

"I just got back from vacation!"

"I'll get you the time."

"Yeah! I know how that turns out."

"This is different. Not like those Patent Office proceedings we've done. This is big. Courtroom trial. This company I've been telling you about is stealing our people—and our trade secrets."

She shook her head in a daze. She wasn't ready for this. "To what?"

"Advanced Systems."

"That's what I'm working on!" she said indignantly.

"What the hell do you think I've been trying to reach you for?"

The receptionist stuck her jaw in. "Mr. Pomerine can see you now."

As they were led through the halls, Mike Hoag began muttering anew about the purported coincidence of Katie's appearing there at the precise time of a scheduled meeting on which he'd been trying to call her for three days.

"Forget it, Mike."

"It's damn implausible."

Her laugh, tinged with bitterness, rang in the corridor. A sound so improbable to its surroundings brought two young lawyers from cubbyhole offices, who stared at their progress down the hall.

Katie was, of course, in a very peculiar frame of mind. She felt like the principal at a sacrificial ritual, who understands, despite being drugged, that she is not going to appreciate the trouble being taken in her behalf.

Francis Pomerine's office was definitely not a cubbyhole. It was elegant and immense. Its furnishings were antique, as was its occupant, in manner and appearance, if not quite yet in age. A tall wispy man in his early sixties, he was sharp-featured but chinless, expensively attired, and courtly in his greeting. He spoke with what might have seemed, at startling first impression, to have been a Brooklyn accent but, on closer attention, was recognizable as old Dutch, New York.

Plaques on his wall declared him to be past president of the American

Patent Law Association, a Fellow of the American College of Trial Law-yers, an Order of the Coif at Harvard Law School and, most importantly, a graduate of Princeton in the same year as Royalle Sloane, USCC's chief executive officer.

"We've only just received," he informed them, "a brief hour ago, the investigator's report on our man." He circled, with a bit of a stoop, to behind his Chippendale desk where, sitting, he crossed his tailored legs and adorned his nose with the sort of half-glasses popular among lawyers and witnesses at Congressional hearings. "I've just had a moment to pe-ruse it," he said, opening the file, "but it appears to contain some rather remarkable information."

"Let's hold that," snapped Hoag. "Have you talked to his lawyers yet?"

"Yes, indeed. He's represented by the Haight firm, here in the city. Peter Haight is one of my oldest friends."

"No shit! Well, that solves everything!" The patrician tone of his out-side counsel rubbed raw in Mike a class consciousness he generally sup-pressed.

Pomerine chose to ignore it. "They make the point, Mike, which is perfectly valid, you know, that Quantum is entirely within its rights to hire our employees."

"But not to steal our damn secrets!"

"Quite so."

"What are they paying these guys?"

"I believe it is largely a stock deal. The stock is not worth much at present."

"They must think it will be."

"So it would appear."

Mike Hoag snorted. "Damn funny!" Turning to Katie, he said, "While you were away, they went right to your area. They got Fowler, Macready, and Rosenberg. Those guys know everything we're going to do for the next ten years—and how we're going to do it."

Katie simply blinked. The people named had worked with her almost from the time she'd started with the company.

"Listen," said Mike, "your friend Haight can claim as much as he wants that they're not interested in our secrets—and either he doesn't know what he's talking about or he's a goddamn liar. There's no other reason to hire these people."

Pomerine cleared his throat. "I would have thought they were among our most competent architects."

"If they'd wanted brains, they'd have gone after Katie." Embarrassed by this pronouncement, Mike refused to look her way.

"Perhaps," said Pomerine with pursed lips, "they intend to."

Now both men stared at her.

"Look," she said, "I don't know what's going on here. I just got back from vacation."

"Of course," said Pomerine. "I have something more to tell you about my conversation with Peter Haight, but first, to put it in perspective, perhaps I should touch upon some of the highlights of this report."

"And they stole the damn blueprint," insisted Hoag.

Pomerine looked impatient.

To Katie, Mike said, "One of our blueprints on a piece of testing equipment showed up at an outside fabricator's with the name Quantum Corp. printed over our logo. Can you beat that? If that's not outright theft, I don't know what is!"

"It is," observed Pomerine, "our best evidence so far."

"Damn good evidence, too!"

"Mike . . ." he gave a gracious smile, ". . . shall I just touch on some of the highlights . . ."

"Go ahead, go ahead."

The investigator's memorandum fluttered in Pomerine's liver-spotted hands. "Let me see . . . yes . . . 'subject' is thirty-six years old . . . unmarried . . . has a net worth estimated at between . . ." he raised his eyes over his spectacles "eighty and ninety million dollars."

Katie looked bewildered. She thought, Subject?

"This is all the more remarkable because, according to this . . ." he found his place ". . . subject *dropped out* . . ." his mouth exaggerated the colloquialism ". . . of high school and never graduated. He joined the United States Navy at eighteen where he took several courses in basic electronics. That appears . . ." again the raised eyes ". . . to be the only formal education in the field he's had."

He flipped a page. "Subject joined Control Data Corporation after being discharged from the Navy . . . hmm, was with CDC four years . . . I'll let you have copies of this, of course . . . let me see . . . oh, yes, left CDC with four men to found Synergistic Systems, Inc. . . . and you both know what that company has done over the last ten years."

He creased the report neatly at the last page. "Subject sold his Synergistic holdings three years ago for an estimated sixty-five million dollars . . . since then has founded three companies, the latest of which is Quantum Corp., whose prospective business, beyond meaningless generalities, is unknown.

"Subject has a reputation for obsessive work, brilliance and . . . it says here, honesty." He removed his glasses and waited.

"The guy's a pirate," Mike Hoag scoffed.

"Who?" said Katie. "Who is? What is this 'subject' crap?"

Francis Pomerine was taken aback, more from this mode of expression by a young woman of standing, then by the question itself. "I'm sorry," he said delicately, "I thought you knew. We've been talking about a man named Briton Bell."

She thought she'd imagined it. "Who?" Her heart stopped, the blood rushed from her head. She heard the name repeated and thought she might faint.

"What is it, Katie?"

"Did you say—unmarried?"

"So it states here."

He had two children at the school. They told her so.

"Do you have a picture?"

They were looking at her very strangely. They did not have a picture.

Of course, he could have been divorced—or the supposed marriage, everything, a trick! But for what, for chrissakes? Pretty damned elaborate just to keep her from hating him for the rest of her life.

Was it to worm trade secrets out of her? She racked her brain and could not remember a single question he had asked on the subject or any information she'd revealed.

"How old did you say this guy is?"

"Thirty-six."

Unconsciously she was pacing. Reality, as she had known it, was coming back into view. How could she have been conned like that? He did make up that song! Of course he wasn't saddened by leaving his wife and children—he didn't have any wife or children. And Hanratty—he must have been in on it. He had gotten to Hanratty on that trip into town. She had broken into a sweat.

"Katie," asked Mike, in a voice wavering between solicitousness and belligerency, "has he approached you too?"

She started to laugh. "You might just say that!" Her laugh became semi-hysterical. She clamped her hand to her mouth. She plunked down in a seat within the embrasure of the window. The men were gaping and silent.

Finally Pomerine said, "That might explain the next bit I was to tell you." His lips pursed again in faint distaste. "His lawyer, Peter Haight, has called for a meeting . . . ah . . . among principals, as it were. Mr. Bell is proposing that he meet, without lawyers, with one representative of your company. He proposes to show this representative certain . . . ah . . . . materials which, he claims, will establish beyond question that he has no intention of using our secrets. There's also a suggestion from Peter Haight, veiled but there, that these materials would support a possible claim by Quantum against USCC."

"Oh boy!" said Katie, coming out of her trance. "I'd give him a meeting all right!"

"That appears," said Pomerine, stroking the sharp beak of his nose, "to be his idea, too. The additional condition he imposes is that the USCC representative be you, Miss Dunston."

"Jesus Christ, Katie, how well do you know this guy?"

Her eyes sparked with outrage. "If I know him, I'll kill him! You tell that to your Mr. Haight!"

Neither Pomerine, by nature, nor Hoag, by affection, wished to test the extravagance of that claim.

CHAPTER FOURTEEN

Katie Dunston drove to Croton in a rented car, getting angrier by the mile. It was a cloudy, humid spring afternoon, and traffic on the Taconic was nearly nonexistent. She stayed in the right lane and looked at the trees. It was a parkway from another era.

She had insisted on going alone and even studied the maps in order to do so. There was a good chance, she was still sensible enough to perceive, that she'd make a fool of herself. Someone both as angry and as much in love as she was very commonly did that.

One night, one whole day, and one nearly endless morning—waiting for this confrontation to take place—she wavered between certainty and confusion.

There had been no listing of his name in any Manhattan directory as far back as she could find phone books. Both *Electronic News* and *Computerworld* had brief references to him, but no photographs. The investigator Pomerine hired had never met him. All contacts with USCC employees appeared to have been made during the three weeks before she and Briton went to Ireland; the defections, while they were away.

Most of the time she thought it could not be he. No one, she fumed, could be that treacherous. The coincidence of name and age meant nothing. And *that* Briton Bell would not have called for this meeting.

But then, she thought—Hanratty's face on the beach. He *knew!* And then she thought of that scene in the park. Some sort of trick. There would have been no need to pull that off unless the whole thing had been trickery to begin with.

You bastard! she thought. You cruel son of a bitch. What really hurt was that it wasn't necessary for him to have done it. She was so besotted, she would have told him anything, gone anywhere he asked.

Stop it! she thought. You are wallowing in self-pity! When you see him, you know what you are going to do—you're going to kick him right in the balls!

The exit led onto a small country road. About four miles east of the town of Croton, a large new sign appeared, reading "Quantum Corporation." Not even someone with her errant sense of direction could have missed it. A gravel driveway climbed a steep hill. On the top of it was a parking lot, also in gravel, and a two-story plant still under construction.

As Katie stepped out of the car, Art Fowler emerged from the plant to greet her, picking his way through the stones, sweating in his tropical suit. His black hair flopped, his pocked skin glistened, his paunch bumped up and down. On his face, as he fingered the new Quantum Corp. identification plate affixed to his breast pocket, was an exceedingly sheepish grin.

"Hi Katie."

"Hello Arthur."

"I tried to reach you." His handkerchief came out to mop his face. He was a good foot taller than she. "To explain why I did it."

"You don't have to explain anything to me." She started walking.

"I know."

"You gotta look after yourself."

He nodded, this big, smart homely man who had worked beside her for three years. It was Art Fowler who had picked her out of the indoctrination course and made her a computer architect.

"I have four kids, Katie."

"Holy Christ, I know you've got four kids! Arthur, you don't owe me! Tell it to Roy Sloane."

"I have."

"Okay then!"

"It's a gamble, this," he said taking in the plant with a wave of his hand. "But the potential payoff. . . ." He shrugged. "We're all getting stock. And the man's a genius."

"Great. With whose ideas?"

He looked hurt. "It's not like that, Katie."

"I'll bet."

They were climbing the terrace stairs to the front entrance, stepping over lumber and associated building materials. "You'll see."

"Yeah."

"Let me take you around. He's anxious to meet you, but he thought I ought to show you the place first."

She allowed herself to be toured from one unfinished room to another, banking little of what she saw. The lawyers would be after her to describe every detail, and she knew she should be more observant, but she didn't care. The hell with 'em.

Okay, here was a pilot line set up, some state-of-the-art diffusion equipment, other apparatus mostly still crated, air-conditioning ducts exposed at the ceiling, workmen milling with technicians, everything a jumble.

In one particularly long and narrow room, extending the width of the main plant and jutting beyond it were unassembled sections of another piece of equipment that did not look like anything with which she was familiar.

"What's that?" she asked.

Fowler's smile was proud and proprietary. "He said to tell you anything."

"So?"

"That's a Hyzinger particles reactor."

"A what?"

Then Macready, Rosenberg and others she knew came in with grins as sheepish as Fowler's. Look, she wanted to tell them, I don't give a damn that you've left the company. That's your business. I just don't want to be made a fool of, see! Either by you, because you've stolen my ideas, or by him . . . because . . . what he's stolen. . . . Shit!

"All right," she exclaimed aloud. "Enough of this dog and pony show. Let's see the great man."

Feet were shuffled and throats were cleared.

"He wants to see you alone," said Fowler, blushing for no apparent reason.

"Well—that suits me. Where the hell is he?"

As in a procession, with each man peeling off silently to his own office, Fowler led her to the indicated door.

"Why don't you just go in."

"What's this, Arthur, you afraid of him?"

He laughed, again coloring. "Of course not. He just made quite a point about seeing you alone."

"Holy Mother," she said, as Fowler took off, but her hand was trembling as she gripped the door handle.

From the raw plaster and concrete of the hallway, the door opened onto the largest and most opulently furnished office Katie had ever seen. Sculptured sofas and chairs, giant graphics that seemed to float from the walls, a carpet that buried one's shoes. Angelo Donghia must have decorated this room. Windows on two walls gave a view of half of Westchester County. A man in a polo shirt and khakis, standing in front of the desk, turned as she closed the door and smiled apologetically. "To impress our new customers," he said.

Ohmigod! The same voice, the same smile, the same aquiline nose!

"Miss Dunston? I'm Briton Bell."

For an instant, a strange doubt. Then none whatsoever.

Her face distorted like a child's, full of rage and hurt.

"Don't you 'Miss Dunston' me," she cried, "you rotten stinking bastard!"

She stormed from the office, roared through the plant, fled to the lot, wailing imprecations, not caring—beyond caring—who the hell heard.

CHAPTER FIFTEEN

The next morning, in her office, Katie's secretary announced a third as yet unanswered call from Mike Hoag.

"No calls," snapped Katie, staring helplessly at mounds of mail collected in her absence.

Her secretary, just nineteen, with eyes made owlish by prodigious glasses, falteringly said, "He sounds kinda mad."

With a sigh of exasperation, Katie picked up.

"I understand," said a voice as angry as advertised, "that you walked out on him. Izzat right?"

"I don't talk to thieves."

"You went there, didn't you? What the hell did you go there for if you weren't going to talk to him?"

"I wasn't sure it was him."

"What's that supposed to mean? You're talking in riddles. The report I get from Pomerine, who got it from Haight, is that you took one look at that guy and went screaming through the plant. What the holy hell is going on?"

"It's a long story."

"All right . . . net it out!"

"Forget it."

"The hell I will. Listen you! I want to know what this is all about."

"Why don't you just sue him?"

"Because, dear lady, before we get hit with some counterclaim that's being bandied about, I want to know what he thinks he's got on us. Understand? And he's willing to tell me—through you. So you damn well better listen! Got it?"

*   *   *

Katie Dunston sat in the dark gnawing at a hangnail on her thumb. She was at home. She was miserable. She was confused.

She could understand—almost—why he hadn't told her who he was in the beginning. But making up a wife and two children? Was he that fiendishly devious that he'd cobbled up this excuse from the start? How'd he get that receptionist at the school to go along? Why that ridiculous trick in the park? And why, after taking all this trouble to deceive her, did he then arrange through two firms of lawyers that they should meet again?

None of this made any sense to her.

If it had anything to do with stealing trade secrets, surely he would have asked her to talk about her work. But he never had. Not in any way that mattered. Not . . . no, she was certain. She would've remembered that. Because she probably would have told him, just to show off. Because she trusted him. How could she not have trusted him? No. Christ. It was something else.

He was obviously playing some sort of game—but what was it? What was it for? Did he really think she was so simpleminded that she'd be taken in by Hanratty's theory that the two of them probably cooked up— and that pretense in his office that they'd never met before? That's what really hurt—he probably did, or why else was he enacting the pretense?

The more she thought about that, the more furious she became. She had given him plenty of reason in Ireland to believe that she *had* been taken in. He was attacking her pride, her intelligence.

The son of a bitch had even put on a wig—his hair was much longer than it could have grown in five days. Oh, if he were here right now, she fumed. She'd pull that wig off his head and hurl it in his face!

She heard a creak on the stairs. As in her favorite line from Keats, it "went through her like a spear." Couldn't be! She thought: Absurd theatricality. But there was someone not resident of this building looking for a door.

Hers opened, and it was he. Her body rioted with the news. He switched the light on and her eyes blinked dumbly at him.

"Get out of here!" she hissed, hair bristling and teeth showing like a cat's.

He seemed to consider, then reject this, as if it were a purely abstract proposition. He was wearing khaki pants again, a blue oxford shirt, and a dark blue windbreaker, which he unzipped. In the other hand he held a file-sized manila envelope. "We have serious things to talk about," he said.

"Like how's your wife and children!" she screamed.

"I'm not married. I have no children." He moved in, settled easily into the Eames chair, which was her sole prideful possession, and observed her for a while. "You must be the only woman in this city who doesn't latch and triple-bolt her door."

In reaction to so much reaction, her body went numb. I don't believe this, she kept saying to herself. I really don't believe this.

He had the actual nerve now to be smiling. "It opens," she snarled, "just as easily from this side."

"Remarkable," he said, with a perfectly affable grin. "Look . . . what should I call you? . . . Katie. . . ."

At this, she again blew up. "What should you call me? Is that what you said?"

"I do have some notion why you are angry."

"That *is* keen of you!"

"But you're wrong. It wasn't me."

"Oh boy! Here we go!" Katie shot up trembling in every limb. "Briton," she croaked, her voice catching now, so strained as to be almost inaudible, "Get out! I've had enough. That was the dirtiest, meanest trick anyone's ever played on me." Because this was far milder than she intended, she screeched, "I hate you!"

He regarded her with maddening calm. "This," he said, "is ridiculous."

"You're telling me!"

"It's not me you're angry at."

Oh, she seethed, the loathsome self-satisfaction of this man! She then sagged to the sofa. "How?" she pleaded to the ceiling. "How could I have let myself get like this?"

"I wouldn't know," he said, pulling a sheath of vouchers from the manila envelope and depositing them in her lap. "Look at these!"

She did so as if they were repellent.

"They came in my morning mail. From what is now my principal creditor—the American Express Company." He resettled in the Eames chair.

"So wha'd'ya expect? You want me to pay'em? Go to hell!"

"Katie, I have never been to Ireland in my life."

"Oh Jesus, Briton, who the hell do you think signed them?"

"*That,*" he said with the first show of emotion, "is what I am trying to find out."

She shook her head sadly. "You bastard! You really are!"

"Will you listen to me for a moment?"

"Get out of here!"

"You," he said gently, "are not the only one involved in this."

"Oh sure!"

"Listen to me! By the sheerest coincidence I got a call this afternoon from a man I've known for years, named Tom Hanratty. In the course of the conversation he mentioned he'd just gotten back from Dingle, Ireland."

"Coincidence, hunh!"

"He told me he had dinner with you there three weeks ago—you and a man who looks like me and is using my name."

She picked up the vouchers and flung them at his face, but they simply fluttered all over the room. "You think I'm going to believe this rotten story?" she screamed. "Just cut it out, Briton! It's just pissing me off."

He grimaced in thought. "If," he said, "I *were* actually the man you think I am, why do you imagine I'd be here?"

"To torture me, that's why!"

"There must be at least a thousand ways to prove you're wrong."

"Name one."

"I can't. But you can. Every one of them."

Her lips pressed white. "Okay! Who are you? Where are you from? Who're your parents?"

He flinched. "My parents are dead."

"Oh?"

"When I was six, they died in a plane crash. The Electra. You'd be too young to remember."

Softened more than she liked, she said, "All right, you meet me tomorrow at that school."

"What school?"

"Oh right! Phony, phony! Heycroft."

"Where is it?"

"Oh boy! Seventy-fifth and Park."

"What time?"

"I'll set it up and tell you. We're going to see that headmaster."

"Fine."

"You bet it's fine."

"This, I assume, is someone who saw you together."

"Don't push me, Briton!"

He shrugged, got up, tossed into her lap a stack of printouts two inches thick. "Now you look at this."

With a deep disbelieving frown she glanced at the first page, then began flipping them furiously. "Where'd you get this?" she demanded excitedly. "Did Art Fowler give you this?"

"You recognize it?"

"Recognize it? Recognize it! You're a goddamn crook! That's my operating system!"

"Be sure, look at the rest of it." He sat on the opposite end of the sofa.

"I can see. You've copied almost every goddamn step. You've even copied unessential features. You may have stamped your goddamn logo on the cover page—but this is my work!"

"Keep reading."

Flipping through, she finally muttered, "All right, you've added on. So what! An entirely superfluous layer."

She put it down and moaned. "Y'know, I don't get it. I really don't. It would have been so damn easy to tell me who you were. It wouldn't have mattered to me! That's what really gets me."

"Read some more," he urged gently.

Sighing, fussing, she continued to flip pages. "All right, what'y need all this crap for? My system works perfectly well without it."

"What you have there," he said carefully, "is *my* operating system, completed December of last year. I have seen yours. An employee of your company showed it to me—and when I realized what it was I threw him out of my office, and didn't hire him. But 'your' system, as you call it, was not finished until February of this year."

"You," she spat, eyes narrowing, "are accusing *me* of stealing *your* operating system?"

"The thought has crossed my mind."

"Boy, you really have balls! There are fifty people who worked alongside me every step of the way. If anybody's stealing anybody's operating systems!"

"The alternative explanation is somewhat more troubling."

"Oh sure! Two people coming up with virtually the identical system, instruction by instruction! Not in a million years!"

"They're not identical," he said offhandedly, troubled by something else.

"Except for that unnecessary layer, they are!"

"It's hardly an unnecessary layer."

"Then what's it for?"

He held her gaze before seeming to decide something significant in her favor. "My hardware."

"Oh yeah! What's so special about your hardware?"

"Well," he smiled, "what would you think of a memory containing a trillion bytes with the processing capacity to use it?"

She laughed out loud. "Where you going to house that? The Empire State Building? Yankee Stadium?"

"I thought I'd put it in a device about the size of a watch." His voice was cool. "At least the processor and main memory."

"You're a goddamn lunatic, that's what you are! Now this whole thing's beginning to make sense."

"Is that what you really think?"

"Of course! The size of a watch! What are you going to use for transistors? Subatomic particles?"

"Isn't that," he said with a wry smile, "an interesting notion."

Katie then had the weirdest sensation she'd ever had in her life.
"Jesus!" she murmured.

"Think on it."

Ohmigod! It was so crazily simpleminded, it was almost conceivable.

"I want to talk about that," she said soberly.

It was, of course, the concept for the ultimate miniaturized computer.
If someone could actually invent such a thing—advance a hundred generations of technology in a single step—it would turn the world on its head.

"You have enough to think about," he said, rising, zipping his jacket.

"No, I really want to talk about that."

"We will. Soon."

She got up too, a bit shakily. "What about my operating system?"

"That too."

She was looking at him strangely, staring at his hair.

He ran his hand through it. "What's the matter?"

She reached up, squeezed a bunch of it in her fist and tugged hard.

"Hey! Jesus girl!" He got free. "Cut it out!" He rubbed his scalp, while
giving her a mystified, semi-amused look. "What the hell was that for?"

She shook her head in astonishment. "Not a wig," she murmured.

The implication was clear enough. "Your man had shorter hair," he
stated.

"Another trick!"

"Katie, you're beginning to believe me."

"Like hell I am! We'll see tomorrow—*if* you show up."

"I'll be there. You just call."

"Tell me this! Do you or don't you own a music publishing company?"

"Good God, no!"

"Another lie you told me. Another whopper."

He held her upper arm and she trembled. "Katie," he said softly. "Until
yesterday, we had never met."

He went out the door with the evident expectation of returning at some
point, since he left his computer program and his vouchers behind him.

She threw the latch and closed the bolts. She was a lot more than angry.
She was filled with rage, confusion and joy.

CHAPTER SIXTEEN

The meeting at Heycroft was, from Katie's standpoint, a debacle.

The new headmaster, Mr. Catchings, was of course gratifyingly pleased to see Miss Dunston again and to meet her friend, Mr. Bell. But as for the purpose of this visit, "That, ah, had not quite been explained on the phone. . . ." Mr. Bell smiled patiently at Mr. Catchings as if waiting for Miss Dunston to begin. Miss Dunston's glance bounced from man to man with mounting perturbation.

"You, of course, *know* Mr. Bell," she said.

"I . . ." he broke into an apologetic nervous grin ". . . don't believe I've had that pleasure, no."

The air itself became hostile.

Katie blurted out, "He was the founder of Synergistic Systems, Inc."

An idea—one closest to the central nerve of Mr. Catchings' existence—then took root and promptly flowered. "Ah, that Mr. Bell!" he exclaimed, believing himself at last to have caught the cue. "May I show you around the school?"

Later, in mid-tour, in the middle of, as it were, Mr. Catchings' "development" patter, he whispered in an aside to Katie's ear, "How thoughtful of you to bring him to us." And when he literally purred to Briton on the way to the new physics lab, "Let me tell you what we are trying to do here at Heycroft," Katie went down the stairs and out of the building, took a cab to her office, and called the school.

"I wish," she said, having difficulty breathing, "to speak with either Edward or Geordie Bell. I believe they are in the fourth and second grades, respectively."

"I'm sorry, we have no children here of that name."

"Thank you," she said, as if having received a sensible answer. It was the same voice, she was positive of that. The one that had gabbed to her two months before about both boys and their class mother.

She paced her office. Logically, she thought, there are only two possible explanations: either I'm going crazy, or Briton has bought the school. There was a third that was not only illogical but likely again to unbalance her mind. Irresistibly impelled, she placed a call to New Haven.

"Hanratty," she blared, when he finally got on the phone, "this is Katie Dunston."

"I've been hourly expecting your call."

"Have you now! Well, let me tell you—this has gone far enough! Okay? The joke's over!"

"What joke?"

Suddenly she couldn't speak. On the one side of her mind was the enormity, the awesomeness, the renewed horror of this possibility. On the other, the cruelty, the sheer viciousness of the trick.

He was saying, "I know what you're thinking . . . all right? . . . but there is no joke. At least none that I'm a party to."

He sounded hostile and this somehow, immediately, cleared her brain. "How do you know him?"

"Which 'him'?"

"Cut the crap!"

"The Briton Bell I know was a former student."

"Bullshit. He never graduated from high school."

"I'm aware of that. He took a special course, sponsored by an industry group, that I and two other professors of physics gave eight years ago. The course was in quantum mechanics and particles phenomena. He was the standout student. We have kept in touch.

"As a matter of fact, and as you may know, I spoke to him yesterday afternoon. If he was the man I saw you with in Ireland, then I, too, am the victim of a hoax."

She was thinking of something else, marveling that she had accepted it before as mere coincidence. "What the hell were you doing in Dingle, Ireland, Hanratty?"

A considerable pause ensued. "Looking for you."

"For me? In Dingle? How'd you know to look in Dingle?"

"Mystifying, isn't it? How does one select Dingle, Ireland, from all the places in the world?"

"What did you do? . . . wait a second . . . you speak to Jeanie Scanlon?"

"Which narrows it to Ireland. Miss Scanlon, however, was not informed of where in Ireland you might go. And I most urgently wished to see you at that point. Particularly when I obtained the passenger list from Aer Lingus and learned who else was on that plane. Imagine my surprise when I discovered a different Briton Bell. If it was, in fact, another person."

"*Your* surprise! Hanratty . . . Jesus . . . you've got a lot to tell me."

"Indeed."

"So talk, damnit!"

"Well . . . the Briton Bell I know is a very clever fellow. Quite capable of a hoax of this sort if it suited his purpose. I rather suspect, for example, that he took somewhat more from that course than I intended to communicate. And I would very much like to know if that were the case."

Hanratty gave a small laugh of unpleasantly sardonic intonation. "It is amusing and perhaps inevitable that the three of us should have come together like this. Or should I say, the four of us? And, of course, that raises the possibility that it was not a hoax? . . . that there is some other explanation? . . . one that I am perhaps the most qualified to give?"

"So give it!"

"Ah. That is asking for a good deal more than you think."

"What, . . ." she uttered, "what is your interest in this? What are you being so goddamn coy about? Why don't you just tell me what you know?"

"Why don't you first find out what he's doing at that plant of his . . . in Croton?"

"What?"

"I should think, in the circumstances, that either one of us might be a bit overfastidious to reject the possibility of a trade."

"A what? What the hell are you talking about?"

"I think you've got the drift."

"Oh my God! Industrial espionage, yet!"

"When the stakes are this high, my dear, the matter moves onto quite another plane of morality. Rather different standards apply. And I suggest you move quickly. I do have other potential sources."

"You're a fucking madman!"

"That estimate, I should think, will be revised quite substantially if you earn the opportunity to hear what I have to tell you."

"What'y going to do? Give me some more of that cockamamy theory again?"

"I'll give you this on account. You *may* have met two Briton Bells. I most assuredly have met two Katie Dunstons. The Katie Dunston I have in mind is a checkout clerk in Mystic, Connecticut. She was once married to a man who still parks his motorcycle on her front lawn.

"Good-bye, my dear. I look forward to hearing from you shortly."

He had hung up. She touched her forehead and realized with some surprise that she was bathed in sweat. She started to laugh. "This can't be happening to me!" she said out loud to the walls of her office.

CHAPTER SEVENTEEN

Katie spent the night in her apartment, listening to the rain. It was sufficiently torrential to be distracting. In the morning, she rented another car
just as the Budget office in her neighborhood was opening. She sloshed it
through the puddles of Manhattan, then onto the Henry Hudson Parkway
and up the Taconic. On the side roads of Westchester County, rainwater
steamed from every leaf and lawn. It was like driving through a vaporizing
reservoir.

Which is, she thought, the condition of my mind. She was a person in
pretty deep trouble.

Everyone depended on illusions, the most cherished being the illusions
of Self and the Uniqueness of same. These, of course, are often attacked
by Reality. It was bad enough having to think about, for example, the
reality of being a speck on a top spinning in the Fathomless Void. But as
hard to swallow as was the reality of Speckness, there was Katie, getting
panicked at the notion of her especial characteristics being boringly mass-
produced upon infinitely repetitive worlds.

And if it were true? If it were proven? If these transferences were
common and the word got out? If she'd actually been at a meeting with

Bell and Catchings, and she saw Briton, and Catchings saw someone else, where the hell was she? Jesus!

What she fumed about, what she could bawl hot tears about, was the maliciousness inspiring her being singled out for this joke—whether conceived by something cosmic or by a single, devious rat.

*   *   *

While Katie was still plying the puddles of Manhattan, Briton Bell was already in his office, at his desk, plowing through the morning's deliveries of Federal Express mail and assorted memoranda. That he was actually absorbing these communications was a fiction enacted entirely for himself. The plant was empty, no phones rang, no meetings were scheduled for an hour. He was dressed in his habitual open-shirted, work pants style. His mind was eons away.

This Briton Bell was exactly who he said he was. If Katie was in trouble, his problem was no less insoluble, his entanglement in it no less bizarre.

There were few people in this world who would have believed Katie's story, no matter how many Tom Hanratty's said it was so. Most people would have thought that she was either lying or suffering from delusions. Briton thought neither, but he was in a fix whether the story was true or false.

It did not help to know about the vagaries of particles phenomena or the theory of multiple worlds. If anything, that made matters worse. It allowed him to accept intellectually that a time-clone of his was walking this world, whereas it did nothing to prevent acute emotional disorientation at contemplating that possibility.

Briton threw down his papers and pushed away from his desk. For a man who saw value in detachment, he was in a highly excitable state. It was not, of course, simply the story she told him. It was Katie Dunston herself.

It was her eyes so large for so small a face, the intelligence in them, the whiteness of her skin, even the freckles on her nose. He had been profoundly affected by those freckles. Though he had tried to conceal it, when he first saw her, his heart took a leap. He suspected, before she spoke a word, that his life had been altered. He suspected this because there had been two other young women in his life to whom she bore a most troubling resemblance.

The first was a girl in his high school class in Morristown, New Jersey, whom he pursued throughout sophomore year. On their first kiss, she confounded him by admonishing, "Let's not become passionate." He was not even clear at that stage what the word meant, never having perceived himself as being in that condition. The perception painfully dawned. Every day after class she appeared at his desk, pert, a little plump, fussing over the collection of his books. She took possession of him in every sense but one. The "no-passion" edict remained unwaveringly intact, as did her lovely young person. His frustration grew boundless. Complaints on his part gave rise begrudgingly on hers to a rather fastidious, mechanical accommodation. In one of these unsatisfying sessions, the idea finally sunk in: that for which he deeply yearned was something of which she was fundamentally incapable.

The second young woman, though slender and tall, had the same Celtic features, which he recognized right away. Again, the attraction was immediate. And this young woman enforced only one rule insofar as passion was concerned, which was to engage in it as often as possible. So their problems were of another sort.

He met her while he was in the Navy, stationed at Berkeley. She was a laboratory technician and candidate for a Ph.D. (She even, he now ruefully reflected, wore the same kind of glasses as Katie.) She also thought of herself as being exceptionally brilliant. This pretension was unfortunately as unfounded as it was large. It was even more unfortunate because their field—quantum mechanics—was the same. In the realms in which Briton's mind worked with special, intuitive creativity, hers was not really at home.

In all events, in the wake of these two, Katie was a thunderclap shock. It was as if, when he met her, he suddenly saw that the potential of human relations was *not* necessarily inadequate to human desires—three centuries of romantic literature, and two decades of personal experience, to the contrary notwithstanding.

There was, he realized, nothing rational in such a conclusion. Her personality was scratchy, her tone, belligerent, her appearance, bedraggled. The fact remained, he'd been knocked for a loop. He felt himself clench.

He got to his feet, stretched his arms upwards and was punched straight in the stomach by love. "Good God!" he cried, sinking back to the chair. His body agreeably shivered, even while his mind still groped for the truth.

*   *   *

If there was a security guard minding the plant, he was not in evidence. Katie simply wove through the continuing construction confusion, breezed past the empty secretarial bay of Briton Bell's outer office, and barged in. Four men in shirt sleeves looked up from their papers, three of them amused. The one not smiling was Briton Bell. They were seated around a glass coffee table on those sculptured chairs and sofa. The room was illuminated only by sunlight from the corner windows, so that the area in which they were seated was relatively dark. At a word from Briton, the men got up, collecting their files. She did not hear them go on the opulently thick carpet, and her eyes, as the three men treaded around her to the door, registered only Briton, in a stance that was grimly determined.

Though his heart was racing, what showed on his face, so far as she could make out, was annoyance at this disruption. She therefore took the offensive.

"Your security," she hooted, pouncing forward, "stinks! Anyone could walk in here."

He said more sharply than he intended, "You're here. Good. Sit down."

"Don't you take that tone with me!" she objected, her knees, to her great dismay, buckling.

"We picked you up on the screen," he said in a manner now affectedly offhanded.

"Did you!"

"Do sit down." He redeemed his own chair. "I'm glad you've come."

She looked anything but, as she sank to the sofa, continuing, disbelievingly, to stare.

"You look tired," he said.

"Of course I look tired. I haven't slept in three days. And how do you know," she said, her voice again menacing, "how I usually look?"

"I don't. And I haven't slept either. I have some things to tell you."

"You bet your ass you do! That's why I'm here!"

"Are you always so angry?"

"No! I'm not. I am normally a very pleasant person, as you well know."

"Do I?"

The more she studied him the less certain she became. In proof of this uncertainty she bit her lip.

"You see?" he said. "Yesterday at the school—"

"There are other explanations for that," she snapped.

"Are there?"

"Stop doing that! You know damn well what they are, too."

"But equally as farfetched."

"*Nothing* could be as farfetched as this story you and your madman buddy have concocted."

"Madman?"

"Hanratty!"

"Oh, I see. He's in on it, too." He reflected on this for a moment. "I'd better tell you right off. After our meeting at the school, I got a report on some checking I'd had done. I suggest you brace yourself."

She laughed derisively. "What've you come up with now?"

"You asked me if I were ever in the music publishing business. I've found out that there's a company called Bell Music, Inc. It's now a shell, a subsidiary of Warner's, but it was once a very successful independent company." He took a deep breath and his expression warned her. "Its office was once in the Chrysler Building. It occupied the same space that Pomerine's law firm is now in."

Her face went blank, her eyes looked through him.

"There's another part of this you're going to like even less. I was brought up, Katie, by a great-uncle who is now eighty-seven years old. He lives in Morristown, New Jersey. I went to see him last night. It seems he had a first cousin I'd never heard him speak of before. His name was Briton Bell." He leaned back and pulled his hair from his forehead. Her heart, involuntarily, turned over. "That Briton Bell founded that company. He died childless thirty-one years ago."

"Oh boy!" said Katie, shaking her head.

"You don't believe it?"

"Just took you a little long to tell me about it—that's all."

"You are making this very difficult for me." He got up and went to the window, this lean, aquiline replica. But his expression was darker and deeper than anything she'd seen on that other face. There *was* something about him indefinably *different.*

"Look," he said ruefully, but with the edge of a laugh in his tone. "Put yourself in my place. Some beautiful girl one day appears in my life and tells me a story—which I *can* check up to a point—about some guy who supposedly looks like me . . . who may in some extraordinary sense be me. From my standpoint that has to be at least as disturbing as it is from hers. And this same girl happens to be the very person who has done an entire computer operating system nearly identical to mine."

"I'm not going to be taken in," she said in a strained voice, "because somebody says I'm beautiful."

He laughed out loud, and at that her mouth twisted. "All right," she said heatedly, "February twenty-second. At four o'clock that afternoon, where the hell were you, Briton Bell?"

He didn't smile now. "Is that when you met him?"

"Just answer my damn question, please!"

His face clouded. He went to his desk, consulted an appointment book and brought it to Katie, opened at the page.

Scanning, she read, " 'Two o'clock, Drexel.' Who's Drexel?"

"One of our investment bankers."

"You had a meeting with them? Where?"

"At their offices, in Philadelphia."

As her eyes filled with hurt, he said very carefully, "You were in Philadelphia that day, too, weren't you?"

"You know damn well I was."

"And at about four o'clock, on the way to my hotel—"

"What hotel?" she rasped.

"The Sheraton—I got stuck in an elevator in the Drexel building for more than two hours. A power failure, brought on by an electrical storm. And that's when you met him, isn't it? At the Sheraton Hotel?"

Katie gawked. "You are either," she hissed, "the most treacherous con man who ever lived or . . . or . . ."

"Let's work on the last assumption."

She threw her head back on the sofa. "If you're lying to me, I think I will probably kill you."

"I'm not," he said, lost in thought. "That storm . . ."

"But I don't believe in doppelgängers. And I don't believe in multiple worlds. Nobody with any common sense can believe in those things. At least they don't happen to me."

"So it's easier to believe I'm lying. Only . . . Katie, look at me . . . you don't really believe that either, do you?"

"I don't know!" she complained. "That's the trouble."

"Let me tell you what I think. I think if I were that guy and I'd been staging a hoax, and I now confessed, you'd probably forgive me, wouldn't you? You'd be so damn happy to have this off your mind, you would—of course, you would! So I wish I could tell you that. I have great incentive to tell you that. But I can't. Because it isn't so."

She eyed him sharply. "What incentive?"

"Oh," he blushed, just like the old Briton Bell, "the normal sort of incentive."

"What's that supposed to mean?" she cried out.

He sat down next to her on the sofa. "That operating system of yours. There really isn't any way you could have copied mine. I had one printout and one reel of tape. They were both in my safe, which has an electronic device that records any time it is opened. No one opened it but me. I *know* you did your system independently of mine. And," he said with some obvious embarrassment, "it's a brilliant, elegant piece of programming. I should know! Katie, there could hardly be a clearer demonstration of the affinity of minds!"

"*That,*" she exclaimed, marveling at the ingenuousness of his expression, "is a declaration of *what?*"

"What do you think?" he said, taking up her hands. She was acutely aware that his shirt was pink and open and his chest was hairless.

"I really don't know. What are you saying?"

"Isn't it apparent? I haven't had much experience at this, I'm afraid."

"Experience! At what?" She was tremendously excited but had not removed her hands.

"Something very strange has happened to you. Well," he laughed, "to me, too. And the situation would be straight farce if it weren't so sad. You are obviously still in love with this man."

"I hate the bastard. It's you."

"I wish it were."

" 'Were,' 'whom!' That's the way you talk, all right. Where'd you learn that—the Navy? You think I'm going to swallow this?" she said, feeling it already mostly digested. "Just tell me—how'd you fix the school?"

"I didn't. And you know it. You know I'm different. But in one way I'm the same."

Somehow she could not retrieve her hands. They just lay in his, hot and imprisoned.

"You tell me," he said, "and look at me when you do! How long after you met this man did you fall in love with him, and he with you?"

"Please let go of my hands," she said, staring at them as if they were appendages of someone else.

"Katie. . . ."

This man was practically a stranger. "I have to go now."

"Please look at me."

"We're in a goddamn office!"

"I know where we are."

"I want to get out of here. Let me go!"

"Katie, for God's sake, I've told you! You are not the only one involved in this!"

"What are you saying? Are you trying to tell me you're in *love* with me?"

"I know it hardly seems possible."

"I don't believe this."

"I almost don't either. But it certainly seems to be so."

"What is this 'seems' business? Don't you know?"

"Well . . . I guess I do. It's just a little incredible."

"It's surely very odd!"

"Yes. It is."

"We've had one conversation for twenty minutes—if you are who you claim."

"Yes. Hurts my case, doesn't it?"

"Well, I don't know! Your case! You think I really care about your case!"

"May I kiss you?"

"You want to kiss me?" she asked dumbly.

"I do, yes."

"You gotta ask?"

"I thought I should."

"Jesus!"

He brushed her lips.

She surged against him, arms around him, almost swallowing his mouth. "Oh God!" she cried, breaking free. He even tasted the same.

"What's the matter?"

"You've done it now!"

"What have I done?"

"It's worked! You have me in your power."

He gave a tense laugh. "You still don't believe me?"

"It doesn't matter. That's the goddamn problem."

"I'll persuade you. We'll figure it out—how it happened."

"I don't want to figure it out. I just want your damn body. Jesus!" she exclaimed. "I've really gotta stop this."

"Katie, let's get out of here!"

"No!" She pounded her fists to the sofa. "Ridiculous, ridiculous!"

"What is?"

"I've been as good as married to you a month. And now I don't even know you. How the hell can I feel like this?"

"How do you feel?"

"Confused!" she lamented.

He stretched his legs out on the table, sat back and folded his hands behind his neck.

"Damnit!" she swore, adopting a similar posture.

"This," he said, "is very frustrating."

"You're telling me!"

"So we're going to sit like this all day?"

"Who knows?"

"Katie, please," he said, hoarsely, "let's go! This is really silly."

"No it's not. It's status quo."

"And that's good?"

"I no longer think in those terms. I no longer think!"

"I'm really . . ." his face broke into a foolish grin ". . . . in a very bad way."

"What do you think is happening to me?"

"Let's lock the door and close the draperies."

"Are you out of your mind?" she cried, horrified.

"All right," he laughed, "move in with me tonight."

"No!"

"Why? Why on earth not?"

"I don't even know you—or I know you too well!"

"You realize, of course, you're not making the slightest bit of sense!"

"You think this makes sense—this . . . this situation."

"So let's talk it out."

She sighed heavily. "Okay."

"Where do we start?"

"Dunno. It's your idea."

"Katie. . . ." He put his arm on her shoulder.

"Go away."

"Katie. . . ." He kissed her neck behind her ear. She shuddered and squirmed. "Don't do that to me!"

"Katie, please!" He kissed her mouth, he moved his hands all over her.

"Lock the goddamn door," she muttered.

*   *   *

Midday. She thought: *his* body, different moves. More hesitant, less venturesome, now and again missing when Katie expected a touch. She had had to open her eyes to reconfirm it was he when otherwise they'd be shut tightly. Instead of giving herself up totally and normally to what her body was shouting, she got lost in thoughts of other worlds, of other Katies, other Britons, and in wonderment at the immensity of this scheme.

The conclusion, however, was eminently satisfactory. In its glow, she both believed and felt very powerful. She felt as if she had given birth—as if she had conceived him miraculously out of her desire that he exist. She felt, not boringly mass-produced, but magnified billions of times. It gave her the startling belief that she could dance on the wind, walk on the water, dissolve into rays of sun.

She raised her head, and these feelings slid from her.

"Katie . . . ?"

This was not at all how she'd expected this meeting to turn out.

"What's wrong?" he asked.

Or was it? She sat up, covering herself with her arms. His were immediately around her. She shuddered.

"Cold?"

She watched the closed draperies burn at their edges. It felt as if the left side of her brain were shutting down.

"What just happened, . . ." he said. "That was . . . truly wonderful."

But it wasn't. It was too much, too fast, and almost entirely nonvolitional. This was a man she might have spoken to only twice before in her life.

"Katie, don't."

She squirmed against his tightening grasp, turned on him, pushed him down on the sofa and inspected.

He suffered this for a time. "You seem immoderately interested after the event."

"Just checking."

"Checking what, Katie?"

"What'y think?"

"And?"

"Not a damn difference."

He sat up slowly. "There must have been some."

"Oh, yeah. That . . . sure." She was driven by her particular demons.

"Katie, what troubles you?"

Her eyes watered with inexplicable resentment. "Nothing!"

"Come on," he smiled. "Tell me. Please."

"I'm getting to be a pushover, that's all."

"If you are, then so am I. For you."

Her eyes scanned the room. She asked in her hardest voice, "You have a bathroom in here?"

"Of course," he laughed. "How about a shower?"

"You have a shower, too?" she marveled, almost jogged from her mood by this prospect.

He held her face in both hands. She glanced down again, withdrawing. "Katie, look at me."

She didn't want to. It made her turn soft.

"I love you," he said. And then, with surprise in his voice, "I really do. It's that simple."

"Pretty simple, all right." Even her tears had turned soft. He kissed them, laughing, and then her mouth. And then her small breasts.

"Oh God," she cried.

"You do, too."

"Twice in three months," she wailed despairingly.

*   *   *

Early afternoon. Nudity soaped. Clinging in steam. Marvelously and deliciously sinful.

The towels were huge, fluffy and white. Wrapped in one, coming out of the bathroom, she took one look at the still-darkened room and let out a small scream.

He tracked after her, still toweling his hair.

"I must be crazy!" She was in all events crimson. "Do you realize that everyone in this place—but I mean absolutely every person—knows what we've been doing in here."

He broke into a grin. "I doubt that."

"You doubt it? With the draperies drawn?"

"No one would think anything so outrageous—and no one would come creeping outside to see if the draperies were drawn or open. But so what? Who cares?"

"I damn well care! This has only happened to me once before in my life, and now I've just broadcast the fact to two companies!"

She fell into his outstretched arms. "And my hair's wet!" she complained. "Everyone will know!"

"Good. And when you move in with me, the world will know, and that's even better."

She pulled away, half laughing and crying. "You're going to hold a press conference?"

"What a fine idea!"

She sank down to the sofa, in a turmoil again of rapture, confusion and horror. "You're the one who is crazy."

"Right. We're going to have lunch. I'm going to tell you about my invention—everything, blueprints, flowcharts and all. Then, we're going to drive to the city in my car, pick up your things, and start living together tonight."

"You're going to tell me how you put a trillion bytes in the space of a watch?"

"I am."

This, to her, was not at all the irrelevant statement it might, to others, have appeared to have been. It was, on the contrary, the ultimate declaration.

"Briton, if you can do that—I'll probably believe anything."

*   *   *

They had lunch sent in—*after* opening the draperies—and while eating, he put his case. He talked explicitly only of his invention. It was, in reality, however, a sort of courting, and understood as such by both.

He told her it worked as she had guessed it must—using atoms (in fact, carbon atoms) in place of transistors. The concept itself was exquisitely simple. Electrons revolve in rings or "shells" around the nucleus of an atom, much as planets orbit the sun. When an energy source is applied to an electron in the shell closest to the nucleus, the "ground" shell, the electron moves to the next higher shell, and it will then emit a particle of light, known as a photon.

"And that photon," he explained, "is detectable on a photosensitive plate, also made from carbon.

"When we want the atom to represent a 'one,' analogous to the 'on' state of a transistor, we add enough energy to the ground-shell electron to move it into the next shell, force it to emit a photon, and recognize that photon as a 'one' on the photosensitive plate.

"When we want the atom to represent a 'zero,' analogous to the 'off' state of a transistor, we do nothing."

"It can't work," she concluded.

"But it does."

She shook her head emphatically. "I don't know very much about particle reactions—"

"No one does."

"—but you're talking about an energy source so narrow it can pick out a single electron without disturbing anything else in that atom or the electrons in any surrounding atoms."

"That's right."

"Well, there ain't anything like that. To *select* a single electron you'd have to use an extraordinary high-frequency wave."

"We do use a wave."

"Well, you'd have to use gamma rays, and they wouldn't just budge the electron into the next shell—they'd knock it right out of the atom."

"So they would," he smiled. "That's why we don't use gamma rays."

"Well, what the hell do you use?"

"Come, let me show you," he said.

*   *   *

They were in a small dark room illuminated by a single red bulb at the ceiling. His face was sepulchral in this light; she assumed hers was too. She was acutely aware the plant was buzzing.

To get inside this room required disengaging three separate security devices. Two guards stood outside. In the center of the room on a black marble table stood a piece of apparatus about two feet high. A narrow tube or pipe extended from it through the ceiling. "The control unit, processor and memory are inside," he explained. "This is the prototype I built before setting up this company."

"What the hell's that for?" she asked pointing to the tube.

"The energy source."

"Which is what?"

"Sunlight."

She frowned. "What'y' have on there?"

"A game. We've just dumped into memory about a dozen available data banks. All the New York Stock Exchange prices for the past fifty years, the Lexis system, whih is all statutory and judicial law, federal and state, the Encyclopaedia Britannica. . . ." He thought. "Oh yes, the records of all players and teams of the major sports . . . that sort of thing."

"How many walks," she asked with a straight face, "did Shoeless Joe Jackson get in 1918?"

With equal solemnity, he punched the question into the terminal. The answer appeared almost immediately on a cathode ray screen: 87.

She read it, blinked, then said, "What was the price of USCC common stock on February twenty-second, 1938?"

The CRT said, "Company not in existence at that time."

"All right," she said, "I have a few thousand more questions."

They stayed in the room two and a half hours. What Katie asked, Katie got. Right or wrong, the thing was working.

"Open it up," she said.

"It won't tell you anything if I do."

"Where's the carbon plate?"

He showed her.

"How do you do it?" she demanded. "What do you use to energize the electrons?"

"It's a wave, as I said. A part of light."

"What's it called?"

"I haven't named it yet."

"*You?*"

"I discovered it."

They spent the rest of the working day locked in his office. He had his secretaries, whom Katie had been chagrined to find lurking at their desks when they exited, cancel all meetings, hold all calls and bar the door.

He showed her everything: every drawing, blueprint, chart, formula, engineering note. Through the extreme complexity of the implementing apparatus shone the beautiful simplicity of the original idea.

The source was indeed solar. Since the initial objective was to produce a series of vertically oriented waves, all waves not so oriented were filtered out by vertical polarizers. The properly polarized waves were directed through microscopic spectroscopes that both divided the rays and eliminated those of unusable frequencies. The remainder entered a miniature bubble chamber which changed the energy content of the particles and reoriented and regularized their spin. The product of this process was then divided into wave-particles destined for "logic" or "memory" functions. Each part was beamed through the tiny openings between atoms of a series of polycrystalline metal foils to produce the equivalent of a trillion photon guns, each aimed at a carbon atom.

The "logic" guns were "hard wired," creating patterns of electrons, in and out of ground state, forming "and," "or" and "not" circuits. The "memory" guns were capable of switching.

"Only they're not photons," Katie observed.

"No," he allowed.

"A photon would have the mass energy at the speed of light to knock an electron to kingdom come."

"Right."

"So what are they?"

"I don't know."

"But they can't have less mass than a photon—a photon has *no* mass."

"Right."

"To have less mass-energy, they must travel more slowly."

"Exactly."

"You've discovered a particle in light that travels more slowly than the speed of light and yet has a high enough frequency to seek out a single electron."

"Or is formed in the trail of light as a result of interaction with photons."

"Jesus Christ, how did you find this?"

He laughed. "Accident. After I left the Navy, I stayed on with a team using the particle reactors at Berkeley."

"And you told no one."

"I did this work on my own."

"You knew what you found. How it could be used."

"I suspected how it *might* be used. I built this prototype last year."

"You're a goddamn genius."

They were sitting at a round conference table, blueprints and notebooks spread over its top, and she was staring at him with unabashed awe. He rubbed his cheek, which was flaming.

"Had you seen," he said, "what I saw on that instrument panel at Berkeley and the photographs later developed, you would have recognized the potential as well as I."

"I seriously doubt that."

"I don't. I know how your mind works."

She grew silent. The sun was getting low in the sky, rimming the hills of Westchester County, and the room was dim.

"Besides there are still bugs. You can't see it when the output is visual, on a CRT, but you get it on a printer. Sometimes—when I've had this hooked up to a printer—it won't stop. It keeps printing the same answer. It might do that for days, unless we take the whole system down."

But Katie had stopped listening. "Do you realize what you have here?" She looked to the ceiling. "Of course you do. But you can't possibly make enough of these systems to fill the potential demand."

"This," he said, "is only a pilot plant."

"So what are you going to do—make a line of these things to demonstrate, and then raise money for more plants?"

"That's one way to go."

"Are you getting a patent?"

"Of course."

"You're going to put every competitor company in the world out of business." She slapped her forehead. "You're going to be a goddamn billionaire! No one could compete with this thing. You're going to put hundreds of thousands of people out of work!"

"I can always license others."

"Boy! That'll make you even richer."

"It might. But after a point, that hardly matters."

"You're sure being awfully cool about this," she said suspiciously.

"It's not going to be that simple, Katie. Those other companies—yours particularly—are not going to be exactly happy over this development."

"So—what can they do?"

He spread his hands out and smiled. "I'm about to find out. I have a meeting with Roy Sloane tomorrow morning."

She thought about this, and there was something in it she didn't like. "You're going to tell him what you've got?"

"Some of it."

Her flesh contracted. "Are you using me, Briton?" The blood was rushing from her head.

"Good God, no! Katie. . . ." He seized her arms. "What I'm going to propose to Sloane is a joint venture, which will get this system commercially developed five times faster than I could do it alone, and a licensing program that will include all comers. It has nothing to do with us. You ought to stay out of it."

"Oh really!" she said wrenching free. "After my entire company now knows that I was the only one you'd agree to talk to. Very clever, Briton."

He stared at her hard. "It's about time you started trusting me."

She opened her mouth to retort she'd never heard of the concept, then clamped down, got up and began to pace. In trouble she was definitely a pacer.

"This morning, Katie," he began, but she whirled upon him. "This morning meant nothing! Okay! What I've learned in all this is that I'm an extremely lustful person. It's got nothing to do with how I operate when I'm not out of my mind."

"Were you out of your mind this morning?" he asked quietly.

"Well, what'y' think? You were there."

"I was out of my mind, too."

"Well too bad for you, then."

"Katie, I am not using you. I have no need to use you, and I wouldn't if I did."

"It fits together awfully well, Briton!"

"All right," he said, standing. "You stormed in here this morning, and you are now working yourself up to storm out again tonight. But it's not me you're fighting. I expect you'll realize that when you calm down."

"Why'd you show me all that stuff, then," she glared, "if not to help you with Sloane?"

"Why do you think, Katie?" He walked toward her. "Isn't it obvious?"

"Don't you touch me!" she enjoined.

"Katie, what's happened, all of a sudden?"

"Everything!" She went to the door. "It's too goddamn much for me. Inventions that turn an industry upside down. People coming in and out of different worlds. Falling in love with people in two minutes. I really don't think it's my kind of thing."

"I thought," he said cautiously, "the idea was that we'd work on it together."

"You just confuse me, Briton."

"Come on, let's get out of here. It's late. There's a decent restaurant we can stop in, on the way."

"No thanks."

"Look. We're both tired. In two or three days we can have everything figured out. Once you know something's possible it's always easier to deduce how it happened."

"You deduce—you're the genius." She opened the door. "See, no storm."

She left and he let her. He pulled out a drawer in his desk, flipped up a screen and watched as she drove down the driveway.

She was bitter, disoriented and now empty. After driving a mile past his cameras, she stopped. "Oh God," she said, "what am I doing?" She thought about that and got emptier and emptier. In some other world, Katie thought, she would return and move in with Briton, and they would live happily ever after. But in this one, Katie was too stubborn to go back.

CHAPTER EIGHTEEN

A special meeting was convened in the boardroom of the world headquarters of the United States Computer Corporation in Saddle River, New Jersey.

The chairman of the board presided from the center of an open, semicircular rosewood table. Interleaved hierarchically to his left and right were the president of the company, the executive vice president, the five group presidents, the vice president and general counsel, and the vice president for technological development. At one end of the table sat Mike Hoag, Francis Pomerine and Katie Dunston, she squirming in her club chair more than she would have wished to have others notice had she been conscious of doing it, which she was not.

The room itself seemed designed to exclude her. It was the one architectural eccentricity of an otherwise starkly modern building, patterned as it was on the sitting room of a London club. Eustace Hull, the company's founder, had chaired the architectural committee, though having previously stepped down as CEO. On basic style, he had acceded to modernity and public relations advice about corporate image. As to the boardroom, however, he had had his way. As a result, the walls were darkly paneled; the chairs, tufted; the rugs, antique Oriental; the paintings, four exquisite oils by Sir Alfred Munnings, including *The Artist's Wife on Her Horse.* Another object of unusual value stood within the circumference of the table: a solid-gold easel used for flip-chart presentations, purchased when the price of gold was still subject to government control.

The chairman, Royalle Sloane, directed the doors to be locked and the meeting called to order. To Katie, he sent down the length of the table a bucking-up smile. She was not bucked up in the slightest. She was wishing she were someplace else.

There were two preliminary matters to discuss. They were noted on the agenda, which was the top sheet in each docket book. Katie watched Sloane manage the debate toward the outcome he evidently favored. He was the sort of man who, left alone in a new group, would emerge as its leader, the decider of its issues, without committing himself openly to a single conclusion until drawing it from the members themselves.

He had led this company for sixteen years. He had taken it from a secondary position in accounting machines and late entry into computers to the largest, most innovative, most efficient industrial complex in the world.

He wore power like his loose-fitting clothes. Exceptionally tall, over six feet six, lanky and wide-shouldered, he looked, with his raw boned features, ruddy complexion and still-dark hair, like a movie star of the forties. He preferred open collars, summer-weight suits in a size too large, old shoes and, even in the coldest weather, no overcoat or gloves. It was rumored he had a sadistic streak and that he'd cruelly mistreated three ex-wives, one of whom was in an asylum. Even if guilty of such propensities, they were not in evidence when it came to his nine children, whom he overindulged, or his employees, whom he dealt with fairly. Senior management feared him even while holding him in admiration and respect. He was utterly intolerant of weakness in people at this level, barbed of wit and a consummate second-guesser.

Four years before, when Katie was working on the operating system for the now-current line of equipment, he had dropped into her cubicle-office unannounced, looking like someone she thought would be trouble to throw out on his ear. To her rising annoyance, he read her a lecture in his midwestern twang on the pitfalls of group programming. He told her that programming errors were increased exponentially by the number of pro-

grammers involved, which was why group projects got mired in "bugs."
He banged on her desk: "Do the hard, innovative work on your own!"
When he left, she found the team hovering at the door to her office. Her
uneasy suspicion about the identity of her tormentor was immediately
borne out in their faces. To them, she'd been annointed for company
stardom.

The tormentor was about to strike again. She'd been warned by one of
his aides of the role she had to play at this meeting, and she didn't much
like it—but neither had she much choice.

Sloane introduced the subject in the ironical tone that senior management had reason to dread. "We've invested to date about seven hundred
million dollars in the development of new transistor technology for advanced systems. We've done this in order to miniaturize even further the
logic and memory circuitry of our central processing units, to increase the
speed of processing, and to use this technology eventually in our periph-
eral equipment."

He looked around the table at every face in a manner that was blatantly
accusatory. "I had a meeting this morning which suggests that investment
may be in jeopardy—if my caller was speaking the truth.

"As most of you know, his name is Briton Bell. What he told me—in, I
might add, seemingly rational terms—would be incredible but for two
things.

"The first is his own track record, with which you've been made familiar by the materials in your docket books. The second is that one of our
principal computer architects, Miss Dunston, has been treated to a demonstration of Bell's prototypical machine."

His eyes riveted on her. "Katie . . . tell us what you've seen!"

Twelve heads turned in her direction—ten of them belonging to the
most powerful men in this company; several, among the most powerful in
the land.

The first word issuing from her suddenly tight throat was too hoarse to
be audible. Furious, she started again. "Actually, I haven't *seen* that
much."

"Whatever—describe it!"

"It's a small machine. It could be anything. It could be a standard microprocessor using monolithic chips of sixty-four thousand FET circuits —that is, it could be a hoax . . . or it could be what he claims it is."

"What does he claim?"

She drew a long quivering breath. Her mouth was dry, and her hands shook as she poured herself a glass of water.

"Basically . . . according to the blueprints I saw . . . it takes a light source. . . ." She shook her head. She hated to do this, but had no choice. "I have to go to the easel," she said.

"Well, damnit, Katie, get up there!" said Sloane.

"Right." Her legs were almost uncontrollable. When she collided with the edge of the table, she got angrier. "Okay," she said, flipping the cover off the large pad of graph paper. Magic marker in hand, she felt better. This is what she did well.

"The concept is to replace standard semiconductor technology with practically the smallest particles known to exist. . . ." She looked at the disbelieving faces around her. "Namely, electrons."

Reactions, from incredulity to derision, were pronounced. Except Sloane's. "Is that possible Manny?" he asked the company's chief technological officer, Emanuel Fleishbach.

This man, chain-smoking, slouched forward, one elbow extended, fingers fisting a grizzled mane. "Theoretically," he said in a nasal voice of unplaceable accent. "How is this supposedly done?" he asked Katie.

"*Supposedly*," she repeated with emphasis, "by recognizing ground state as 'zero' and second-shell state as 'one.' Second-shell state is recognized by the emission of a photon onto a light-sensitive plate."

"An electron," explained Fleishbach to Sloane, "will discharge a photon if pushed beyond ground state. A laser works on essentially the same principle. And simply heating an atom—what element's *supposedly* used?"

"Carbon."

"Simply heating an atom—adding energy to it, will do that. But I take it, Miss Dunston, that this Mr. Bell is not talking about heating all atoms in a piece of carbon undifferentiatedly."

"No, selectively. One at a time."

"That's quite a trick."

"I'll say!"

Fleischbach smiled, sympathetically. He had once held the Einstein Professorship of Physics at MIT and had been chairman of the department. He was a kindly man, used to dealing with enthusiastic students and did not believe a word of what he was hearing.

"So, Miss Dunston, there is a selective energizing of specific electrons."

"That's right."

"By what?"

"You realize, Dr. Fleischbach, I am simply reporting on what I've been told."

"Naturally. What have you been told?"

She cleared her throat. "I've been told . . . that this selective energizing is brought about by a wave-particle found in light."

"A photon gun, yes," he said dismissingly, "there are such things."

"No. Not *a* gun. Trillions of them. And not photons. Something else."

Emanuel Fleischbach grimaced. "What? Not gamma rays, surely?"

"No, not gamma rays. A wave-particle that has a lower frequency and a lesser speed than normal light-wave particles."

"What is it?"

"He doesn't know."

Fleischbach lit one cigarette with the remains of another. "Perhaps you'd better explain the selectivity aspect."

Katie, then reproducing in schematic form what she could recall, took them through the series of polarizations, bubble chamber reactions and atomic screenings that Briton Bell had described in his office; and when she concluded, the room for a moment was quiet.

The silence was broken by Sloane. "Well, Manny—is it possible or isn't it?"

"Almost anything is possible." He inhaled deeply and released smoke in a thin, deprecating stream. "This, however, is extremely improbable."

"Why?"

"The unknown wave-particle. I doubt its existence. There are, conservatively speaking, several hundred reasons why it cannot exist."

"If it did?"

The man frowned, "The rest would follow."

"All right, Katie, what do you think?"

She had already returned to her seat, exhausted and somewhat frightened by her responsibility in this. She merely nodded.

"What does that mean?"

"I think he's a genius," she heard herself say.

"You mean he has what he says he has?"

"Yes," she murmured.

"I think so, too."

Sloane sat back, folded his arms across his chest, and let that register. It did. "I'll tell you why in a moment. Mike—is this thing patentable?"

"If it exists? Hell yes!"

"Francis, what do you think?"

"Well . . . yes, if it exists. You can't patent an element of nature—but the use of it, the overall system . . . yes, subject to analyzing it, seeing the drawings, I'd say it was patentable."

"How valuable?"

"Well . . . potentially, if it's reducible to commercial practice . . . quite. A generic patent. Quite strong."

"What does that mean, Francis? Compare it to something!"

"That's hard, without having seen it . . . but if it's as described . . ."

"Edison?"

"You'd probably have to go back that far, yes."

"That's what I thought. Sam? What does it do to Advanced Systems and the present line?"

Sam Sheffield, President of the Systems Group, had his glasses off, his pencil out, and was figuring. He was a large man with a huge head, who radiated excessive energy. A former salesman, he was brilliant, tough and compulsive. Ten years younger than Sloane, he was expected to become the next CEO when Sloane, three years later, would step down.

"His problems," said Sheffield, "are productivity and manufacturing capacity."

"Assume he can get out a product with an eighty-percent yield, and hooks up with two or more of our competitors for existing plant?"

"They'd have to retool—it's a huge gamble, but if he has what he says he has, there should be enough money for that."

"What happens then? To us? Existing line?"

Sheffield's face contorted. "Gutted. Obsolete. We can't compete with those memory capacities or processing speeds."

"Advanced Systems?"

"Same thing. Down the tubes."

"What's our loss?"

"Billions." He turned over his large hands. "The company."

"Yeah. That's what I think, too. All right, let me tell what the offer is. We get a free look. At everything. Test whatever we want. If it tests out and we opt in, we deal on his terms. He gets the entire treasury stock of the company—value at today's market, about two billion dollars . . ."

The reaction was near pandemonium.

"Listen to me!" shouted Sloane. "Calm down. There's more. We develop jointly, splitting costs. We use our plant and equipment for manufacturing. When the patent issues, we license all comers at two and a half percent of gross sales, which is damn low.

"If we opt out, we pay nothing, owe nothing. He will simply go to another company—probably two or three. Then *we* wait our turn for a license.

"That, unfortunately, is not the offer of a man who is trying to pull a fast one. If this thing were a sham, we'd learn that in two days. The downside is all his.

"All right, who's got something to say?"

For a moment there was silence. Someone muttered "two billion dollars," to which Sloane said, "He'll use up half of that in the development." He then looked down the table where Leland Brooks, V.P. and General Counsel, was pinching the corners of his mouth. "Leland, what are our alternatives? How do we fight?"

Leland Brooks was a slight, trim, thoughtful man in his early sixties. He had washed blue eyes, a lumpy nose, and a thinly haired head shaped like a bullet. He'd been the head of his firm, a United States Court of Appeals judge and ambassador to The Court at St. James's. He was known more for his savvy and judgment than for legal brilliance, but he was adequately endowed with that too. When he left the government, he rejected all offers and went back to his firm. But Sloane, needing a general counsel of stature, extended an offer that made him very nearly the richest man in that room.

Now he was plainly troubled. "If," he said, "we were to fight, we should do so on two fronts. The most direct would be a declaratory judgment action to have the patent, when it is issued, ruled invalid."

"On what grounds?"

"All grounds. Noninventiveness, lack of novelty over prior art, everything the statute provides. We should also by that time have developed a competing system—and would sue to declare ours noninfringing."

"How long could we keep a suit like that going?"

"A very long time. Ten years, anyway. Maybe twenty. Even thirty is conceivable."

"It would be a large drain on him."

"Yes. That's the point."

"What's the second front?"

"A trade secrets suit. Based on the blueprint of apparatus we found and anything else that turns up in pretrial discovery. We'd go for an immediate preliminary injunction which we should win. We've got him dead to rights on the blueprint."

Brooks sighed heavily. He obviously did not like what he was saying. "To the world, when we won, he'd look like a crook. Particularly to the financial and business communities. It might cripple him."

"Katie," asked Sloane, "how important is that piece of apparatus?"

Surprised to be called on again, Katie took a moment before answering. "It's a piece of testing equipment. Nothing earth-shattering, but it did take a long time to develop. There's a patent pending on it."

"Does he know we got the blueprint from the fabricator?"

"I don't think so."

"Is he aware that one of his people sent it in?"

"I doubt it."

"Go on, Leland."

"That's it. Except . . . Roy, either of these moves would be of highly questionable morality, if this man has invented what he claims. There's nothing wrong with the trade secrets suit as such—but . . ."

"The preliminary injunction motion."

"Yes. That would bother me. If we showed his lawyer both blueprints, ours and their copy, there's little doubt they would agree to some procedures that would ensure against his company using any of our secrets. The

only purpose of having a preliminary injunction tried in these circumstances . . ."

"I understand, Leland."

"I thought you did."

"We have to think of it. We have to think of everything right now. We
have six hundred thousand stockholders around the world. Most of those
people own fewer than a hundred shares a piece. They are not rich people.

"Well . . . I take it there are no objections to our having a look?"

There, of course, were none, and the meeting broke up with various
groups, having differing responsibilities, leaving at different times. Out in
the hall, Sloane, towering over the rest, asked Katie to join him alone for a
moment in his office.

He had one call to return first, which kept Katie waiting for a few
minutes in the outer reception room of his office compound, where she
talked briefly with Hoag and Pomerine. But at the sound of his buzzer,
one of his secretaries let her in.

The office was nearly the size of the boardroom but spartanly furnished.
Sloane had a large, ancient oak desk. He faced an enormous, intricate
Escher painting which was behind her as she took her seat. Outside,
behind him, and in her view, was a Japanese garden of raked pebbles and
miniature trees.

He was already in shirt sleeves rolled to his elbows; his collar was open;
his bony knees jutted as he tilted back in his chair with his heels jamming
the desk edge. He wore a white oxford button-down shirt, a thin rep tie
that hung like two ribbons, and suit pants that had faded with too many
cleanings. Katie wondered who bought these clothes—which of his many
assistants—for he hadn't the time to go shopping and hadn't been married
for years.

"Well," he said, grinning, "quite a fandango."

"Yes," she agreed.

That smile continued winningly. A weapon in the arsenal of a complex
man, it merely increased in her the unease of this meeting.

"Katie, would you like some coffee, tea?"

She declined.

"How long have you been with the company?" He opened a desk
drawer and drew forth a packet of gumdrops.

"Six and a half years."

"Right out of school?"

"Yep," she said, determined to be natural.

"Want one?" He held out the box.

"No, thank you."

Surprisingly, he blushed. "Keeps me from smoking," he said, popping two in his mouth. "Guess the hospitality in here's not too lavish this afternoon."

She now realized with a jolt the source of the tension, and could think of nothing to say.

"I kind of think of you as a fixture around here, young lady. You're a very important person." He chomped away on his junk candy.

"Mr. Sloane—"

"You know, most people around here call me Roy. Makes me feel even older than I am when they don't."

She shut her eyes. "Roy," she forced out, "I will help on this every way I can. And I will not tell Briton Bell anything that happened at that meeting."

"I know you won't."

"I mean it. You didn't have to ask."

"I didn't," he noted with that same engaging smile.

"Well, you were going to."

"Nope." He shook his head for emphasis. "Wasn't going to. Was going to ask something else."

"What?" She drew back in her chair.

He sprang to his feet and walked about with nervous, quick movements and gangly grace. It was like watching someone proficient on stilts. She was fascinated. For a sixty-two-year-old man, he had extraordinary vitality and—she couldn't think of a better word—"youth."

"Katie," he said, landing on the front of his desk, right before her, "are you emotionally involved with this guy?"

She instantly turned crimson. After a brief moment of meeting his glance, she looked to the floor.

"I wouldn't ask, you understand, in other circumstances."

"I understand."

"So . . . what's the answer?"

"It's a complex question."

"You're used to dealing with complexities."

"Not this complex, I'm not."

"Katie," he coaxed, intercepting her wandering glance.

She sighed heavily and stared back. "Let's just say—you're right. On reflection, I shouldn't have anything more to do with this. I may not be entirely objective."

His lips pursed. For a moment he looked almost his age. Slowly he returned to the chair behind his desk and draped his long legs over its corner.

"You understand why I had to ask?"

"Yeah."

"Sorry."

She shrugged, looking sidelong.

"And you really think this guy's honest, huh?"

"In his work, yeah."

"But not with you?"

Her lips pressed together, and she got up.

"It goes together, you know," he said slightly wincing.

"Yeah, I suppose."

"Okay," he said, getting up also. "No more of an old man's prying."

Her head snapped up. "I don't think you're an old man, and neither do you, Roy Sloane!"

The famous grin again, from the covers of *Time*, *Newsweek* and *Fortune*. "Well, I've accomplished something at this meeting."

Out in the hall, she started to breathe. Jesus, she thought, he really makes you believe it.

CHAPTER NINETEEN

At one o'clock in the morning Katie was lying in bed with the lights out thinking about Briton Bell. Her Briton Bell. The one she fell in love with and went to Ireland with. She missed him terribly. She could now indulge herself fully in that feeling since she no longer believed the two to be the same.

She conjured up her favorite scenes. She went back to the elevator encounter and replayed the scenes like a movie. She wanted him awfully. She did not want to be in love with two identical people. She would go crazy soon—if she were not already—unless this was cleared up.

And she did not mean cleared up to some physicist's intellectual satisfaction. It was all very well for him to treat this as a problem in physical science, but she didn't operate that way. This was her life. She got very self-protective and emotional where her life was concerned. There was not a bit of the mathematician or scientist about her on that subject. Mathematics and science were for things that happened to objects, machines, plant-life and other people. Her solutions meant touching and feeling. If the man was not of this world, if what had happened was something no one of this world could otherwise possibly believe, let him come back for a moment and tell her.

The telephone rang.

She jumped from bed and switched on the light. Why was this always happening?

"Hi," it said.

"Who is this?" she rasped.

"Briton, who do you think?"

"Which one?" She knew.

There was a long pause. "The unmarried one."

"Not funny!" she yelped, slumping back into bed.

"Not so intended."

"Damnit, Briton, don't you see? I'm not going to be able to handle this. I'm going absolutely nuts."

"Stay calm for another moment."

"Look. I walk down the street. I see a person, I see a tree. Suddenly I see many persons, many trees. I see an infinity of persons and trees. You think I can stay calm in those circumstances?"

"I'm working on a theory."

"Oh fine! That's just what I need." She struggled to a sitting position. "Where are you? You sound far away."

"I'm in Los Angeles. Waiting for a plane."

"What's the matter? Don't you have your own plane?"

"I do, yes," he laughed. "That's what I'm waiting for. It's being refueled."

"Terrific! I had to ask."

"Where are you going to be the day after tomorrow, late afternoon?"

"Why?"

"That's when I'm getting back. Will you be in your office?"

"You can't possibly come to my office."

"Why not? I'll pick you up then. About five o'clock. We'll drive to New Jersey. I want you to meet someone."

"Who?"

"My great-uncle."

Long pause.

"Got to run," he said. "Plane's ready."

"No!"

"No, what?"

"No, I don't want to see you anymore."

"We'll talk about it when I get back."

"No, Briton, damnit! I mean it."

"You'll like him."

"It's not your great-uncle I don't want to see. It's you!"

"Go to sleep. And lock the door."

"Briton, don't you dare show up in my office!"

"Katie, listen to me! I'm not letting go, just because something strange has happened. We're going to deal with that."

"Oh yeah. How?"

"Do you love me?"

"How should I know? I hardly know you."

"Well, that's progress."

"Not for me, it isn't. It's confusion."

"Katie, be serious."

"I am! Give me a hint."

"Okay. You want a hint?"

"Yes!"

"Neutrons, protons and electrons go out of existence."

"What?"

"They go out of existence. Every instant. And in the place, say, of a single neutron, weird new particles appear. They may be leptons or mesons or neutrinos or photons. But they have a different mass in combination from the particle they replaced. And then *they* go out of existence and another neutron or such emerges. It's a dynamic condition; the switching back and forth goes on constantly. When you look at any physical mass—the Empire State Building, for example—it is constantly being reconstructed by different elementary particles. It's a new building every minute fraction of a second."

"That's a hint? I know all about this stuff. It's my project for Hanratty."

"The question is: when a neutron goes out of existence in our world, where does it go?"

"This is bullshit, Briton. It has nothing to do with me."

"I'll send you some books. I've got to take off."

"Wait a second!"

"Hold on! I'll be right with you."

"What?"

"I was talking to the pilot. We've got to get on the runway."

"Why didn't you tell me you were going to hold my whole damn company up for ransom?"

There was another pause before he spoke. "Is that the way it looks to you?"

"What would you call it?"

"I thought I made a fair offer."

"So did Attila the Hun."

He laughed. "If that's what they think, they're free to turn me down. Bye, Katie, I'll see you on Thursday."

*   *   *

Katie checked into her office the next morning to glance at her mail and telephone messages. Having endured the pleading, somewhat desperate look of her owlish secretary, who took the brunt of unanswered calls, she ran off to the New York Public Library, the big one at Forty-second Street with the lions in front. She spent a half hour with the card catalogs, musing offhandedly about lions and owls, and called for eight books. Two of them were currently in print, and when the library closed she marched to Scribner's and bought them both.

She spent the night reading one, and the following morning, the other. She should have done this two months ago, she thought, but had left this technical side of the project to physicists within the company. That night Briton called again. At first she told him she couldn't talk, she was too busy reading about quantum mechanics. Then she thought better of that and asked him some questions. He really knew the subject. It was just as he said, and Hanratty before him. Nothing in the world was as it seemed. Every object, every person—that is, every particle comprising every person and object—was constantly disintegrating, with new particles forming in its place.

"If you could do it fast enough," she said, "you could pass one building right through another."

"That's right."

"Your invention is based on this, isn't it?"

"A simple application, yes."

"And the bug—the repetitive printouts?"

"That too."

"But you can control that."

"We're working on it."

"What you need is another polarizing screen."

"I knew you were a quick study."

Her anger flashed. "Don't you dare patronize me!"

"Listen you!" he said, laughing into the phone. "It took me a hell of a lot longer than one day to figure that out."

Partially mollified, she changed the subject. "Do you realize you may be in for a very big fight?"

"I'm aware of it, yes."

"So? What are you going to do?"

"Do you want me to tell you my contingency plans?"

She bit her lip. How stupid. She wasn't ready for that commitment. "No."

"I'll tell you anyway."

"Briton, don't. I have a conflict."

"At least you recognize a conflict. That's something."

"Don't build on it." Why did she say things like that?

"The fact is there's nothing much I can do. Either they take my offer, or we fight."

"You might lose."

"I understand that."

"Some of those people you hired from USCC may have taken things they shouldn't have—trade secrets."

"I'd be surprised if they didn't, but I'm certainly willing to agree to any measures to prevent those things from being used."

"Maybe I should tell that to Sloane."

"Taking sides?"

"That's not taking sides, that's taking a message, clearing things up."

"Don't get involved, Katie. I have lawyers for that."

"Suit yourself."

"Look, I'm grateful for the offer. I don't want you getting hurt. If there's going to be a fight—"

"Sloane'll listen to me faster than any lawyers."

"Katie, I've got to get back to my meeting. Stay out of it. I'm flying to Westchester airport in the morning to be at the plant. I'll see you at your office, late afternoon. We'll talk then."

"What kind of plane do you fly in?"

"A Lear jet, why?"

"Where do you get your pilots?"

"Katie, for chrissakes!"

"Well, go ahead—hang up, then!"

"I'm sorry. If you were flying all over the country, I'd be worried too."

"I'm not worried."

"Fine. Is your door locked?"

"This is getting sappy."

"You started it."

"Yeah. That's the damn trouble," she said and hung up.

*   *   *

Mike Hoag was in Katie's office, feet propped on the opposite edge of her desk. His face wore an expression of bemusement and dismay.

"It looks like it's going to check out," he announced.

Anything else would have surprised her.

"We got there at eight-thirty this morning. Bastards were ready for us, Fowler and that crew. Everyone but Bell." Her heart jumped; did the plane land? "Son of a bitch comes strolling in, calm as you please, at eleven-thirty."

Katie grinned.

"What are you looking so pleased about?"

"Me? Nothin'." Her face was all innocence. "Did you find the bug in it?"

"You mean the multiple printouts? Didn't have to. It's the first thing they told us. Doesn't amount to anything. Be a miracle if there weren't bugs at this stage. Christ! The whole damn thing's a miracle. Son of a bitch has leapfrogged at least fifty separate generations of technology. It's unheard of. We're just going to have to deal with him or try to destroy him."

"And?"

"That's not my decision."

"What would you do, if it were?"

He shrugged. "Too big for me. That's what Sloane's paid for, making decisions like that."

"Would it work? Brooks's plan?"

"Sure. Catch him red-handed with his hand in the till? That's what the media would believe. A preliminary injunction then would be the end of him. He wouldn't raise a cent."

"He'd still get a patent."

"Maybe. Depends on what we can prove. If there's any trail from stuff those guys stole from us to this invention, maybe we can knock it out on that ground. Or at least tie it up in litigation so long that the patent would run out before it's over. Patent's only seventeen years. No one would take a license while we're litigating."

"I think he made the invention, Mike, before he hired anyone."

"Yeah, well, we'll see. Nothin's ever that obvious in litigation."

Katie was frowning. "It sounds like a dirty trick."

"Does it now? Which side are you on, anyway?"

"Roy Sloane told me to stay out of it."

"*Roy* Sloane, hunh?"

"Oh yeah. We're like that," she laughed happily, holding up two closed fingers.

"I'll bet. Why'd he call you off?" He looked at her suspiciously.

"Private."

"Is it, now? I must say, you seem to be bubbling over today, with our company coming down on our ears."

At that moment, Jeanie Scanlon barged in. "Say, what the hell's going on here? There's some crazy rumor going around about some new fantastic invention that's going to obsolete our whole line."

"Where'd you hear that?" snapped Hoag.

"Jesus, man. Just walk through the hall. You'll hear it too."

"Bloody hell! Well, you scotch that!"

"Why? Is it true?"

"Jeanie, where'd you hear it?"

"Okay Mike, don't get so mad. I only heard it from Pete Simmons, who got it from Art Fowler. Art and a bunch of others from that new company, Quantum, worked on Pete yesterday."

"And—what did they tell him?"

She shrugged. "It was all very mysterious but that's the idea he got."

"Is he going?"

"Christ, Mike, you'd better talk to Pete about that directly."

"I damn well will!"

Katie's secretary came in, glasses at the tip of her nose. "There's a person at reception, Miss Dunston. For you. A Mr. Bell?"

"Well, Holy Mary, Mother of God!" exclaimed Mike Hoag.

Katie's face was aflame. She looked helplessly at Mike.

"Well, get him in here!" Mike ordered. And when the secretary left, he said, "Katie, what is this? I thought you said Sloane told you to keep out."

"He did. And I am."

"So what's Bell doing here?"

"Why don't you ask him?"

"Jesus Christ, the whole damn world's out of whack."

"Yeah. That may be so."

Briton was shown in. He was wearing a blazer with gold buttons, a maroon tie and medium-gray slacks. It was the most dressed up Katie had seen him.

"Hello, Mike," he said affably and he introduced himself to Jeanie, while Katie stood mute. "Making any progress?"

"Enough. You want to see me for anything?" Hoag asked gruffly.

"Not at the moment, Mike, no." His smile reminded Katie of Sloane's.

As Mike and Jeanie took themselves off, the latter flashed Katie a crude gesture, shaking a limp hand at the end of her wrist.

The door closed, but it was hardly quiet. Both of them could hear the murmurings outside.

"You've embarrassed me, Briton," said Katie in a bit of a daze.

"So let's get out of here," he suggested.

She came from behind her desk with stalking movements. Eyes fixed at the approximate level of his chest, she shoved him against the wall and dove her hands inside his jacket.

He kissed her on the mouth. She kissed back somewhat more

voraciously than she intended. When finished, she stared at him hard.
"Don't think I enjoy this!"

"I wouldn't be that presumptuous."

"Good. Now, we can go."

"Let's."

"And next time," she said astringently, "you fly somewhere—anywhere!
—you understand?—when you land, you call me!"

*   *   *

The car was sitting in a no-parking area in front of the building, open
and ticketless.

Ten blocks down Fifth, Katie suddenly asked, "What is this car?"

"It's—" he glanced at the dash where no name was in evidence "—a
Cadillac, I think."

"He thinks!" She folded her arms and commenced muttering to herself.

"What's wrong? Too ostentatious?"

"Yes, I think it's ostentatious!"

"I'll have it changed tomorrow."

"Briton, don't you realize you left an open, thirty-thousand-dollar car on
Madison Avenue with the keys inside?"

"Well . . . not really." He took a deep breath and pulled up at a light.
"It's leased by the year with a driver. He was watching it. I just gave him
the night off."

"Oh, for heaven's sake. Then what's the point of changing the car?"

"Other than your dislike of it, there isn't any." The light turned green
and he went.

"Jesus, we really are in different worlds!"

"Katie, I need that service."

"I know, I know. You are very busy and very important."

"At least, busy."

She shut her eyes and sank into the corner.

"What's wrong now?"

"Nothin'!"

He drove carefully, giving rise to the impression he was not terribly
good at it. Ten blocks later she said, "Where are we going?"

"I told you, to visit my great-uncle."

"In Morristown?"

"Right."

"Why are we doing that?"

"You'll like him. And I want him to meet you."

"You're not suggesting I'm to be taken there on inspection."

"Of course not."

"Of course not," she repeated. "We're going to talk about his first cousin."

"We don't have to."

"Not much!"

"Katie, it's up to you."

"Yeah," she muttered and again closed her eyes. He turned west on Thirty-ninth Street and for several blocks, sporadically, the muttering continued.

"Are you saying something I should hear?"

"No."

"Then why are you sitting there mumbling?"

"I am saying I do not understand what's going on."

"Well, don't get all excited. We are simply paying a visit to an eighty-seven-year-old man."

"That's not what I don't understand. What I don't understand—one of the *many* things I just don't, at the moment, understand—is how I could possibly—how I could conceivably—" she pressed her lips together, then blurted it out "—how I could be in *love* with you."

The car screeched to a halt, throwing her against the seat belt, bouncing her back to the seat. They were at the entrance to the Lincoln Tunnel.

He sat there staring at the tunnel mouth. "Would you mind saying that again?"

"Are you crazy?" Her panicked glance went back and forth between him and the rear window. "Those people are going to kill you! They're blowing their horns."

He shrugged, looking very childish.

"Briton, you're out of your mind! Start the car."

He simply smiled at her.

"All right! I'll say it! I love you. Now, go! Jesus!"

CHAPTER TWENTY

A. G. (for Algernon Guthrie) Bell looked like a painting Katie had once seen of a splendidly elongated, notoriously promiscuous sixteenth-century cardinal. Taller than his nephew, with narrower shoulders and aquilinity more pronounced, he took an amazingly strenuous grasp of her hand, staring down from his height with Jehovically fierce blue eyes. His hair, shock white, was tonsured to youthful bristles in an almost ecclesiastical style. There was some bagginess beneath his eyes; a piece of flesh-colored tape kept his right upper lid from drooping; his neck was leathery and strung. But he made her feel that these coverings belied a capacity equal to a more conspicuous inclination. It must be, she concluded, the family resemblance.

Over cocktails, which A. G. mixed, moving around a lot as he did so, the conversation developed mainly between Katie and himself. He was quick to disclose in short, barbed sentences that he had been an auto worker, a labor organizer, and one of the founders of the CIO. For these activities, he revealed with bitter pride, he had spent more than five years in prison. He married a schoolteacher when he was nearly fifty and she twenty-five. She died of a combination of pneumonia and undiagnosed tuberculosis when Briton was a child, by which time he had already lost his own parents. As for his nephew, A. G. was at pains to conceal an immoderate fondness.

They sat in the parlor of a small cottage situated on several acres of land, A. G. managing to imply he was as much a guest here as Katie.

"He bought it," said A. G., nodding in Briton's direction. "I was happy enough in some rooms I had, but it didna' suit him! To get along with people . . ." another nod ". . . y' best humor 'em—even bearin' inconvenience to y'self."

"Not when they try to bully you," Katie asserted.

A. G.'s laugh barked like his speech. "Y'speak from experience, lass?"

"I do."

"And you're not one to be ordered about, are y'?"

"I'm not."

He studied her appraisingly and at unpardonable length. There was little doubt in Katie's mind that in his she was being ungarmented.

She asked simply, "Are you quite finished, A. G.?"

"You wouldna' by any chance," he burlesqued with grinning ribaldry, "have a slightly older sister?"

" 'Fraid not."

"More's the pity."

As A. G. got up to mix another round, Briton said, "Shouldn't we have dinner?"

"Why?" he asked in a rough, biting voice. "Y'in a rush to leave?" He handed out martinis.

"We have to drive back to New York."

"So? If you're too enfeebled, I'll drive y' m'self. Y'think I'm going to let this lass out of here so quickly? I have things to find out."

"What things?" asked Katie uneasily.

"What do y'think?" exclaimed the old man. "Things you're na likely to tell me. Things I must observe for m'self."

Dinner, when finally called, was served by the middle-aged woman who cooked it, A. G.'s housekeeper, also furnished by Briton. She was a plump, short widow, also of Scotch ancestry, with a sweet youthful face, blue eyes and a bead of sweat on her upper lip. She moved about with her head cast down, smiling silently at any reference to herself or the meal. At A. G.'s rude remarks on the quality of the cooking, her smile never wavered, particularly since his appetite was not affected; he ate everything on his plate. In fact, it was rack of lamb and delicious.

Dessert was fresh fruit on raspberry sherbert, and then there was port wine. A. G., lighting a cigar—one of three he was permitted per day—said bluntly, "I gather you've had a run-in with a man calling himself by this fellow's name and claiming to be in the music business."

With a sharp look at Briton, Katie said defensively, "That's right."

"Look here, lass, y' need na' be close with me. Or embarrassed."

"I'm not embarrassed!"

"Then why," said A. G. with amused asperity, "are y' blushing up to y'roots?"

"Because—" she wondered at the rapid familiarity she had fallen into with this man "—you've plied me with so much alcohol since I've stepped into your house, it is rising like blood to my cheeks."

"Ha!" he barked, the laugh rattling into a cough.

Briton said, "Tell Katie what you told me the other night."

"Is that what y' want, lass?"

"About your cousin? Why not?" It was bravado, for she felt goose bumps also beginning to rise.

"Y'quite sure?"

"A. G.," said Katie, "stop playing around!"

The old man smiled. "He was in the music business, all right. Damned successful at it too, for a while. Until he drank himself to death. N'r had any children, so far as I knew. And the business went to a partner. This man you met was probably a liar."

Katie breathed deeply. "Perhaps."

"Of course, that Briton, my cousin, this fellow's namesake, did na' come here until he was about thirty. I suppose he might have sired some brats over there."

"Why don't you tell us what he was like?" said Briton.

A. G. shrugged, tipped an ash into the tray. "A gambling man, a piano player, boozer. I suppose y'have to give him the fact he had some charm. That sort usually does. Womanizer, too."

Katie wanted to tell him to stop.

"Unlike anyone else in the family," Briton dryly noted.

"What's that supposed to mean?"

"Nothing whatever."

Their glances locked. A. G. made a noise of withered patience and went on. "He was educated—sent to the University at Edinburgh, impoverishing his father—the damn fool. Our family—his side of it anyway—had pretensions to nobility, in case you did na' know. But he took a job as a schoolteacher, as I recall, someplace in Ireland. There was trouble there over some lass. They threw him out, which is when he came here."

Katie said, barely audibly, "Where in Ireland?"

A. G. observed her intently. "Do na' remember. Are you all right?"

She downed her wine. "Perfectly."

"Then why have y' turned green?"

"Have I?"

"Well, y' look better now."

"May I have some more wine, please?"

He reached across to pour. "It was what I said?"

"Do you have a photograph of him?"

The family album provided nothing insofar as the first cousin was concerned, but unearthed a sufficient number of snapshots of Briton in various stages of growth to keep A. G. going, anecdotally, for an hour.

"A. G., we've got to go. Big day tomorrow."

"What?" he expostulated, taking a watch from the pocket of his brown cabled cardigan. "I thought so! It's na' even ten o'clock."

"Sorry. Next time we'll get here earlier."

"And I slept all afternoon!" he complained, suddenly looking as forlorn as a child, as Briton had looked at the mouth of the tunnel.

He badgered them all the way to the door. Katie kissed him on the cheek, promised to come back to visit him, and got a rough bear hug in return—with, if she did not entirely imagine it, a slight squeeze on her bottom.

They drove silently for several miles on poorly lighted country roads. On the parkway, Briton said, "You were doing pretty well until he mentioned Ireland."

She did not respond. She sat transfixed by car and highway lights and the white lines darting past them. Finally, with great effort and a sigh, she told him. She told the story Freddie Doyle had told about her grandmother and the Scotsman, and then, about the two old men in the hardware store in Dingle. She told it flat and strained to keep her voice from quivering. They drove another mile in silence.

"Are you certain he couldn't have been their grandson?" Briton ventured.

"Are you kidding? My grandmother lived in Dingle another two years before coming here. You couldn't have kept an illegitimate child a secret in that town for two minutes, let alone two years. Besides—we are not talking about someone who just resembles you, Briton."

"All right."

"I don't think you fully grasp that. I really don't. I—" She bit down on the thought and huddled in the corner.

"Don't be frightened."

"Who the hell's frightened?"

He pulled out to pass a car. "Would you like to stay at my place tonight?"

"No."

"Would you like me to stay at yours?"

No answer.

"If there are parallel worlds—"

"Briton, you're doing eighty miles an hour!"

"Am I? Sorry." He slowed down.

"And this is not the place to talk about this."

"Look, he's either from this world or he isn't. That's a straight, logical proposition. If he's not, the theory of multiple worlds is true. And if it's true, if there's travel between them—if those two seemingly impossible things can happen—then it is equally possible that transfers between systems can be influenced by will. That's what I wanted to say."

"Terrific."

"Go to sleep."

"Oh, sure."

An hour later, when they arrived at her building, she was deep in slumber, her head thrown back on the seat. He parked in a questionable spot close to a hydrant, then found the keys in her bag. In the light of a street lamp he studied her face. Her glasses were off, her mouth open, her eyes closed like a cat's. She looked about eight years old. He awakened her with a kiss.

"Very romantic," she derided, shaking herself crankily all over.

Upstairs, after she'd brushed her teeth and thrown herself into a nightgown, she did not protest overly much when he joined her in the small bed.

"Just hold," she murmured.

"Okay."

She squirmed a bit and said sulkily, "You really believe this crazy stuff?"

"Katie, that time . . . when you saw him at that school . . . he was a member of the board. The headmaster we met had never even heard of him. Where were you at that meeting? The 'you' you're conscious of?"

She shuddered and turned over on her other side.

"You asked," he said.

"And now I'll never get to sleep."

CHAPTER TWENTY-ONE

Briton and Mary Jo and the two boys were at breakfast in their kitchen. Geordie, while spooning his cereal, was trying to read upside down the cover of a box of doughnuts.

"Do whales give milk?" he pondered aloud.

Edward glanced up from the Science section of the *Times*. "Of course. They're mammals, aren't they?"

Geordie considered this, his small brow furrowed. "Do people *make* things out of whale milk?"

Briton, putting down his own section, said straight-faced, "Pretty hard to milk a whale."

Edward, reading the box right side up, let out a yelp. "That's *whole* milk, stupid!"

Everyone laughed, even Geordie, who turned the box around. "I thought it was kinda peculiar!"

Edward said, "I had a funny dream last night. I dreamt I was all grown up."

"And?"

"Nothin'! Just funny."

As the boys ran off to dress for school, Briton had a sudden thought of

Katie. This would happen pretty often. Guilty thoughts, because unsharable. He tried to shut them out. Day by day. Like forming a habit. Sometimes, often in the street, with strangers so certain of their space, he felt like shouting at them. And to her. The truth. They'd lock him up, of course.

Mary Jo said, "To look at you and your son—"

"Edward?"

"Yes. It's weird, the way you both sit there reading your paper, the way you laugh . . ."

"He does resemble me."

"Resemble you! Briton! He's the very image. There's never been a father and son who looked and acted so alike."

He thought so, too. It was his pride, his soaring joy. This love for both his sons, so much a part of what he felt for Mary Jo, had brought him back, he thought.

He said, "Strong genes. But Geordie looks like you."

"Like both of us."

"Well, some of me, I guess."

Mary Jo poured them both another cup of coffee. Briton resumed his study of the *Times*. It was like hundreds of other mornings.

"I had a call yesterday," she said, "from Mr. Catchings. About Edward."

His head picked up.

"I didn't mention it last night. I . . . don't know whether to be happy or disturbed. He's been saying and writing things in science that seem to have his teachers terribly excited. They think he has . . . 'special gifts,' is the way Catchings put it."

"Do they!" His pulse was racing. "Why should that be disturbing?"

"I don't know." She gave a half-laugh, anxious, almost wistful. "They want to give him special instruction. Take him out of his regular class. He's so young to be singled out like that, don't you think?"

Briton thought nothing of the kind. "Let me speak to Catchings. In that school, it will probably make him a hero. Those kids are all bright."

"It doesn't worry you? Our son being a genius?"

"We're not going to treat him any differently. He's still a nine-year-old kid. He's got a way to go before he's a certified genius."

"I suppose," she said resignedly.

"Mary Jo, this is really marvelous news!"

"You think someone's happier with 'special gifts?' "

"Of course. It gives one focus, a center."

With a brief exchange of looks, each glanced down, having a different reason from the other's to be embarrassed by this thought.

She said abruptly, now staring at him hard, "I've been thinking of starting a business." She added, "A travel business. There are so few good ones."

He blinked at this transition; so obvious, it wrenched his heart.

"Hard to break in," he said softly, with caution. "And you'd have to be away from home a lot."

"Would you mind?"

"Sure. But . . . I suppose we could travel about together . . . with the boys on their vacations."

"Yes. That would be nice. Summers and spring and Christmas. Only rarely without you."

"Okay. It's not a bad idea. You'd be good at it. In fact, the more I think about it . . . you'd be sensational. Need some capital?"

"No. Very businesslike. I'll get a business loan. Oh, Briton, you'd like to travel with me, wouldn't you?"

He colored, knowing, too, where this was coming from. "Yes," he said, and meant it.

CHAPTER TWENTY-TWO

It was a chilly, damp Friday afternoon in May. Katie sat huddled in her white Irish sweater atop the USCC world headquarters building.

The building was a five-story octagonal. Its inner court was divided geometrically into gardens characteristic of the principal countries in which USCC did business. The most elaborate was the Japanese garden outside Roy Sloane's windows. It was at those that Katie peered.

The roof of the headquarters had been made into an observation or lounging deck, itself divided into gardens replicating those of the inner court. The wind now and then whipped across the deck, stirring stones and leaves, whirlpooling dust from the planked crosswalks, making bramble of her hair.

This was the place in which company employees would gather in fair weather to think large thoughts about "firmware," cybernetics or "conscious" machines. On this day of penetrating wind and steely sky, Katie was alone.

A meeting in Sloane's office was in progress. She had been told of this and summoned to stand by. Standing by was not something she was good at. After fifteen minutes of thumbing company magazines in Sloane's outer chamber, she had told his secretary where the great man might find her.

Inside his window, she could make out shapes around half the conference table. Someone would speak, then slump back, then another. Sloane's stance was firm. He appeared to be getting his way, as usual. Whatever that was. They were deciding the future of USCC. More importantly, to Katie, they were deciding what to do about Katie's once and future lover.

Katie cared about the outcome of this meeting but not as much as she cared about the great problem of her life. It was this paradox that still obsessed her.

She did not really believe that Briton, the one they were discussing, was lying. She only wanted to believe that when the thought of two Briton Bells made her feel she was losing her mind. Between losing her mind and losing her lover, the battle inside her was fierce and close.

As she watched the blurredly observable portion of the meeting, her thoughts of her dilemma eddied with thoughts of Briton's invention, and in both instances, some underlying, unrevealed concept nagged. It was quite some time before she became conscious of the nagging sensation. When she did, she could not define it. Since it persisted and grew more insistent, she concentrated hard. Her mind cleared, then opened. And finally it came.

There was a connection! A connection between the invention and the paradox of two Briton Bells. In fact, a connection between the two Briton Bells and the bug in the invention. The bug in the invention generated multiple printouts like nature generated multiple Briton Bells.

My God! She leapt to her feet. "I've got to think this through!" But there was no time left; the meeting was breaking up.

*   *   *

As she stood outside Roy Sloane's office, Katie got what she regarded as fishy stares from the line of departing executives. Maybe because she had forgotten to comb her hair. She ran her fingers through it. But maybe it was something else.

"In here, Katie!" barked Sloane.

He sat her at the same conference table she'd been watching for more than a hour, took his accustomed seat and looked at her grimly.

"That," he said, "was quite a session."

"You're going to sue and go for an injunction," she surmised, color leaving her face.

"What do you think we should do?"

Her throat was dry and she swallowed. "Settle."

"Why?" His voice was hard.

"It would be the moral thing to do."

He nodded his agreement.

"I know you have the blueprint—"

"There are three now. Three have turned up at different outside fabricators."

"I can't believe he knew about them. I can't believe they're significant. And he would agree not to use anything anyone has taken. He would agree to a monitoring system. He told me. And besides—it's a great invention. It's probably the greatest invention ever conceived."

"So it now appears."

"It does!" she exclaimed, eyes very wide.

"Quite categorically."

"So—you'll make a deal?"

He sat back, arms folded, and an ambivalent expression came over his face. "I think I should tell you what's been happening. Last night I decided to make your Mr. Bell, at age thirty-six, one of the four or five richest men in the world."

"Ohmigod!"

"Wait. This morning a call came in my aides insisted I take."

Her stomach was sinking.

"The man I spoke to made a prior claim to this invention. He also claimed to know you and Bell quite well."

Her lips curled.

"I've now confirmed he is what he said he is."

She was up and pacing. "The man's a crook!"

"Katie, he's a full professor of physics at Yale."

"Hanratty!" she spat out.

"So you do know him."

"You bet I know him! He's a maniac as well as a crook."

"He knows a great deal about this invention."

"Yeah? Well lemme tell ya how he's found out. Y'know I've been workin' with this guy on a project? . . . They've got a Model 7600 at Yale? . . . Well, he calls me last week . . . no, that's wrong . . . I called him on something else . . ."

"Calmly!"

"Calmly? *Calmly?*"

"Katie!"

"Jesus! I can't believe this."

"Will you sit down for a moment!"

She stopped in her tracks, flapped her hands at her sides, and took a very deep breath. "He tried to get me to spy for him."

"On Bell?"

"Right. To learn about this invention . . . only I didn't even know then there *was* an invention . . . and to tell him all about it."

"How do you think he knew there was an invention?"

Her mouth gaped for a moment, then closed. "He said he had other sources. But he knew nothing about it then. That's why he asked me to spy."

"He told me Bell was in a course he gave eight years ago and that he started working on the invention even before then. He thinks Bell spied on him."

"The hell he does! Roy, when he talked to me last week he knew nothing! He must have found out from those other sources."

"Possibly."

"Roy!"

He looked unconvinced. "What did he offer you?"

"Offer me? The man's a lunatic."

"Is he?"

Her face revealed the recollection that Hanratty's offer was the most disturbing thing that anyone had ever said to her in her life.

"Katie, in this whole farfetched affair, your story about Hanratty is no more fantastic than anything else. But—"

"It's not fantastic. If you knew Hanratty . . ."

"I will certainly have the opportunity."

"What's the 'but?' "

"I've got to turn this thing over to the lawyers."

"Oh Christ! Just cause some maniac calls you up on the telephone."

"He may be as you say—but the man is a chaired professor at Yale. I cannot deal with him lightly, certainly not on something like this."

*   *   *

Katie expropriated someone's vacated office and immediately dialed Briton's plant. While she waited on the line, she noticed, staring at her, photographs of the office occupant's wife, his children, dog, house and boat. In the ashtray lay three pipes of various bores. How neat, self-satisfied and smug, she thought. How normal!

Briton finally came on.

"Have you heard," she exploded.

"Yes. Where are you, Saddle River?"

"Right."

"Stay where you are. In a half hour go to the helicopter pad on the north strip of the grounds. I'll pick you up there."

"Where we going?"

"New Haven."

"*What?*"

"I've spoken with Hanratty. He'll be waiting for us in his lab."

"Briton—you're not going to make a deal with that bastard!"

"I want to hear what he has to say."

"He's trying to cheat you! I completely forgot to tell you. Last week, he tried to get me to spy on you."

"Did he really? That should be useful. You'll tell me about it on the way up."

"Wait a second—I'm not going on any helicopter."

"Be there Katie! Half hour!"

*   *   *

She lurked in the rear corridor of the building and heard it land. As she came out its blades were still turning, like a Waring blender for people. He spotted her, took her hands and almost dragged her aboard. It was a genuinely terrifying thirty-five-minute experience. From the New Haven airport, a waiting limousine drove them to Payne Whitney labs.

"I can't think or hear," she complained, pumping her ears as the elevator brought them to the attic floor.

The Sterling Professor of Physics waited jovially on the landing. "Good of you to come," he dryly greeted, and threw open the door to the lab.

A single lamp illuminated dimly from a corner of the room, projecting on the walls and ceiling lengthened shadows of equipment.

"Now I can't see," she said. "What is this? Why don't you turn on some lights in here?"

Hanratty affected a pretense of concern. "At five . . . when the staff goes home . . . we do our bit for conservation. Come. Be seated."

Two high stools stood—had obviously been placed—in front of a laboratory table against which Hanratty leaned.

Briton approached one of these chairs, gripped its back and stared at Hanratty for some moments. "Thomas . . . I am having considerable difficulty associating you—my friendship for you—with the events of the last several hours."

"Only because you lack the facts, my friend. Yet I have things to tell you that will strain your credulity even more . . . although, at the end, you will know them to be true. I . . . ah . . . trust we will be speaking in confidence?"

"I hope, Thomas, this is not a threat of litigation."

Hanratty waved his hand in dismissal. "I have more important things to offer you than forbearance from litigation. But . . . do I have your word?"

Briton frowned unpleasantly. "Go on. Speak."

"Yes or no?"

"Yes!"

"You are not . . . by any chance . . ." he had the grace to blush ". . . wired?"

"Don't be ridiculous!"

"You will not mind, then, if I . . . ah . . . check?"

"Thomas, are you feeling quite all right?."

"Perfectly well, thank you. You will understand my caution in a moment."

With a wry face, Briton raised his arms mockingly, allowing Hanratty to feel along his trouser legs, chest and back.

"You're not putting those filthy hands on me!" Katie snapped.

Hanratty shifted an inquiring glance to Briton, as if permission were his to grant.

"Forget it."

"Take off your sweater, my dear."

"My sweater, Jesus!" Frowning furiously, she ripped it over her head. Had she been equipped, the nylon blouse she wore would have revealed the wires, for she was braless. "If you think I'm stripping down any more for you, buster, you got another think comin'!"

"So. . . ." Hanratty shrugged. "We will not embarrass you further." He leaned back again against the table.

"The point of that little exercise was not as you might think. I am not going to threaten, admit or extort. I have no fear of being recorded on those grounds. On the contrary, I am going to share with you a great discovery—one of which your little invention, my friend, is but a minor application . . . and of which you, uniquely, will see the value. You may even, with my compliments, publish it as your own—if you dare. I do not. That is the limit of the obligation of secrecy I place upon you. I do not wish to be associated with this discovery. It is not provable empirically, except to you. And though it is without question—and I say this with full appreciation of the seeming extravagance of the claim—the most extraordinary discovery in the history of mankind, to publish it would not enhance my reputation as a serious scientist, but destroy it.

"I see I have your attention. Good. Let me begin this way.

"Approximately eight weeks ago, you, Miss Dunston, had a troubling experience. I suspect you have thought a great deal since about this experience, and certain subsequent events have even suggested an explanation, which is more troubling still.

"I, of course, was not there and cannot describe it in precise detail. But I know for a fact it occurred. I expect it began with a feeling of . . . ah . . . disintegration? Disorientation? A feeling not . . . shall we say . . . of this world?

"And in the place in which you found yourself . . . people reacted

220 ALAN HRUSKA

somewhat strangely, I should imagine . . . in a manner difficult to put
your finger on . . . eh? And you were different, too, were you not?

"I will speculate more here . . . did you find yourself, perhaps, to be a
right-handed person? Suddenly? And the people around you right-handed,
too? Does that hit home? I see it does.

"Now let me tell you how I know all this. I have met a young woman—
although, I would guess, several years older than you. She does not have a
chip on her front tooth, nor, I should add, on her shoulder. She is not very
bright; indeed, lamentably dull. But for all that, she is unquestionably the
most fascinating young woman I have ever encountered.

"I think you know who I mean. She is a checkout clerk in a supermarket
called Almac's in a town called Mystic, Connecticut."

"Bullshit! You think I believe this? You got this from Marcel."

"Did I? You judge. Approximately eight weeks ago this young woman—
as she told me—was sitting quietly at home watching her favorite afternoon soap opera, and what do you think happened? The next moment,
without warning, she found herself in front of a large convention, lectur-
ing on a computer system for checkout applications which was entirely
unknown in her world—and certainly to her. About an hour later, just as
suddenly and inexplicably, she was again in the living room of her own
home.

"Regrettably, from her standpoint, she retained a recollection of the
schematics she had used, hastily drew them out to convince herself she
hadn't been dreaming, and sent them to the manufacturer of the system
installed in her store. She became the recipient of a prize, a pending
patent and nationwide media publicity. In short, she is now widely regarded as something of a freak—and I doubt seriously whether her sanity
will survive this experience much longer, if she hasn't snapped in the week
since I saw her."

"Why should I believe this story?"

"Please, Miss Dunston. You already do. What you should find remarkable in this story is not that it happened, but that I should know it
happened."

Briton finally seated himself on the high swivel chair. "You are claiming, I take it, the existence of another world. And . . ." he exhaled audi-

bly in resignation, ". . . the ability to transport your not inconsiderable bulk to this place."

"At will, my friend. That is the key."

He came away from the laboratory table with a glare in his eye. "Listen to me! Physicists have known for more than fifty years that multiple worlds exist. It has been proven in space flight and in a thousand thought experiments. All over this earth must be people who have done it—do not understand what they have done, and may be going insane as a consequence.

"I have discovered *how* to do it. And the *how* is almost ridiculously simple. You will forgive me my metaphor when I say, I have discovered the doorway of time."

"And this is what you will share with us?" said Briton.

"I am prepared to do so, yes."

"In trade for my invention."

Hanratty clucked his tongue.

"Why else are we here, Thomas?"

The large man smiled. "One might say, to help me solve a moral dilemma. I have, you see, been deeply affected by the plight of the young woman I spoke of. I should think you would be, too, Miss Dunston, for you are more directly responsible. Yet to help her in any meaningful way, I should have to spend considerable time in her company.

"I could, of course, go to her, but I should tell you, when you travel in this fashion, it appears you leave behind a most distressingly incongenial nerd of a fellow—no fun at all, I am told by my wife. So . . . would that really be fair to her, to say nothing of my associates here, my staff, my students?

"The alternative would be to bring the young woman here. Quite possible. The apparatus, as I say, is simplicity itself. She certainly has the ability to journey in this fashion, and I have little doubt she may be persuaded to do so. The poor girl is desperate for help, and gaining her confidence has been no very large matter.

"There is, however, a rather significant catch. Should she come here, my dear, you would go elsewhere. It does seem as if this sort of travel has a dramatic domino effect. You would have to occupy your . . . ah . . . counterpart in some other world, or if, in that world you had no counterpart, you would perhaps become . . . what? . . . a school of fish . . . a colony of ants . . . foam on the waves? Who knows?"

Hanratty laughed out loud. "Yes, yes. I quite realize it sounds preposterous. Quite certifiable! But not to you. Which is why I seek your advice on this . . . as I say . . . moral dilemma."

Briton was not laughing at all. "This will require some thought."

"By all means. Yet . . . time is of the essence. I cannot wait indefinitely, or this poor girl will be beyond help."

Katie looked from one to the other. Stunned, she said to Briton, "You gonna fall for this?"

"What are your terms, Thomas?"

"Ah, as you will see, I am not a greedy person. Full pooling of information. I will demonstrate and explain the means of . . . ah . . . travel. And, of course, a full partnership between us."

"And the young woman you referred to?"

"Well . . . once you possessed the means, you might do with her what you like?"

"This man's a crook!" Katie declaimed.

"Right," said Briton. "And I can just see us going to the district attorney and accusing Professor Hanratty of Yale of extortion. 'What did you say he threatened you with, Mr. Bell?' "

Briton turned again to Hanratty. "There is one more thing. If I am the counterpart of the man you saw in Ireland, his visit here had no effect on me."

"So I surmised. There are, however, three possible explanations. This . . . ah . . . displacement may not be invariable—which I seriously doubt. Or, you are not in fact his counterpart, despite the identity of names and appearance—another doubtful conclusion. Or . . ."

"I was the man in Ireland."

Hanratty shrugged, which drew to Briton a fierce look from Katie.

"I'll call you Monday," said Briton.

"No later, please."

CHAPTER TWENTY-THREE

This time Katie paid little notice to the helicopter ride to the city, the pilots or drivers, except that they were reasons why nothing that just happened could be openly discussed. She did not, in fact, wish to discuss it with Briton, at least not for a while. She had plenty of discussion going on in her head. It seemed the left side believed him; the right side did not. And they were locked in furious debate.

His apartment, where they went, was a twelve-room penthouse suite with a large flowering terrace on Eighty-fifth Street and Park Avenue. It was decorated almost entirely monochromatically. The walls were ice blue, the upholstery French blue, the draperies, cerulean blue, a few accent vases and cushions, Prussian blue, and the Oriental carpeting, apart from a dash of lime yellow, a combination of the foregoing. The total impression was a blue haze. Katie felt for one astounding moment that she had landed in heaven. Every piece of furniture in it was antique, except for an étagère and two side tables of stainless steel and glass.

He showed her the kitchen, a super-bright room of blue, white and stainless steel, on which easily sixty thousand dollars had been lavished. She said, momentarily distracted from the issue at hand, "I suppose you lease this too."

"Sublease. With an option to buy."

"You're not actually going to buy something!"

"That depends." He caught her glance, feeling the elation almost leap out of him. "On whether you like it."

She looked down—into a lagoon of blue vinyl.

"If," he said, "we are going to spend the rest of our lives together, we obviously need someplace in which to spend it."

"Big 'if!' " she said scornfully, blowing up her cheeks and turning away fast.

His bedroom was thirty feet long with a door to the terrace. In the center stood an oversized double bed with a blue velvet canopy and draw curtains at the end and sides.

She plumped down on a Louis XV chair, auctionable for thousands, and stared disdainfully at that bed. She recalled a similar symbol in a Philadelphia hotel. There was no hiding it, at least from herself. Once again, despite everything, she was ready: love had done her in. But though her body was ready, her will was otherwise determined. The ascendancy was on the right.

"Hanratty's playing you."

"Obviously."

"But you can't let on, can you? You can't concede this other-world crap is preposterous, because that's your excuse for the masquerade."

"Oh Christ, Katie, you're back on that! What about *your* experience?"

"Things like that . . . can happen! They can! The mind plays tricks."

"How could Hanratty have known about it, then? And tell me this . . . your other friend . . . surely he must have done things and said things that struck you as different . . . he must have known things that we don't know."

Katie thought of the song that Briton had played to the bewilderment of two hundred experts at the Killarney singing bar.

"I don't believe it."

"I'm afraid I do."

"I don't believe *you!*"

"Because you don't want to believe *it!*"

"You got a piano in here?"

He glanced at her steadily. "I don't play the piano, Katie."

She got to her feet. "It ain't gonna work!"

She began to pace between a chaise lounge and the sliding doors to the terrace. "You think I can live a rational life with you? I haven't lived a rational minute since I met you."

"When was that?" he asked with an expression now grim.

"In Philadelphia!" she stubbornly proclaimed, throwing open the terrace door and marching outside.

The terrace was flagstone and huge, at least forty feet by twenty in its largest rectangle, and it embraced three sides of the apartment, all well lighted. The edges were planted in dogwood, evergreen and, among the now flowering plants, rhododendron and tulips. The latter were a match for the tulips growing below on the Park Avenue dividers, which reminded her of the matching gardens atop the USCC building in Saddle River. The rhododendron reminded her of Ireland. From here she could see down the avenue to the tallest buildings of Manhattan, including the Chrysler Building spire, and she could see into the park, the dark meadow at Ninety-eighth Street. Although the sky was cloud-laden, the night air had turned warmer. It felt as if it might rain.

She was powerfully affected by these associations.

"Katie," he said from behind her. His arms crossed over her and squeezed her back to his chest. Though the contact was pleasurable, she squirmed. He put his hands on her breasts, and she thought she might faint from this pleasure. Trembling, she ripped away.

"It isn't fair what you do to me!" she protested.

"And you to me," he said hoarsely.

"So let's stop it!"

"Right now? Just like that?"

"Yes!"

He spoke with controlled calm. "It is difficult—I mean it is very, very difficult—to conceive of anyone so ornery, anyone so self-defeating as you. The evidence is staring you in the face. If you'd think clearly, you'd accept it."

"Never!"

"It's something else, too, isn't it? You talk about my renting things. All right! I know what you're saying. I concede it. But do you think you're any different? You're afraid to show that anything matters to you, things or people. How many people have you let into your life?"

"I let you in!"

"Up to a point."

"I let him in," she said, looking down to the flagstones.

"And how comforting it was he was married."

Her face smarted as if slapped. "You bastard!"

"Because I'm right. Why do you put people off all the time? Why are you such a little terror? Why do you live, on *your* income, in that tiny apartment with furniture thrown away by Goodwill?"

"I have an Eames chair!" she pouted.

"Nobody's that consistent."

"This has nothing to do with that!"

"You're wrong. It's another form of denial. Another product of guilt. Why do you feel guilty, Katie? I know why I do. Because my parents died and I lived. It's perverse, but at least I know it. What are you guilty about?"

"Nothin'!"

"The hell you aren't. Is it because you're the only one in your family with brains? Because you don't love them?"

"I do! You're so goddamn smug! You don't know anything about it."

"Don't I? *Use* your brains, Katie."

"On what? This situation? This situation is lunatic!"

Peremptorily, he wheeled her inside and plunked her down on the chaise where she sat like a bundle. He went back to the terrace door and closed it. He said, "I want you to listen to me for about a half hour."

She moaned. "This is impossible."

"We're going to deal with the problem."

"Are we?" she said bitterly. "You're going to talk it away? Do you have flip charts?"

"No charts."

"Well, there you are. I can't concentrate without flip charts."

"Try!"

He opened by stating it was self-evident that only one world existed in our space because we could see in that space only one world. He said that it was therefore deemed to be nonsense that this space could be occupied by a multiplicity of worlds, much less credited that people from one world could travel to another. But concepts no less nonsensical than this, he said, have been the basis for every discovery in the new science since Einstein and even before.

He took for an example the famous speech given by Lord Kelvin in 1900 to the Royal Institution in England. Kelvin, a distinguished physicist of his time, was actually trying to discourage graduate study in physics because so few problems remained to be solved. To him, Newtonian laws explained everything. According to Kelvin, there were only two "clouds" left to deal with: Planck's experiment in blackbody radiation, which supposedly proved the "nonsense" conclusion that heated objects give off energy discontinuously, in separate "packets" or "quanta"; and the Michelson-Morley experiment which "proved" the equally absurd proposition that the speed of light is constant.

"Everyone knew," lectured Briton, "that nothing could move at a constant speed in relation to a individual who's also in motion. If I am moving toward an object at one hundred miles an hour, and that object is moving toward me at five hundred miles an hour, the speed of that object in relation to me is six hundred miles an hour. That's just common sense.

"But Michelson-Morley," he went on to say, "proved that, while that was true as to everything else, it was not true as to the speed of light. That speed in relation to anything else, moving or not moving, is 186,000 miles per second.

"It was this so-called 'cloud' on Newtonian physics that led Einstein to prove mathematically his theories of relativity. And relativity scraps the preponderance of Newtonian physics, except for the large-scale world— the world," he added, "we think we see.

"As for the Planck paper on discontinuity, the effect on Newton was even more devastating. Everyone 'knew' that a heated object gives off energy continuously until it cools down—that's exactly what they could see as they watched it smoothly change color from ultraviolet to blue to red. And that accorded with their preconceptions that light was caused by 'oscillating' electrons that smoothly ran out of energy. In fact, the physicists of the day dubbed the Planck experiments showing the opposite the 'Ultra-Violet Catastrophe.'

"But proof that energy came in specific amounts, in specific 'quanta'—

that objects absorbed or emitted it only in tiny, discontinuous 'explosions'
—gave rise to the laws of quantum mechanics.

"In other words," he said, "Newtonian laws work for the large-scale
world, but not for the world of elementary particles. And everything—
every rock, insect, human being—is made up of those particles. It is the
laws of quantum mechanics and relativity which these particles obey. So
the 'clouds' of 1900 have by now reduced the entirety of Newtonian
physics to a footnote—to a set of exceptions to the general rules."

He then reminded Katie of what he had told her, and she had read,
about the characteristics of elementary particles or quanta—that at speeds
at or near the speed of light, each proton, neutron or electron will somehow go out of existence, to be replaced by combinations of particles of
light, called photons, and strange new particles called leptons and mesons,
which then themselves go out of existence to be replaced by new protons,
neutrons or electrons, and so on, ad infinitum.

"Where do those particles go?" he asked.

"They decompose!" she insisted stubbornly.

"Not that simple! The leptons, mesons and photons have a different
mass-energy in total than the particle they have replaced. Something else
is happening in this world of particles. Something else is happening to us.
Every instant.

"You put together Einstein's thought experiment on the paradox of
twins, the bug in my invention and the appearance of your Philadelphia
man and you reach exactly the sort of 'nonsense' conclusion that you are
refusing to accept—but which is probably very close to the solution to this
problem."

Einstein's twin paradox, she recalled as he related it, was what Hanratty
had described—one twin traveling from this planet at or near the speed of
light will return younger than his brother. He has literally been in a different time world. "It is no more fantastic to conclude," Briton asserted,
"that a proton disappearing at or near the speed of light is similarly traveling to a different time world.

"Every object," he emphasized, "and therefore every person and particle exists in not only the three observable dimensions of length, width and
height, but also in the fourth dimension of time. If a particle can travel up

or sideways, it can also travel in time, and so can the conscious being who is composed of those particles.

"The problem is how—and the answer," he explained, "may be intuitable. When a proton, for example, emerges in the place of leptons, there is little reason to suppose that it is the very same proton which went out of existence in that spot originally. What may be happening is that each proton and each other elementary particle may exist as an infinite succession of such particles, circling sequentially—like a bicycle chain at light speeds—among infinite systems of time-space.

"Therefore, while every person and large-scale object in this world may be stationary from a time-space standpoint, every particle of that object and person—which we already know is constantly changing—may also be both constantly new and constantly supplanted by particles from a different time world.

"To get an entire person to time-travel without accelerating his speed to that of light—or without moving him at all—would require switching every particle in that person to another time dimension.

"Here," he said, "is where two new 'clouds' of physical science come in."

The first one he described involved an experiment on particle pairs. "Some particles exist only as twins—part of a two-particle system. Change the spin or other characteristic of one particle and you change the same characteristics of the other. The experiment in question demonstrated that this could be done even if the paired particles were separated by great distances—those, in relation to their mass, many times greater than the distance between the earth and sun.

"If the bicycle chain theory of the existence of particles is valid, the particles in that chain may be 'paired' in the same fashion. If some force could be exerted in one time dimension to change the time characteristics of one particle in that chain, then all particles in the chain would similarly be changed. And if you can do that to one particle of a human being or object, then you can do it to all particles comprising that person or thing —and switch him or it to an entirely different time system.

"The problem here is what could that force be? It could not be something common, or the phenomena of time travel would commonly occur. The second new 'cloud' may suggest at least part of that answer.

"And that," he said, "is the double slit experiment. It is the strangest experiment ever conducted. It has been done again and again. Always with the same result. And no one knows how it happens. Not even Einstein could figure this one out. Because the answer seems to be the biggest piece of nonsense ever conceived. The answer seems to be that elementary particles are 'conscious.'"

"What?"

"Listen." He then explained. "You put a screen in a dark room between a light bulb and a wall. You cut one small slit in the screen with a razor blade, turn on the light bulb, and the light waves fan out behind the slit, like ripples in a pond, and produce a circle of light on the wall. Cut two slits in the screen, one above the other, and there appear on the wall, not two circles of light, but nine alternating bands of light and dark, the middle band of light being the brightest. There is nothing shocking in that," he assured her. "The pattern of alternating bands is caused by the interference of the two ripples of waves fanning out behind each slit, like interfering pond ripples.

"Now, you take a pencil and trace on the wall each of the five bands of light. Then you cover the lower slit on the screen with some material impenetrable by light. Next you take a photon gun and shoot a single photon of light—a single light particle—through the top slit. It will go directly to an area on the wall that was a dark band when both slits were open and the source of light was a light bulb. In a dark room you can see that photon land in a tiny splash of light *between* the pencil markings. And you can mark where it lands on a photosensitive plate.

"Now here comes the punch line. If you open the bottom slit, aim the photon gun exactly as before, through the top slit, and shoot—the photon will not go straight to the wall. It will not land in the same dark band or any dark band. It will change its direction and land only in one of the bands penciled in for light, even though there are no interfering waves to have caused that change in direction.

"In effect, the photon 'knows' when the bottom slit is open and when it is closed. It 'knows' where to go under each condition, and acts accordingly. It is somehow 'sensing' information and acting upon the information it has obtained. But a photon is nothing but a particle of energy. It is nonsense to say that any particle is organic or conscious. Yet that is what it seems to be."

Katie, who had been listening to this without expression, now said rather dazedly, "So you are saying that some form of consciousness of particles is the force—the force that does the switching. All one's particles simply get together and decide to switch."

"No. I don't know what the force is. I'm saying that if particles have consciousness, their receptivity to switching may be a necessary condition."

"Oh I see." This was almost flippant. "And what about the bug? You said there was a connection there, too?" It was, of course, exactly what she had intuited on the observation deck at Saddle River.

"There may be. The way the invention is engineered, there is no apparent or familiar explanation for the multiplicity of printouts. There is, however, a 'nonsense' explanation: that the time characteristics of each carbon atom in the final plate are constantly being switched."

"Yes. Of course." She felt strangely at ease, almost as if she were floating. And slightly giddy. But this was tenuous. She felt, beneath the surface of this mood, an incipient hysteria. The ascendancy was on the left.

She said as calmly as she could with only the slightest revealing quiver, "I have to go, now." She got up, trying to remember the direction to the door.

"Katie!" He was on his feet, too.

"I have to think, Briton. I have to think this through."

"Together!"

"No, I can't think this way, you just confuse me."

"Stay here. Take a room. Take *this* room. I won't disturb you."

She laughed out loud. "Being within a hundred yards of you disturbs me."

"I'll take you home. We can talk on the way."

"No talk!"

His expression, as she left him, was as vulnerable a sign as she had ever seen him give.

*   *   *

It stayed with her as she sat in the dark on her living room floor, thinking with intense concentration. She was in the same lotus position in which his predecessor had found her some six weeks before. In the midst of emotional storms and gales of nonsensical improbabilities, she made a pocket of calm.

Systematically she then sifted the facts. It was fact, for example, that eight weeks ago, for at least one hour, she became a right-handed person. It was fact that this experience was both preceded by, and concluded with, sensations of disintegration. She had told no one of this experience; yet Hanratty had known. Everything else could be attributed to chicanery. Not, however, that.

Like a programmer at a terminal, she talked to her brain. Okay, she said, if you're so smart, how do I get out of this?

I want him, she said, I want his kids. I don't want to think about other worlds, much less travel to one. But if that bastard from New Haven is not bluffing my ass, that is exactly where it is going.

Okay, she said, let's focus real hard. Let's assume it's all true. If he can do it, so can I. Jesus, if he can do it, *I have done it!* If I get there first . . .

How?

How did I do it?

How do I do it again?

She repeated this inquiry, like the utterance of a prayer, into the early morning hours. She did not recognize time passing. Finally, before dawn, the conversation became two-sided. Her brain started "talking" back.

When Katie devolved into this sort of abstraction, which she did often enough in her work, solutions, whatever the problem, appeared veritably in the form of telecast images from one part of her brain to the other. Physiologically, this process is commonplace. One part of the mind normally thinks verbally and quantitatively, while the other, more imaginatively, in pictures. What was uncommon in Katie's case was the ability of the more methodical part to "see" the other—the sharp lines of its distinctiveness—and to correspond directly with it.

This was useful, because the "other" had a will of its own. It was also used to operating surreptitiously. When it was tracked down, found out and directly confronted, it would shy back, and had to be entreated like an oracle to speak. If so induced, the product could be particularly rewarding —in inspiration, even epiphany.

It was on this that Katie worked through the night.

As dawn cracked, the solution at last materialized, and she struggled to keep the picture intact. In the manner of oracular pronouncements it was Delphic and difficult to read. What it looked like to Katie was something as ephemeral as a state of mind itself; hallucinatory perhaps, imprisoned in a sphere of light—a sunbeam perhaps—recumbent, receptive and chimerical. She saw it first as an infinitesimally small glint far, far off, like a window in the distant skyline, and then, zooming closer, as this sunbeam, clear and luminous, resting on—of all things—the top of a small hill.

No more, but it was enough. It is, she concluded, coming out of her trance, a matter primarily of relativity. As if returning from the cleansing of mythic-sized stables, Katie fell soundly asleep.

CHAPTER TWENTY-FOUR

Three hours later Katie sat on top of the hill in the meadow at Ninety-eighth Street. It was a day in which sunbeams sporadically bounded through clouds like a strobe show at a disco. The air smelled of cold grass and cinders. She waited for a really good beam.

*　　*　　*

"Who's that?"

"Ohmigod!"

"Oh no!"

"I did it! Jesus! Did it! First shot!"

"I'm going crazy again!"

"Easy girl."

"You! Get out of my head!"

"Don't make a scene!"

"I'm gonna fucking scream!"

"There are people in this store."

"I don't care!"

"Don't you dare come apart on me!"

"I don't want to go away again."

"Sit down! You're not going anywhere. I've got to think about this."

"You're a voice in my head, that's all. A voice in my head."

"That's right. Hanratty was wrong. I didn't have to bounce you at all."

"I'm not gonna listen to you."

"Look, girl! If you could talk to me all the time, you'd be a genius."

"I don't wanna be a genius."

"Okay, you see! We're talking to each other now. Not much of a conversation, but talk. Nothing bad's happening."

"This ain't bad?"

"What's so bad? You're in control. Come on, get up now and take a break. No one'll be at this counter for ten minutes. Let's get outside for a bit.

"That's right, she'll cover. Thank you very much. Now move your butt! Good. That's better. We can breathe out here. Just walk around for awhile. See you're doing it—I'm not. I go where you go."

"That's the goddamn trouble!"

"Think of it this way. I'm like a part of you you never use. A power you have. I'm your potential."

"For the loony bin."

"Hey! You won a prize didn't you?"

"That's why I'm going to the shrink."

"Will you stop with the shrink. I can help you more than he can."

"You're the problem!"

"Boy, are you screwed up! I'm the one who's going to get your life in order. Now look. First of all, you've got to get away from this town. You go to that company that gave you the prize. They'll offer you a job, if you ask them. I know how these companies work."

"They already have."

"Well now!"

"I can't do that stuff."

"What the hell do you think you did?"

"That wasn't me! It was you!"

"Wasn't me, kid. I slipped in someplace else. Bounced whoever was there, here, and you went elsewhere. See! There are lots of us. You must be the only one in our line who's not using her brains. You wouldn't have remembered that stuff if you didn't understand it—some of it, anyway."

"Lots of us!"

"Trust me. It's true. I know it's hard to believe . . ."

"Oh God! That guy on the beach, the professor. I thought he was nuts."

"Large man with a beard? Okay. He's someone I came to warn you about. Listen to me, will you! I don't have very long. Your attention's wandering."

"He said the same things as you."

"I'll bet."

"He's a famous man. I seen him on TV."

"That right?"

"I see his picture all over now."

"He's a prick. I know him better than you. You get mixed up with that guy, and he'll send you out of here so far you'll never get back again. Katie!"

"I'm getting very tired."

"Keep walking!"

"Are you going now?"

"In a minute. And I'm not coming back. So you'd better listen to me while you have the chance. Just remember two things. One, stay away from that guy with the beard. If you ever see him again, run in the opposite direction.

"The other thing is—take that job. They'll send you to school and you'll be amazed how easy it's going to be. You've got a knack you don't even know about. Use it!"

"You say you're never comin' back."

"Right."

"Suppose I need you in that school?"

"Listen to you! Two minutes ago you were pleading with me to get out of your head."

"Yeah. That's what I want."

"Okay, then."

"If I could believe I wasn't just hearin' things . . ."

"All right. It just hit me. I'll tell you what. There's a man you ought to try to find. He may live in New York. His name's Briton Bell. If he exists in your world, he'll help you."

"How?"

"Don't worry about that. Just find him!"

"Briton Bell."

"Super guy. You'll love him."

"Really?"

"Pretty sure. Now I'm going."

"Oh look in that store! I told you! That man's picture's all over the window."

Katie saw. It was Hanratty to the life. And it was the way to send him here, so he'd never bother her again.

* * *

The same morning Briton awoke in a dangerously volatile mood. It fluctuated radically from depression to elation, from anger to indifference, from joy to despair.

He would have been less than human not to reflect on the facts that he had just made one of the world's great inventions, was on the verge of driving the largest individual bargain in the history of industrial society, and had theorized a solution to the many-worlds problem which, when confirmed by the mathematical calculations now made possible in a lifetime by his own invention, would command a Nobel prize. All this, he had laid, as it were, at her feet—to be interrupted in mid-brilliance.

And he had much more to explain. For example, why particle chains might be the physical implementation of the concept of cyclical time, as espoused by Far Eastern religions. How other heretofore untheorized forces might contribute to the time switching of particles. How light itself might well be composed of a continuum of particles, from the slow photon that powered his invention to those traveling at conventional light speed.

He was not any longer in the least distressed by the implications of this construct. Nor was he overly disturbed that it gave reality to Hanratty's threat. That, he was confident, he could deal with—at worst by cutting him in.

The problem was Katie. She was not taking this well. And for that he had no ready solution.

In the shower, his worry got deeper. With his breakfast, peanut butter spread on slices of apple, a chill attacked his gloom, sending goosebumps over his body. Never had he felt so intensely the depths of incipient loss. He was totally unprepared for such a reaction.

He walked out onto the terrace and peered through the park, as if he might see her. He considered racing to her apartment, before she awakened, before she went out. Before she went out of his life? Not likely! He shivered. It was freezing, and he came back in.

He lectured himself. When she is ready, she will be here. She understands we are inexorably bound. This, somehow, was not reassuring. It had an underside to it of warning. Did he himself actually comprehend anything important about their love? He thought about that most of the morning.

Every clue was itself an impenetrable puzzle. This other Briton Bell, for example. How he got here he thought he understood. But that didn't explain his own bond with Katie; it merely restated the question. And the nearly identical programming work? Highly suggestive, but that—he didn't even have a theory of how *that* was done.

He made himself lunch and couldn't eat it. He tried to read the *Times*, then tried to nap, and couldn't do either.

The warning became more specific. Their love was different. The problem lay in that. He thought of her face; it might have been there—fresh, freckled, touchable on its cheek. He thought of the softness of her body, the clean, fresh smell of her hair, and he grew dizzy. Yet this was not, ultimately, what his love was about. His love relied on her honesty and toughness. On her being stubborn, being rebellious. That much he understood. And this was uniquely the sort of situation—this seeming direction from on high, its implacability, its predestination—she would be most impelled to rebel against.

Did she really even like him? He had opened up to her more than to anyone—but, he had to concede, he kept a reserve. Yes, a detachment. Fear of failure? A legacy from his former loves? From the loss of his parents? Was that, also, what this was all about?

The doorbell rang at precisely one-thirty. He bounded like a madman into his own front hall. You want the opposite of detached? he raved to himself. But a reflex checked him, one triggered by this kind of excitement. His opening of the door was studiously, stagily offhanded.

It was not she but an apparition to stun him, wild and beatific, in a rakishly worn, purplish heather cap. Her hair sprang and coiled from beneath it; her face freshly shone. In her black sweater and gray skirt she leaned provocatively in the doorway, one hand against the jamb, the other waving—with a single swoop of fingers—hello.

He felt that life itself had been restored.

"We are going," she announced, "for a walk."

He took an unsteady breath and coolly agreed, even while the joy of this life stretched before him.

* * *

Two o'clock. Saturday. Katie and Briton sat atop the same hill in the same meadow in Central Park.

Only, the day was now cloudy and gray. The strolling families, the children wielding skateboards or bikes, the old men walking their mutts, did not linger long in any one spot, nor did anyone long occupy benches. It was too unexpectedly cold.

Briton was bubbling, but not over the top; this he had effectively bottled. He said, "I know what you think is represented by this place, but is there any particular reason we must sit here?"

"Yes," said Katie, "there is."

"You will at some point, before we freeze to death, tell me what that is?"

"Better, Briton, I will show you."

In his present frame of mind of grateful acceptance, he was magnanimously prepared to talk this out.

"In short, we are to sit here indefinitely until something happens which you can identify as being the purpose for coming here in the first place."

"Yes! If you're cold, I'll put my arms around you."

"I would welcome your arms and the rest of you as well in the warmth and privacy of our apartment."

"*Your* apartment. It will not become 'our' apartment, unless what we are doing here works."

He smiled; nothing could jar him.

"Hanratty will be here any minute."

"Hanratty!" he exploded.

"Yes. I called him. At eleven. He agreed to meet us here at two."

"Katie, Katie, what are you doing?"

As she took off her glasses and peered at the park entrance, she saw the large man waddling toward them as he had once done on the Dingle beach.

He repeated Briton's sentiments on arriving. "Must we sit here and chill our respective behinds?"

"Hunker down!" Katie directed.

"This, as the incipient pneumonia victim once said, better be good."

Katie scoffed as he lowered his body, "You can't cross your legs!"

"One of my many reasons for preferring a seat . . . ah . . . somewhat more elevated?"

Briton did not share her ebullience. "Katie, I have no deal to offer this man."

"I know. I have."

"I'm afraid, dear girl, that offers from you are not what I'm after."

"Wrong, buster. You just don't know it yet. For one thing, I've just returned from a little trip to never-never land."

"That is a reference to . . . what?"

"To the land of your friend—Katie at Almac's."

"Bosh."

"Think so, huh! I'm even going to tell you how I did it. You gave it away. Why was that meeting last night in your lab? And why were the lights out?"

"I believe I answered that."

"You wanted us to see that thing in the corner, didn't you? But not too clearly. That bell jar contraption. I guess you thought it might add some credibility to your claim."

"I had no such thought."

"Bull. And not too smart, Thomas. You're working with photons—you told me so the first time I met you. The heart of Briton's invention is the slow photon. It comes right from the sun, separated out by polarizing screens. There are tubes from that jar in your lab to the ceiling, and I'll bet polarizing screens in those tubes. Just like Briton's prototype machine. And it's the slow photon that sends particles to another time dimension, which is the bug in that invention—and for a conscious being—a conscious bicameral being—the way to travel in time."

"Dubious. But I'm listening."

"You bet your ass you're listening. I've been in that world. I don't need any bell jar. I can get there on my own. *Any time I want.* And I, Thomas Hanratty, can send *you* flying. All I've got to do is find your counterpart—and that ain't going to be very hard."

"Not if I get there first."

Katie looked gleefully on this now dour professor and a stunned Briton Bell. "You can go there right now, for all I care—because you can't travel like I can. I can control it! How do y' like that, fatso! I can go to any world I want. I can *sort!*"

"Like the photon in the double slit experiment," mused Briton out loud.

"Damn right. In worlds where there's no Katie Dunston, I can go there intact. And in worlds where there are—I don't have to bump anybody. I can get in their heads!—and warn them of bearded professors!"

"Very bold claim," said Hanratty. "Particularly for someone who can't find her way across the street."

"You think I'm bluffing, hunh?"

"I'd say the odds favored such a conclusion."

"Like to call me on it, would ya?"

"I should warn you, my dear girl, that if I do—and if you have concocted this story, as I fully believe—your journey will be long and irredeemable."

Reverting in her excitement to childhood insults, Katie showed him her tongue.

"As you wish," said Hanratty, arising with difficulty.

"Long drive to New Haven."

"I . . . ah . . . happen to be associated with . . . Rockefeller Institute on York Avenue? The . . . ah . . . necessary apparatus is there. So . . . bon voyage dear girl."

"You too, Thomas. Long, happy trip."

Briton watched Hanratty waddle back over the meadow and Katie smiling at the sight. "Is there," he demanded to know, "the slightest truth to what you've just told him?"

"It's all true, baby," said Katie happily, never having so addressed him before. "And that is the last we're going to see of Mr. Hanratty."

"Katie, go back! What happened last night and this morning?"

"It was just as you said. It works like a charm. It's incredible—fabulous —it's great fun! You're gonna love it!"

"Why isn't Hanratty coming back?"

She smiled with immense satisfaction. "Because he's a vain son of a bitch."

"You mean—he'll have the invention to himself? He's known that all along."

"Yeah. There's that. But I'll tell you—when he patents that invention, they're going to fall all over him in that world. They're going to think he's another da Vinci. He'll never want to leave."

"Katie, for chrissake—will you tell me clearly what's going on?"

"Shh! I'm going to show you. There's the sun now," she said, looking up at a scarcely brightening chink in the clouds.

"That is not," he said, " 'the sun' as we know it—as in, for example, 'the sun is coming out.' "

"Don't be prosaic. What I think we are about to demonstrate is that, if he can do it, and I can do it, so can you."

"What?" he expostulated, with an expression at once humoring and besotted.

"Listen to me," she said in a rush. "If particles are conscious and can move in time, there must be the possibility of a link—the possibility that something in the mind can trigger the particles to switch. That something must generally be unconscious, but I can bring it out—and so can every Kathleen Dunston, or whatever they're called, in my line. And so can everyone in yours—I verily believe. And under the agency of slow photons, and God knows what other forces, we can do it! We can move ourselves wherever we want."

Dubiety clouded his face.

"Concentrate, Briton!"

But then the sun "as we know it" shot through that chink, picking them out like a celestial spotlight.

"This," said Briton, with more assurance than he felt, "is ridiculous."

"A bit showy, I agree."

"I think I should like to see *his* world."

"Then that's where we shall go."

For a few warmth-luxuriating moments, they said nothing more.

Then something quite strange indeed occurred. First, they gazed upward, directly at the sun, and saw its beams separate like colors in a prism, then come toward them, long drawn-out filaments slightly bent, as with the curvature of space. Next, they felt the separation in themselves. Initially pleasing, the sensation became nearly ecstatic, like the state induced by a sodium pentathol injection before being plunged into unconsciousness and dreams.

The circle of light, of which they were the center, got wider and wider, as did they like dispersing gas. In each such surge materialized beings who were not there before. Soon the whole meadow was drenched in light and bustling with people who were lightly dressed for fine-weather activity or just a lazy day in the sun.

CHAPTER TWENTY-FIVE

As in a magic show with rabbits or flowers, Thomas Hanratty finds a glass of scotch in his hand. He is dressed in a bathing suit and draped in a towel. There is a David Hockney painting in which the artist's friend stands on a tiled slab at the edge of a pool perched high above the green growth of a rain forest or jungle. He watches himself swim under water. The scene reminds Hanratty of that.

He is seated with two men, also drinking, under a poolside umbrella table. They are dressed almost identically in cream slacks and silk shirts, both open at the top three buttons. Their clothes and deep tans in no way mask the fact that they are accountants transplanted from New York.

The elder congratulates Professor Hanratty on having leased Beverly Hills' most spectacular estate, in his estimation. He wears aviator sunglasses on a broad, spreading nose. His hair looks like whipped cotton. The younger, a moon-faced man with virtually no forehead, recites a history of the estate, recently learned. He refers to the other man as Erik.

Erik says, "We understand, of course, that much of your time will still be devoted to serious research." His voice has become very soft.

Hanratty gestures with his glass, noncommittally.

"The two need not be inconsistent. I gather some of your most powerful images come from your . . . other work."

Hanratty appears to reflect. "A fair statement."

"So . . . we think a package can be put together."

"Do you?"

"We believe in track record, here," says Erik.

"The only credential."

Erik thoughtfully sips his drink. "Are you certain," he asks, "that you are not already represented in any way? No previous commitments?"

"None at all."

"It seems remarkable. But very wise, from your standpoint."

"I thought so."

"It's incredible the impact your book has had on the public."

Hanratty's eyebrows rise slightly.

"Well, perhaps not to you, sir. But there are almost no precedents for sales at this level. Even before the film."

Hanratty modestly inclines his head.

"We want to act fast," Erik says.

"Always best."

"A series of books and films. We thought—the creation of your own production company. Highly leveraged. It would cut costs considerably and offer interesting tax opportunities—apart from the deduction of our ten percent. Accelerated depreciation and the like. We would propose to make a distribution deal with one of the majors, who would also publish the books."

"And . . . ah . . . up front? I believe that's the term."

"Of course. We thought . . . perhaps . . . five million, not including the services we offer—legal, accounting, representation, naturally."

"Hmm. I had thought . . ."

"The figure's negotiable," Erik says quietly.

"I see. Well . . ."

"We would, of course, wish to represent the present book."

"I assumed that."

"And, let us say, a five-book, five-film deal."

"There have been . . . other offers."

"Would 7.5 million make it easier?"

"Not quite so much as ten."

"Say ten, then."

"Yes. We'll consider ten. Let me ask you. About the book itself . . ."

"Professor Hanratty—normally I don't allow my private opinions to interfere with my judgment about the public taste. But in this case—yes. I liked the book. I liked it enormously. The combination of genuine scientific brilliance and literary skill—it is a privilege even to be talking to the author, let alone to be talking about representing him."

Hanratty unabashedly glows. "Most gratifying. Your . . . ah . . . agency, again?"

For a moment the man appears taken aback. "Famous Artists."

"Ah, yes, of course. Gentlemen, if I am correctly informed, I believe that deals are made out here by handshake."

They solemnly shake hands, Erik proclaiming, "The beginning!"

"Indeed."

"Will you be staying on here long, professor?"

"This estate?"

"You could not find better."

"Why—I believe you're right. I think I'll buy it."

"Wise choice. A permanent residence."

"Quite permanent. Yes!"

* * *

A young Irish schoolteacher, bespectacled and pretty, emerges from the Guggenheim Museum, blinks at the sun, and pulls off the jacket of her good Irish tweed suit.

She is much more self-conscious in New York than in Dingle. In New York, everyone appears to believe he is free to study her impersonally, as if she might be a mannequin or a bug, and so she is constantly acting a role she has in her mind of a superior person. She pins up her hair, dons stockings and makes her expression aloof. In Dingle, her expression and hairstyle take care of themselves. She goes around, when not working, in jeans and T-shirts, like those of her own age do here, and almost never wears her best clothes.

Now, all dressed up, she stands on the corner, wondering why she is here at all. Of course she knows the answer; it makes everything worse.

Let's face it, she says—for Kathleen Taggart is forever facing up to the odd consequences of her whimsy—I'm a little bit different. A little bit fey, her mother would put it; or, as her new friends, that writer chap from America and his wife, would say, just plain "kooky" or "off-the-wall."

But this current piece of whimsy, she ruefully concedes, this impulse to cross the ocean, exceeded her range and her pocketbook. No one of her acquaintance could possibly understand it—which, in a sense, was the real reason for the trip.

One day, about a month before spring vacation, there came into her mind the picture of a special person—in fact, a man—along with the notion that such a person lived in this city. She has not been able to rid herself since of notion or picture. The reason this man appeared to be special had little to do with the image she had of his face. Indeed, this was vague and changed from time to time. What persisted was the impression that such a person in fact existed; that she had met him or seen him, perhaps when she was very young; and that his mind worked as hers did—although how that *precisely* differed from others was another obscure subject on which she had puzzled without clear result. If she tried to talk about the pictures flashing about in her head, people tended to get very nervous. Relations with people who did not imagine what she imagined were therefore never entirely satisfactory. Thomas and Faith came closer than others—but a young woman of twenty-five needs more companionship than that.

Let's face it, she concludes, crossing to the park side of the avenue, I am a lovelorn person—for someone I have never seen, will doubtless never meet, and certainly have no objective basis for believing to exist, much less to be in this city. Rational people, she thinks, may suffer from intuitions of this sort, but only silly people act upon them.

She is about to become sillier still.

For one thing she is walking north, when it had been her definite intention to go to the art museums located downtown. For another, she is getting a little disoriented. Her mind is filled, not with great canvasses and sculpture, but with a crowded, sun-flooded park.

At that moment, a shock tremors through her; next a thump so convulsive she thinks she's been shot. She is standing wide-eyed on Fifth Avenue, feeling herself all over, and people are eyeing her as if she were mental.

Then a voice pops into her head. "Keep walking!" it says.

Pictures and impulses are one sort of thing; voices are quite another. Sane people do not hear voices. Schizophrenics hear voices!

She knows this one; it is her own. Yet it is so sharp while distant—so "other"—it seems to be coming from someone else. I'm imagining this, she thinks. It's the loneliness of a week without friends. She puts her hand to her head—maybe I'm feverish. But that's not what she feels. She is fighting thinking about what she is feeling. Rational people do not believe they're inhabited by spooks!

She begins thinking about finding a doctor, calling her mother, or simply taking the next plane. Yet her legs are responding to another command —and her brain to another picture. It's him! she thinks with fearful excitement. *That man is in this park!*

*   *   *

Edward Bell, in mid-pitch, lurches suddenly to a halt. Geordie lowers his bat. He moves the gum in his mouth like a wad of tobacco. Frowning, he taps the dirt from the treads of his sneakers.

Mary Jo pulls up from her catcher's crouch to peer with concern at her son. "What is it, Edward?"

His chin tucks in, eyes inspecting his body. He gives a lopsided grin. "I guess it's a balk."

"What's that?" complains Geordie, sensing some new trick of Edward's being perpetrated through the elder's superior knowledge of the sport.

But his father, laughing, calls out from first base—"Means I go to second, slugger!"—and trots across the base path.

Geordie resumes a ferocious stance. On the next pitch, he whacks the tennis ball they are using with the sweetest part of the bat. Giving a yelp, he begins circling the bases. Edward observes the ball soar through the trees and bound off the top of the rocks.

Geordie stomps on the imaginary plate. "My first home run ever!"

Edward feels oddly magnanimous. "Good hit," he says, which stuns his parents. Then his eyes roll up as if concentrating on some inner voice.

"I'll get the ball," says Briton, loping off. To reach it he must scale the rock pile in center field which is as momentous and smooth as a glacial desposit.

She stands twenty feet from the ledge, a ball held out in her hand. "Is this yours?" She is a bit disheveled, her head tilted to one side, both amused and perplexed by some thought way in the back of her eyes.

For Briton, it is like having a hallucination. For both, in one world, there is an eternity in this moment; in others, it is too pleasurable and too fearful to last.

"Katie," says Briton, barely breathing her name, "is it you?"

The sun halos her hair. She gives him a smile as wide as the meadow.

"Ohmigod, Katie!"

"I know."

He wraps her up in his arms. "You're real, it is you!"

She kisses him hard on the mouth to prove it. He drowns in this kiss, then pulls back, the better to see her.

"It's me," says Katie, "don't worry."

"Worry!" he says. "I've never been so relieved in my life."

"You'll want to know how."

"I want to know *where!*"

"Your world, Briton, Just this once."

"It's true, then. These last months I've started to wonder . . . was it a dream or a trick or delusional."

"It's true."

"God, it's fantastic! Beyond anyone's belief. How did you do it? How did *I* do it?" He'd been waving his hands and now stops. "Later. Let's go. We have to talk. We have to work this out. You've got to meet Mary Jo."

She puts her hand to his cheek. "I'm on borrowed time, baby."

"You're staying!"

She shakes her head.

He's thinking fast. "There's a girl," he says. "Katie Taggert from Dingle."

"Not me. You just missed her."

"You've taken her place? You can do that?"

"If I want to."

"So!"

"I wanted to see you . . . one more time."

"Katie, that's not fair!"

"You left me, Briton."

"Tell me, for chrissake, how to get back to you!"

"You can't any longer."

"Do you want to see me go mad?"

"Briton, you can't come to me, because you don't want to. We *have* worked it out."

"Not seeing you ever again! That's working it out?"

"Yeah. It is. For all of us. For Mary Jo and your kids. And Katie Taggert. And a man, Briton, in my world. I know. Don't look like that! He's just like you."

"Oh Jesus! You've met *me* in your world?"

She shakes her head. "In my world, Briton . . . don't be upset. In my world . . . you were older."

"*Were?*"

She bites her lip. "I'm sorry. But it's a different world, Briton. It can't affect you."

"In your world, I'm dead?"

She nods, with a look of extreme bemusement. "At least I think so."

"Then who is this man?"

She is staring past him, for there has emerged onto their plateau a nine-year-old boy who looks just like his father.

Although Edward can seldom remember much from his past, when he sees the young woman talking to his father, he has a memory which goes back to his earliest childhood. It is not a memory of a real person, at least not of anyone he has ever seen in the flesh. It is the memory of a vision who once curled in beside him and warmed him and made him feel especially good.

He blurts out, "I'm Edward Bell."

Her smile is radiant. "I was watching you playing," she says. "I hope you don't mind." She realizes she still has the ball in her hand, and she tosses it to him.

He stares without speaking, allowing the ball to bounce down the rocks. "Dad," he says, "I'm feeling kind of funny."

"My son," says Briton with a look of pride and concern, putting his hand to Edward's forehead.

"Good-bye, Briton."

"Katie!"

She cups his ear. "I'll always love you. I'll always love you both."

Then she shudders and alters. Edward stares and stares as one might at a train of identical cars in which the same face appears in all passing windows. The effect is hypnotic. He remembers, for he now has the same feeling, the instant after the needle went in his arm, when they took out his tonsils, hearing the voices of nurses and doctor as he whirled off to another sphere. Only this time the voice is in his own head. "I have a brother," it says, and it is the last thing for some moments that Edward will hear.

Briton watches his son go down to his knees. In Edward's face and in Katie's shines an understanding so pure as to obviate words and his own hesitant presence. Yet thoughts are exchanged; and to Katie and her fellow journeyer, they are clearly discernible, even as their hold on this world evanesces.

"Do you see!" he exclaims, this man in the form of a child. "That's my father and mother!"

"Yes, I see!"

"Katie, Katie, we did it!"

"Oh, I know!"

"Ohmigod! Ohmigod!" he commences to blather.

"Calmly, baby!"

There is no sun now, no earth—these have fallen away.

"I'm here," she says, kneeling down with him, holding him close, though there is only space on which to kneel.

This, too, begins curving and turns into spirals which wring themselves inside and out.

"You see that? You see that?" he is shouting aloud.

What they see is themselves in infinite progression, like images in two facing, curved mirrors.

"Our future and past!"

"And one!" he proclaims. "In those worlds we are one!"

"It's our children!" Katie exultingly cries.

Edward comes down from the rocks, as if bearing the Tablets—as if, indeed, he has seen them inscribed.

"Where you been, fella?" Mary Jo asks, her grin anxious, protective.

"Oh . . . up there. Talking to some woman. Saw some stuff."

"Ball lost?"

He holds out his hand, pincering the ball like a globe. "Is there another space here?" he asks, raising the ball to the sun.

With a glance toward her husband still on top of the rocks, Mary Jo says to her son, "What does that mean, honey?"

"You know," Edward says, now eclipsing the sun, "something we can't see?"

"Like what?"

"Dunno. Like . . . a blurry thing in my eyes?" He shrugs, blinking. "A singing in my ears?"

Katie Taggert finds herself sitting groggily on the rocks and observes a man in her sun. "Are you all right?" he asks gently.

She says, "I must have been sleeping."

"You've an Irish accent," he says.

Her smile is startling for its unfamiliarity. "Natural enough, in my case."

There is a pause of unusual awkwardness.

"Well," he says.

"Well, indeed."

"May I help you in some way?"

She shakes her head which tugs at his heart.

"I suddenly have the most powerful urge," she says, "simply to go home."

For a moment he fantasizes the conversation which might occur to detain her—and to change this life, this world to another.

"Have a good trip," he says.

She is on her feet looking at him more intently. "I will," she says. "Thank you."

"And a good life."

She laughs. "Do I know you?"

"Common face," he says, waving, and begins his descent from the rocks.

Mary Jo, Edward and Geordie stand waiting and rapt. Mary Jo says, "Who were you talking to up there, Briton?"

"Oh. A young woman. From Ireland."

"Someone you know?"

A sad smile comes over his face. "No. She's a tourist who's on her way home."

Geordie pounds his mitt. "C'mon, you guys, play ball!"

"Right," says Briton.

And as the unseen observers are returned rapturously to their world, the game in others happily, if somewhat repetitively, continues.